ANNIE IN PARIS

CARMEN REID

B

Boldwood

First published in Great Britain in 2024 by Boldwood Books Ltd.

Copyright © Carmen Reid, 2024

Cover Design by Rachel Lawston

Cover Illustration: Rachel Lawston

A CIP catalogue record for this book is available from the British Library.

Paperback ISBN 978-1-83751-693-3

Large Print ISBN 978-1-83751-689-6

Hardback ISBN 978-1-83751-688-9

Ebook ISBN 978-1-83751-686-5

Kindle ISBN 978-1-83751-687-2

Audio CD ISBN 978-1-83751-694-0

MP3 CD ISBN 978-1-83751-691-9

Digital audio download ISBN 978-1-83751-685-8

Boldwood Books Ltd
23 Bowerdean Street
London SW6 3TN
www.boldwoodbooks.com

For every dedicated Annie fan, who kept on asking for a new book.

AUTHOR'S REMINDER
ANNIE VALENTINE IS BACK!

For everyone in need of a little refresh, here's an introduction to the characters from the series.

Annie – our heroine, 40-something mother and fashion makeover queen. After many years as the top personal shopper at London fashion heaven, The Store, she's currently star presenter on popular TV show *How To Be Fabulous*. She's the eternal optimist, on a quest to make every day and every outfit just that little bit better.

Lauren – Annie's oldest daughter, now a young adult out in the world, currently working at fashion label,

Perfect Dress, in New York. Fiercely opinionated and independent, artistic and so into fashion, Lauren looks like her late father, Roddy, with his raven-black hair and steely blue eyes.

Owen – Annie's oldest son, now a 17-year-old in his final year at St Vincent's School. Tall and gangly with his mother's lighter hair, Owen has a big sense of humour and is totally into all music. He plays violin, drums, glockenspiel, guitar – electric and acoustic. He's trying to decide what to do after school.

Ed – Annie's huge-hearted second husband is sporty, outdoorsy, scruffy, and tragically, couldn't care less about clothes. He's head of music at St Vincent's School, plays violin, guitar, loves every kind of music and is a fantastic dad to all four children.

Minette and Max – Ed and Annie's twins are adorable, when they're not fighting, screaming, or having a complete meltdown, obviously. They're walking, talking, four-year-old pre-schoolers in need of a lot of parental time and energy.

Svetlana Wisnetski-Roscoff – the fabulous multi-millionairess former wife of many important men, including oil baron, Igor Wisnetski. A former beauty queen from Ukraine, she has her own house in Mayfair, a daughter, Elena, two sons, Michael and Petrov, and a new English barrister husband, Harry. Annie was once her beloved personal shopper, but over the years, they've become close friends. Svetlana owns Perfect Dress and films regular financial advice slots on *How To Be Fabulous*.

Elena – Svetlana's secret love child, who was estranged from her mother previously. She is now all grown-up into an extremely determined and ambitious young woman. She helps to run Perfect Dress in New York.

Dinah – Annie's younger sister. Dreamy, creative, artsy Dinah, who is always lovely to everyone. She gave up her day job to become nanny to Minette and Max during Annie's busy TV filming schedule. She's married to architect, Bryan, and they have a daughter, Billie.

Connor – Annie's oldest, 'cashmere sweater' of a best friend. Once her late husband's bestie. He's an actor who has enjoyed TV, film and now West End theatre fame. He's single, yet again, and more than a touch diva-ish, but he's family.

Fern – Annie's mother. A retired podiatrist who brought up her daughters as a hard-working single mum and instilled the love of a quality piece of clothing. She lives outside London now and suffers some health issues, including early-stage dementia. She's well looked after by her daughters and carers.

* * *

Fashion plays a huge part in all the Annie Valentine books, the shows, the stores, the labels, the excitement around designers, new collections, and new styles. This is for entertainment and inspiration! In reality, I'm a total jeans-and-a-shirt person, who wears the same things forever.

I'm very aware that we're living in environmentally precarious times and we all need to do what we can to help. I shop as cost-consciously and sustainably as I can and I donate or recycle everything I've worn out. I love fashion classics and basics because you can re-wear and re-invent them and I love buying second-hand and borrowing from my Mum's treasures.

I hope you'll get all the retail therapy you need from reading Annie's adventures and won't feel that you don't have enough or need to rush out and splurge once you've finished the final chapter. The best 'invest-ment wardrobe' is the one you already own.

Thank you so much for reading, loads of love, Car-men xx

PROLOGUE

LES TISSUS NATURELS – NATURAL FABRICS

Elegant French women are obsessed with clothes made from natural materials. Pure wool sweaters and coats, cotton denim jeans, shirts made from creamy silk or crisp linen. The best accessories are boots, shoes, handbags and belts crafted from supple leathers and suedes.

Natural fabrics allow their wearer to move, to breathe, and to warm up or cool down more easily. Well cared for, these fabrics last a long time and at the end of their lifespan will return gently back to the earth.

— FRENCH DRESSING, BY MADAME
MADELEINE MOREAU

* * *

Right now, Annie Valentine was supposed to be somewhere else. At this exact moment, she was meant to be 1.5 kilometres away, sipping at a glass of Evian and calmly preparing for her interview with a major-league star. Instead, where was she? She was trapped in a beautiful 19th century courtyard in St Germain in the heart of Paris.

Yes, this courtyard was paved with worn limestone slabs and co-ordinating gravel, home to clematis-be-decked trellises, not to mention vigorous plants in old terracotta pots, and even the quintessential metal garden table and chairs. It was gorgeous, but she was still trapped!

The door she'd come through had locked behind her, the wooden courtyard gate was barred with a rusty bolt and chunky padlock. Surrounding the courtyard were walls three metres high and there was no obvious escape route.

Even worse, she was fully dressed up for her important interview in her pale suede boots, a fashion-forward 'vegan' leather dress, full make-up, hair done, toting an up-to-the-moment handbag. This was not the outfit for climbing onto bins and scrambling over stone walls. In fact, this was not the outfit for being trapped, stressed half to death, in a relentlessly sunny, stone-paved space. Encased in plastic leather, she was cooking like a chicken in a bag, sweat running in rivulets down every one of her crevices, her make-up sliding off and her hair wilting like a lettuce.

This was absolute torment! And why? Why was she here in this courtyard off the Boulevard Saint-Michel? To be honest, it was because she was trying to spy on the woman that she suspected was getting far too close to her husband.

She glanced hopelessly at her dead phone, hammered once again at the building's locked back door and gave another loud, but dispirited, shout of: 'Hello! Can anyone hear me?' Then she went over to the tall apartment window and pressed her face to the glass to take a glimpse inside the bedroom. An old mahogany double bed with white pillows and duvet took up one side of the room. But she didn't want to stare at that bed and wonder what had or hadn't been going on in there between her husband and this other woman, so she cast her gaze over to the other side of the white-walled room.

Standing there was an antique wardrobe in the same dark mahogany wood as the bed. One of the solid old doors was hanging open and inside – Annie pressed her face right against the windowpane to get a better look – was a row of wooden shelves, neatly stacked with piles of clothes. The glimpse of a dress peeking out from beside the shelves suggested that the rest of the wardrobe was packed with items on a rail.

Despite her trickling sweat, melting make-up and general sense of panic, Annie could not stop the thought bubbling up that right here, inside this mahogany armoire, she may possibly have located the Holy Grail of French style. This antique piece of furniture contained the complete wardrobe of an effortlessly chic *Parisienne*. The whole shebang, the full monty, the real deal – tops, dresses, jeans, blouses, shoes, skirts, trousers, jackets, scarves and accessories – it was probably all in there. Just an hour or two of sifting through that closet would probably reveal all those elusive French Girl secrets.

But there was nothing she could do about that right now, especially as the secrets belonged to *her*. No, right now, she had to concentrate on how to get out of this baking courtyard, this absolutely broiling dress, and somehow salvage something from the wreckage of the careful plans made for today. Oh dear God, everyone was going to be absolutely furious with her.

And if she thought back through all the steps that had brought her here to this locked courtyard nightmare... well, it was definitely Ed's fault. And it had all kicked off back in August on the night of that supposedly Romantic Dinner Date.

1

La Lingerie – Underwear

Even in the smallest provincial French towns, you will find boutiques with top quality underwear because this is an essential ingredient for being well-dressed. Smooth cottons, pretty laces and sexy sheers all feel perfect next to the skin. They make you look and feel better. The best way to wash your exquisite Lejaby bra? Wear it in the shower!

— M.M.

* * *

It would be fair to say that the 'cosy' Italian restaurant chosen for their dinner date was not nearly as nice as Annie had hoped. She had imagined dimmed lights, mellow music, plush chairs and generous glasses of fruity wine, so that she and Ed could steal a brief evening away from the mayhem that currently passed for family life.

While she had been hoicking herself into extra-strength Spanx and applying lipstick for the first time in weeks, she'd imagined enjoying a relaxed meal and uninterrupted conversation with her husband. As she'd fiddled about with earrings, applied one too many blasts of perfume, and fussed about to bangle or not to bangle, she'd even thought about coming home later to a romantic rekindling.

But instead, the only thing about to be rekindled was her almighty temper as Ed was twenty minutes late so far and there had been no word from him since a brief message nearly two hours ago:

Not forgotten dinner, still caught up in handovers.

Handovers... endless handovers... meanwhile, she was stuck in a below-par diner at a sticky table, even though she'd already asked the waiter to wipe it down for her, with a heavy smell of fried onions in the air and a huge TV screen on the wall behind her showing a blinking football match. And why was the TV draped in red and green tinsel? It was the tail end of August. Was this something to do with the football and showing Italian colours?

She picked up her phone with the intention of sending another message to Ed, this time to tell him that she would never be taking restaurant recommendations from him again. Maybe he'd been tipsy when he'd last eaten here, or maybe he'd been planning to keep up with the football during their 'date', but this was just not the setting for a romantic dinner and Annie couldn't get up and go somewhere else because this place was tucked away down several side streets and she'd not seen any other restaurants nearby.

As soon as the phone was in her hand, she could see a new flurry of messages had landed and, for a moment, she hesitated. Yes, she should check to see if there was a message from Ed, or any kind of family emergency, but, on the other hand, this was supposed to be an evening off, and if she opened her messages, the chances of being drawn into some kind of urgent family drama were high.

The waiter appeared by her side.

'Another glass of wine for madam, and how about some appetisers while you wait for your companion?'

She looked at her half-drained wine glass and decided more chilled white was probably needed. Then she added bread, butter and olives to her order, but she wasn't sure if the waiter heard her because a goal had been scored, cheers erupted, and off he darted to watch the action replay.

Annie sighed and opened the messages.

Nothing from Ed, she saw as she scrolled.

She opened the one from her teenage son, Owen, first. He was away for another night at some sort of 'music camp' that he had begged and hassled her to go to, but he seemed to spend most of the day there on his phone begging and hassling her with all other kinds of requests.

Can you top up my phone plz?

Followed by:

Didn't pack enough pants. Can you send?

Followed by:

Back at school at 6pm tmz. Can I get lift? Bag
and instruments too heavy.

She sighed, took another gulp of wine and
tapped out:

Will top up phone. No! Can't send pants! Just
re-wear. Will see what I can do about lift. Hope
you're having fun. Love you xx

Then there was a new message from her oldest
daughter, Lauren, in New York:

I have found a room, but it's v v small and they
want a deposit of $2000. Is that OK?

Annie sighed again and took a bigger gulp of wine.
Lauren in New York was currently just one v. v. big, expensive headache.

Out for dinner. Will call later and talk it through.
Love you xx

A message from the babysitter looking after the
twins tonight had also dropped:

Max says he has a sore stomach. What should
I do?

Sigh. Swig.

Liesel, from Owen's year at school, was not hugely experienced, but she had been available and Annie hadn't anticipated any problems. Her four-year-old twins, Max and Minette, had seemed absolutely fine when she'd left the house earlier.

Give him some water. Maybe a teaspoon of
Calpol (main bathroom cupboard) and let me
know if it gets any worse. Thank you x

She put the phone down and couldn't help the flashes of angst that now popped up... Could Max possibly have appendicitis? Was Lauren about to be scammed out of her hard-earned money? Shouldn't Owen be old enough to count his pants?!

There was so much that she absolutely loved about being the captain of the Starship Family Enterprise, but sometimes, just occasionally, it would be wonderful to have a few hours completely off. But then her thoughts were interrupted.

'Annie! There you are! I'm not too late, am I?'

And here was her husband, unruly, curly hair all

over the place, clothes looking rumpled, and as he bent down to kiss her, she got a blast of heat, damp upper lip and sweat.

'Did you *cycle* over here?' she asked, as he settled down into the chair opposite hers. When he nodded, she had to add: 'But that's absolutely *miles*, babes, no wonder you're late! And now you'll have to cycle home...'

He nodded, helped himself to a piece of the bread and explained between chews: 'Yeah, but that is me bang up to date with school. I didn't want to have to go back for the bike and get dragged into anything else, so... it sort of made sense. I am completely starving. Have you ordered?'

'No, I've been waiting for you, in this cosy, romantic bistro,' she said, heavy on the sarcasm.

She thought about the time she'd spent doing her hair and make-up, choosing the dress, booking the babysitter and now she felt even more annoyed. Look at Ed, he wasn't even wearing a clean shirt!

'What's the matter, Annie?' he breezed. 'Let's order the food and then you can tell me all about it.'

* * *

So, they called the waiter over, selected a generous spread from the menu and, as the dishes began to arrive, Annie started to unload the list of current family woes – how would they know Lauren's flat was OK and that she wasn't being ripped off? When would Owen learn to look after his things, pack properly, and stop making fifteen different requests a day? And many other incidental things that had cropped up recently, not to mention – did Ed think Max could possibly have appendicitis?

One of the very good things about Ed being a teacher was that he was endlessly experienced and reassuring about children and young people: 'Lauren will be fine – as long as she's not expecting us to pay that deposit'; 'I'm sure it's just a phase with Owen'; 'don't fret about Max, it will be a bug' – were the calming phrases he provided that she needed to hear.

The food arrived and it wasn't brilliant, but her second glass of wine was going down well and for a short time between the olives, baked aubergine and fried prawn dishes, she tried to relax and enjoy herself.

OK, well, just as soon as Ed had calmed down about how much onion there would be in these dishes... the topic of Ed's temperamental digestion seemed to crop up just a little too often these days.

But never mind, he was now telling a funny story

about the St Vincent's headmaster, Mr Ketteringham-Smith, and as she listened, she tried to imagine the three-and-a-half-month stint without Ed at home that was about to begin. He was going away the day after tomorrow on a teacher-exchange programme to Paris. For *him*, she loved that he was going. He would have the most exciting, stimulating term in years. Ed probably needed this – something new and different that he could throw himself into completely. But for Annie, managing her work, the family, the home and everything else without him by her side was daunting. No, make that downright freaking terrifying.

Although she kept assuring him to go because everything would be absolutely fine without him, she really had no idea yet how it would all work, although plans were beginning to come together. She would be back at her TV job, the twins were going to start nursery, plus her sister Dinah would still do some part-time nanny duty to cover gaps. But Ed did a lot – he grocery shopped, he was the main cook, and he did so much evening and weekend parenting. And without him, how would she cope with all those unexpected things that cropped up with children, despite the best-laid plans?

Right on cue, in came the text from the babysitter to let her know:

Max has been sick.

'Uh-oh,' she said, picking up the phone, 'Max has vommed.'

'Just the once?' Ed asked, perhaps hoping that maybe one random puke was not enough of an emergency to leave a dinner straight away.

'I'll find out,' Annie said, standing up to make the call outside.

* * *

In the quiet of the side street, Annie quickly established that it was three pukes in rapid succession and Liesel was struggling to cope.

'OK,' Annie told her briskly, 'keep him propped up on the sofa with towels and a big bowl from the kitchen. Just give him tiny sips of water if he wants them. It'll take me about thirty minutes to get home. Do you think you can manage until then?'

Liesel didn't sound entirely sure.

'I'm sure it's just a bug,' Annie said, to reassure them both. 'I'll take a cab, so you can phone me anytime if you're worried.'

Back in the restaurant, Ed protested.

'You're going to go home because he's been sick?

But... it's probably all up now and he'll be fine. What about we at least finish the food?'

'No, I have to go,' she insisted, annoyed with him for suggesting otherwise. 'Liesel sounds upset. She's young and a bit hopeless, so I don't think she can cope and, anyway, I can't say I was loving this.' She gestured to the food and the place.

Picking up her bag, she packed away her phone and prepared to go.

'Enjoy the football,' she added.

'Annie!' Ed exclaimed. 'That's not the reason I chose it and I don't think you should rush off.'

'Well, I do.'

So, just five minutes later, she was being driven past the picturesque canal where she had imagined strolling, arm in arm with Ed, after their romantic dinner.

'OK, phone if you need me,' had been his parting words. 'I'll finish my dinner and be back as soon as I can.' But she knew his long cycle ride home would take some time.

* * *

Once she was back, the next hour passed in a blur of crying Max, crying Liesel, sending Liesel home in a cab, soothing Max as he puked some more, rinsing towels in the bath – Liesel had unfortunately picked the brand-new fluffy white towels for Operation Mop Up – loading the washing machine, sponging carpets, and finally putting a much more settled four-year-old into his bed with the baby monitor on beside him. Somehow, his sister Minette had slept through the entire drama, but Annie knew enough about twin ailments by now to suspect that it was only a matter of time before she woke up with a sore tummy too.

When everything was calm, she went into her and Ed's bedroom, all beautifully tidied and arranged for the romantic rekindling she'd hoped would be happening here later. The bed was freshly made, the fairy lights draped around the headboard were on, and she'd put flowers on the bedside tables along with new tea light candles in little glass holders.

As she stood there, admiring her handiwork, she heard the front door opening as Ed finally made it home. She waited for him to park the bike, take off his shoes and then pad gently up the stairs.

'All quiet?' he asked in a whisper as he came into the room.

'Yes,' she whispered back, 'he's sleeping. I think he's going to be fine.'

'It looks lovely in here,' Ed added, 'very romantic... look, I know it's not been the perfect evening...'

'No,' she agreed, trying to swallow down her annoyance and disappointment.

'But are you thinking what I'm thinking?' he asked with a smile. 'We could try to kiss and make up?'

'Well... maybe I could be persuaded, but you definitely need to go and have a shower first,' she said, pointing to the damp sweat stains on his shirt.

'OK, you get into that very comfortable bed while I shower. Then I will be right back beside you...'

* * *

'Annie?'

Annie opened her eyes to see the twinkle of the fairy lights above her. She realised she'd taken off her clothes, slipped into bed and, almost instantly, fallen fast asleep. Beside her was a freshly washed Ed, his damp hair brushing her shoulder.

'Sorry to wake you... you look very tired,' he sympathised.

She turned to him and, not sure if she really believed it, said, 'I think I could rally... if you made some of your best moves.'

'No... go back to sleep,' he told her gently, 'to be

honest, I've done about twenty miles on the bike today and I'm completely shattered.'

She sighed. 'OK, well, tomorrow,' she said, 'definitely... it's your last night.'

'That's a deal.'

Just as she closed her eyes again, half-wondering, *did I take off my make-up? What about brushing my teeth? So much for a romantic evening...* her phone bleeped.

Oh, for goodness' sake... now what?

She got up onto her elbow, groped for her mobile and saw Lauren's message:

Mum? I thought you were going to phone me back?

Oh no.

And then through the baby monitor came Minette's voice as she said in a pitiful whine, 'Mummy... feel sick.'

Oh no, no, no!

2

Les Accessoires – Accessories

Coco Chanel famously told us to remove one accessory before we leave the house. But she was advising women who wore hats trimmed with flowers and ribbons, plus earrings, multi-strand necklaces, elaborate corsages, bracelets, rings and brooches, all with highly decorative dresses. Nowadays, I look in the mirror at my staple outfits and wonder what I can add to bring them to life – eye-catching earrings, or a bright scarf? My new belt, perhaps, or a brooch? Often, modern women need to add a little more!

— M.M.

* * *

The following afternoon, when the recovering twins had been fed, further entertained and were now drowsily enjoying their slot of allotted TV time, Annie went upstairs to see how Ed's packing for Paris was progressing. The marital bedroom was now in a state of disarray because Ed was in deep prep for his departure tomorrow.

This was not a scene that would 'spark joy' in the heart of any Marie Kondo fan. Ed's clothes and other belongings were scattered across the bed, where his half-packed suitcase was lying open, while shoes, trainers and various electrical wires were strewn about the floor. Ed had not long ago rushed out declaring that he had to buy a new phone charger, an adaptor plug and various other last-minute items.

Annie looked into the suitcase and was surprised to see a lot of nice clothes in there – his newest shirts and T-shirts, plus crisp, recently bought pairs of chinos and two of the latest tweedy English-gent jackets to join his wardrobe. Good grief, even that unopened bottle of cologne she'd bought him months ago was in there. In fact, she had bought most of these items for him, but they'd mainly been left unworn, as he continued to get full wear out of his other older, saggier 'Dad' clothes.

Well, he was obviously planning a whole new look for Paris.

The neatly folded pile of cycling clothes at the foot of the bed beside the open suitcase puzzled her. Surely Ed wasn't planning to cycle in Paris? 'Proper' cycling was his new thing. He'd always cycled to school and back most days, but for the past year, he'd joined a cycling club and begun going on much longer excursions at the weekends. This commitment came with Lycra shorts and tight-fitting zip-up jackets, eye goggles, time trials and the ridiculous carbon fibre monstrosity parked in their actual bedroom because Ed was worried it would be stolen from the shed or scratched up in the hallway.

On the plus side, Ed was incredibly fit, but the downside was that she seemed even less fit by comparison. As their ages slowly but surely ticked upwards, Annie was only too aware that wrinkles and poundage were both creeping gently up on her, meanwhile her husband seemed to be getting more sinewy and muscular by the day and, to add insult to injury, totally suited the slight grey peppering of his thick wiry hair and the craggier face he was developing.

'Ageing like a fine bloody wine,' she hissed as she

pulled on a summer dress with a smocked top but did not feel pleased with the effect at all. She glared at the pile of cycling clothes, then immediately wondered why she felt so annoyed about her husband taking his fitness seriously, and going to bloody Paris on an exchange with a suitcase full of his best clothes. Paris... Paris! Just the thought of Ed in Paris was making her feel unreasonably annoyed and maybe even jealous.

Not far below the surface of these feelings, lurked another thought. Ever since they had first become life partners, she had always absolutely counted on Ed. He was always there, supporting her, helping her to hold family life together, making her feel like she was the most wonderful woman he'd ever met. But lately, she had found herself wondering if their relationship was struggling.

They were so busy with all the demands of children and work, so wrapped up in the day-to-day stuff, that there seemed to be nothing left over for the two of them. Well... maybe their time apart would be a good thing, she tried to console herself. Maybe they would appreciate each other all the more when he returned from his Paris teaching adventure.

Tonight, she was going to make sure that she paid him full attention, no matter what. She was going to cook a lovely farewell dinner and instigate a romantic evening in the bedroom. Nigella Lawson cookbook, tea lights, fairy lights and silky undies at the ready – Ed was going to leave for Paris with only good thoughts about her on his mind.

* * *

So, after dinner, the twins' bedtimes and the last of the packing, they did make it to the fairy-lit bedroom to give a romantic farewell their best effort. And afterwards, it was lovely to lie side by side feeling closer than they had done for some time.

'I think we're a bit out of practise,' Ed was the first to admit. 'We didn't shoot the lights out.'

'Agreed,' she told him. 'Still very nice though. A bit like washing the car...'

'What?!' He turned to her with a slightly horrified expression on his face.

'I just mean, I wasn't too keen, but once I got going, I was completely involved and now, I'm glad we made the effort.'

'And was this a bucket and sponge, a hosepipe, or a jet wash?' Ed couldn't help asking.

'Ed!' she laughed. 'You know what I mean.'

'Yeah... I'm glad we made the effort too.'

And then there was some practical chitchat about

his departure time and whether or not she would give him a lift.

'No, honestly, I'll be fine with the train,' he insisted. 'And thank you, for such a nice evening, for dinner, which was...'

Now they both laughed. Dinner had been a noisy family affair with the twins, still tired out by their tummy bug, all cranky and picky about what they would eat. Meanwhile, Owen, back from music camp, had tried to scoff just about everything in the entire kitchen while talking non-stop about his great, big, looming decision – what he would do after school.

'To study music, or to study economics? That is the question,' he'd said before putting almost an entire bread roll in his mouth. 'And if music – should it be classical? Or contemporary? Playing skills or sound-editing skills? Do I need the School of Rock?' he'd added, although it was hard to tell with so much bread roll in the way.

'That dinner!' Annie began. 'Please don't remind me. How was I supposed to know there was oil from a can of tuna on the cream whisk? How did it get there? It must have been Owen...'

Annie had a simple tried-and-tested meal that she could almost always pull off. So that was what she'd gone for tonight: roast chicken, creamy potato salad and a green salad with vinaigrette. Dessert was home-made pavlova topped with cream, raspberries and passion fruit.

But tonight's pavlova cream had come with an unmistakable hint of fish. Ed had insisted he couldn't taste it and ate his whole portion, but Owen and the twins just needed one mention of 'does this taste a bit fishy?' to be completely put off.

'I'm sorry about the tuna oil,' Ed said now.

'And another thing—' she began.

'Uh-oh... was it the music comment?' he wondered.

'Yes, it was. Did I really need to be teased by you and Owen for not knowing my— what was it?' she complained.

'Your Mozart from your Mendelssohn.'

'Exactly!'

'Annie, you live with two musicians and you know literally nothing about classical music.'

'Ed,' she countered, 'Lauren and I work in fashion and you wouldn't recognise a Fendi Baguette if I served it to you for breakfast!'

Although she had expected him to protest, Ed sank his head back onto the pillow and told her, 'You're right, we should both try and do something about our knowledge gaps.'

'Yeah, well,' she turned out the bedside light on her side, 'as soon as you find time to study the fashion greats, let me know, and I will do some homework on the musical classics.'

In the darkness, as they prepared to fall asleep, Ed asked, 'Did you manage to speak to Lauren?'

'We've been messaging, but I've not had time for a full chat.'

'OK... try and speak to her tomorrow, check everything's OK.'

'Yeah...' And then Annie heard herself add quietly, 'We are OK, aren't we, Ed? Going to Paris isn't about running away from me... from us?'

She could hear him lift his head from the pillow to turn to her.

'No, of course not,' he replied.

'Then why are you going?'

'You know why. We've talked it all through to death, Annie. This decision was made months ago!' he exclaimed. 'It's about having a new experience, being in a different city. I'm a bit desperate to do something just for myself. It's a reset, a refresh,' he added. 'A chance to really focus on what I do and get even better at it. I want to get absorbed in the music and come back a better teacher. St Vincent's is a very demanding school. You've got to keep right up there. So, this is distraction-free time, grown-up time even. Because yes, I have to admit...'

She suspected she wasn't going to like this next bit so much.

'I absolutely love my family, you know that. And you love family life too... but... we're in the same old routine and it can be boring. You know it can.'

'Yeah...' she added in a whisper.

'And I feel desperate to do something just for myself,' he added. 'I think it's important to do this for me... and for us as a couple too. I'm really looking forward to it and I think some time apart should let us all appreciate each other when we get back together again.'

She reached for his hand. It didn't matter that they'd discussed it to death and both agreed to this plan. Now that it was here, now that he was going off to be busy and do exciting new things, while she was left holding the fort, she could only think of all those years after the death of her first husband, Roddy, when she was a single parent to two small children. It was grindingly hard work; it was house arrest once they were in bed, and worst of all, were those moments when you wanted to say, '*Look what they did! Aren't they so clever?*' and there was no one to say it to. That parenting loneliness was what she was frightened of.

'We'll phone a lot, OK?' she asked.

'We will be in constant contact, I promise.'

After several moments, Ed broke the silence again to ask: 'Washing the car? Really...? Is that how you feel about...?'

'OK... I'm sorry. But a bit...' Annie admitted. 'Things are a bit... lacklustre.'

He took his hand away from hers.

'Maybe some time apart...'

'Maybe...' she said.

Then there was silence again.

Now that it was really here, their last night together for weeks, maybe even months if they didn't get a visit organised, Annie felt much more worried than she'd expected.

3

Le Rouge à Lèvres – Lipstick

A whole cabinet packed full of make-up is not necessary. A light foundation, a blusher or bronzer for the days you feel washed out, an eyeliner and two lipsticks are enough. One lipstick can be more natural for every day, and one can be the dramatic red, burgundy or pink that you wear for special days or nights.

— M.M.

* * *

There was a pause on the other end of the line and Annie realised she was meant to make some kind of reply. But this was such a surprise that she was struggling to come up with a good response.

'I realise this is so *not* what you wanted to hear... I didn't want to hear it either,' Tamsin added.

Annie had a tight grip on the phone as she tried to digest this news. She also had a tight grip on Minette's swimsuit straps so that Max could enjoy just a few more moments in the garden paddling pool without being tormented.

Although she had tried to instil a rule of 'Silence When Mummy is on the Phone', she sensed she only had precious seconds left before Minette broke into a roar of outrage.

It might only be a few seconds before Annie broke into a roar of outrage too. This was such disappointing news.

Tamsin was the executive producer of the TV show *How To Be Fabulous* and for the last eight series, Annie had been the programme's star presenter. The show was a solid success, having moved from a small TV channel to a more mainstream one, and those all-important viewer figures continued to grow. But the news from Tamsin today was that two of the carefully planned episodes for the next season, due to start filming just six weeks from now, were going to have to be binned. One of their main competitors was apparently about to air with topics that were far too similar.

'I've seen the previews,' Tamsin went on. 'A friend got hold of them for me. It's almost eerie how alike they are: celebrities turned designers, the step-by-step making of a legendary handbag, even the "one dress, six ways" idea. It's all there. And they're really going for our look and feel. So, I've had to alert the big channel boss, who has hauled me in and said we have to come up with new, much better, much fresher ideas, or... we are in trouble.'

Tamsin had already spelled it out earlier in the call. The next, essential slice of funding was in serious doubt. If their new ideas weren't good enough, the next series might be pulled.

'How long do we have to come up with all this?' Annie wanted to know, because this wasn't just about jotting down some thoughts and sending them over. This was about having a whole smorgasbord of delicious new ideas, enough to fill two episodes, plus doing the research to make sure they were viable, and even, ideally, organising some test filming to give the production team plenty of time to set up crews, locations and permissions in time.

'Well...' Tamsin was thinking it through, 'if we can

get two brilliant new episode ideas through the door in the next month – enough to get our funding secured and the series greenlit – then we can start by filming the six episodes we've already planned first, and that should give the production department time to plan out the new episodes. That's how we'll do it.'

'So, a month, basically,' Annie summarised. 'We have one month to come up with enough ideas to create two series-saving episodes?'

'Yes, that is basically how the land lies,' Tamsin confirmed. 'And not just ideas, Annie, entire themes, directions, major wow factor. It's not just on you, Annie,' Tamsin assured her, 'everyone involved will be thinking about it, but *you* – you're the one who's always had the best ideas so far. So, if anyone can pull us out of this hole, it will be you.'

Annie sighed loud and long. She relinquished hold of Minette's swimsuit straps with the hissed instruction to 'Play nice!' and Minette pinged over the burnt-out, very end-of-the-summer grass to the paddling pool.

Annie already knew that she would, of course, give it her very best shot, but why did TV always have to be like this? One minute, you were a breathlessly exciting success and everything you did was 'uh-mazing!' and literally, the very next second, everything you suggested was 'old, has-been and done-to-death'. It was exhausting.

She was still supposed to be on holiday and adjusting to life without Ed at home. It was just ten days before her toddlers were due to start nursery and next week, Owen would begin his final year at school. She wanted to enjoy the last remaining time with all three of them, not be rushing about trying to decide what was hot and what was not.

'What are you up to right now, anyway?' Tamsin asked. 'I always imagine you off on exciting fashion research.'

'Oh no... school holidays, so we've been taking it easy.'

Annie looked down at her overflowing boob tube, baggy shorts and flip-flops. She was not feeling very *How To Be Fabulous*. No, she was definitely not in TV-glamour mode. Her current vibe was more *How To Look Like A Burst Couch*.

'And Ed has just gone off to Paris...' she added, trying not to feel the inevitable pang of jealousy that struck whenever she thought of where her husband was spending the upcoming term. The whole term!

'He's landed this teaching-exchange scholarship,

so he's off to a very prestigious music school in Paris. And believe it or not, he gets a beautiful Left Bank apartment, thrown into the deal by the wealthy bene-factors.'

'Oh, that sounds fantastic,' Tamsin agreed. 'And meanwhile, you're left at home with all the brood?'

'Exactly!' Annie said. 'Well, Lauren is still in New York and planning to stay there... as long as she can find something interesting to do,' Annie said of her el-dest daughter, 'but yes, Owen and the twins are all mine until December. But don't worry, as soon as you hang up, I'm going to start brainstorming for those episodes.' Annie tried to lift her voice to the level of dynamic enthusiasm required. It wasn't that she didn't love the show, or being on the show, or banking the generous TV presenter's fee. She did, of course she did. But it felt so disheartening to have to start on those episodes all over again.

'And what about your friend, Svetlana?' was Tam-sin's next question. 'She will come back to do her guest slots on the next series, won't she?'

'You know... I'm actually not sure,' Annie admitted. They both knew that Svetlana, the Mayfair-based former Miss Ukraine, the multiple-divorced, multi-millionairess, and her *Tips from your Rich Best Friend* was one of the show's most popular slots, along with the Annie Makeover segment, when Annie pitched up in a straight-out-of-Frumpsville outfit and made herself over. (So much less awkward than making over a shy and awkward, fashion-blind guest).

'Have you seen much of her since filming on the last series?' Tamsin asked.

Annie answered vaguely, 'No, not really, she's been away for most of the summer...'

The truth was more clear-cut.

The two women had not, in fact, seen each other since the last day of filming back in May. The reason for this? Well, just a few days after filming wrapped, Svetlana had phoned Annie with very surprising news. She had announced that she was 'stepping back' from the day-to-day running of her fashion company, Perfect Dress, and employing a new CEO. Unfortunately, according to Svetlana, the new CEO had already identified where 'business transformation' needed to happen and this included making Annie's daughter redundant and replacing her with someone much more experienced.

Annie, who was a partner in the business – admittedly a very small shareholder, but still – had felt completely blindsided. She'd not expected any of this, especially as Lauren had only just returned to New York after an extensive and expensive visa application process.

The exchange that followed between Svetlana and Annie had been heated. Annie was pretty convinced the words: *'playing at lady of the manor'* had left her lips along with *'what Svetlana wants, Svetlana gets – as usual'*.

So, Lauren had left Perfect Dress and was currently doing short-term, bitty jobs as she searched for something else. Annie and Svetlana had not been in touch again all summer long.

Annie hadn't gone so far as to delete Svetlana from her social media sites, so she'd seen the posts:

enjoying summer with my boys in St Tropez!

She'd even occasionally given them a like or left a comment to let Svetlana know that she was around and maybe they should think about getting in touch and talking things over. But there had been no hint of any acknowledgement.

Svetlana, Annie had to admit to herself, was often a bit too much. Her extremely wealthy lifestyle could be hard to cope with when Annie had all those much more mundane problems to worry about: paying for the twins' nursery, not to mention Lauren's flights to New York, or the repairs needed to the grade-blinking-two sash windows at home, or the tragic and unexpected death of the fridge-freezer, let alone the tragic and unexpected vet bills in the last days of Dave the family dog, and on top of that – now the worry that her TV career could possibly come to an abrupt end.

Sometimes, Svetlana's advice, which always involved throwing huge amounts of money at every problem, wasn't very helpful. Plus, it was usually delivered in slightly brusque and dismissive tones.

The worst thing was that Annie, despite all her personal success, still felt like Svetlana's low-rent friend. Annie couldn't possibly keep up with Svetlana's lifestyle, and although they had grown close over the years and both Annie and Lauren had worked in Svetlana's business, there was no forgetting that Annie had once been Svetlana's personal shopper and they didn't ever feel like equals. They had enjoyed many good times together, but then, Svetlana would retreat, for months at a time, to her rightful place in the jet-set crowd. That's where she was now, summering on yachts and jet skis, in designer swimsuits, while staff, no doubt, hovered at her elbow with plates of chilled, sliced melon and mango.

Would Svetlana come back to do her very popular

slots? Currently, there was no chance. If Annie wanted Svetlana back, she would have to find a way to repair the damage done by that argument.

'We have to have Svetlana back,' Tamsin told her now. 'She's a star attraction. I know it's not about money with her, so whatever it is that she needs – if you can find that out – we'll sort it to make sure she returns. Everyone loves her slot. *Loves* it.'

And there was the other thing. How could Annie not be jealous when she worked all year long to re-search new topics, develop ideas, butter people up to interview, while Svetlana breezed in, recorded a handful of five-minute 'rich tips' and everyone thought she was *wonderful*?

Oh my God, Annie told herself off, *what a prime, grade-A diva I'm turning into*. Here she was in the sunny garden of her lovely north London home, with her de-lightful babies, talking to her TV producer about how to make the new series better than ever. Really, she should be eternally grateful for her charmed life, not thinking bitter thoughts about the very wealthy and successful woman she had been lucky to count as a friend and business partner, even if there had been a parting of the ways. But to be honest, Annie would find it hardest to forgive Svetlana for taking Lauren's work away.

'OK, Tamsin, babes, leave it with me,' Annie assured her producer now. 'I will pull out all the stops. I'll come up with two new episodes to *Blow Your Mind!*'

'In six, well, four weeks, ideally...' Tamsin reminded her, 'and there is one last thing... I've been told that they want us to think "older" demographic. The people watching your show are forty-plus, and they want us to draw in the fifty— even sixty-plus audience. More affluent, more likely to book the Saga cruises that fill up the ad breaks, so we need to keep that in mind – not go *too* fashion.'

'Right, well...' she hesitated. *An older audience and not too fashion?* Good grief, this was a lot to keep on top of. And didn't people watch shows like hers for entertainment and inspiration? They weren't all about to go off and buy this season's new Chanel jacket, were they? But that didn't mean she had to start doing segments on this season's cosiest slippers! TV was such a tightrope. It was not possible to keep everyone happy all the time and that was a fact.

'OK, well... and no problem to all of that!' Annie insisted, sounding more confident than she felt, but she would have to try and pull this all together. And right now, she had noticed that Minette had a small bucket, full to the brim, right above her brother's head and was trying to get her grip right to tip it over, so Annie had to go.

'Speak soon, byeeeee,' she told Tamsin as she leapt from her deck chair, popping out of her boob tube in the process, and grabbed the bucket to prevent yet another distressed Max-wailing-at-top-volume incident.

4

La Peau – Skin

Basic skincare is something everyone can learn from a young age. Always take your make-up off, clean your skin gently, moisturise and guard against the fierce sun of the summer. Don't use anything harsh on your skin or your hair. Treat these precious parts of your body like a delicate silk negligée.

— M.M.

* * *

The Bentley purred gently through the slow-moving traffic on the clogged Euston Road, but Svetlana sat calmly in the back seat with her teenage boys and did not fret. They'd left in plenty of time and anyway, trains to Edinburgh seemed to go once an hour at this time of day, so if her boys missed this one, they would just catch the next.

Michael and Petrov were both on their phones messaging the friends they expected to meet on the long train journey north. The handsome young teenagers were casually dressed, but it was the very smartest side of casual: designer jeans and trainers, polo shirts from the currently most fashionable teen label and everything ironed to within one inch of its life by Svetlana's long-serving housekeeper, Maria.

Both boys were making the long journey up to Edinburgh, then Aberdeen, then Elgin, to their famous Scottish boarding school, Gordonstoun. The elite school Prince Philip and all his royal children, including King Charles, had attended. After her divorce from the boys' father, Igor, Svetlana had endured huge fights with him about where their boys would be schooled once they outgrew their exclusive London prep school. Igor had insisted they should attend a disciplinarian military academy in Eastern Europe, as he had done, while she had been desperate to keep them near her in London, so had campaigned for Eton. Finally, after Igor had attempted to force the boys into the military academy, Svetlana had come up with the compromise of Gordonstoun – still in the UK, although a long way from London, but with plenty of sporting and outdoor activity and the exclusive royal cachet that had brought Igor round.

Svetlana looked with deep love at her boys, their dark hair in sharp new cuts for school, their skin conker-brown from a long summer on the waters around France and Greece. She felt a dull physical ache in her heart that she knew was sadness. They were leaving again. Yes, there would be half-term visits and Christmas holidays and all the usual beats of the boarding school year. But her beloved boys no longer spent most of their lives at home with her. She only got them in the holidays and she had to share some of that time with Igor. There were all sorts of small things she didn't know about their lives any more and maybe big things too. A verruca on 13-year-old Petrov's foot had almost reduced her to tears because he'd told her, quite unconcerned, that 'it's been there for ages', but this was the first she'd heard about it.

Whenever one of the boys glanced over to look at her, she smiled brightly. Her make-up was beautifully applied, her hairdresser had come to the house this morning to personally wash, blow dry and then sweep her long blonde locks into her favourite high chignon bun and she was wearing a pale Chanel skirt suit because there were no clothes as effective as Chanel's for tenderly holding together on the outside what felt as if it was falling apart on the inside. So, Svetlana smiled as if she didn't have a care in the world because she didn't want her boys to worry about her.

Now here they were, driver Freddy pulled into the drop-off zone, opened doors, then took out the kind of soft, lightweight, supersized bags on wheels favoured by the elite teenagers who would be travelling up and down the country this week to return to school.

They had made it with just twelve minutes to spare before the 9.45 a.m. train. So, the boys pulled their bags quickly through King's Cross, spotting friends as they went, while Svetlana hurried behind on high heels that clacked loudly against the concrete floor.

The train to Edinburgh was already on the platform and she knew her boys were keen to get on board with their friends. They already had strict rules about station goodbyes. She was allowed a hug and a kiss on each cheek, as long as she did this as 'quickly as possible'. She was allowed to watch them settle into their seats, but she was not allowed to stand there on the platform on the brink of tears, watching and waving until the train pulled off. No, she'd done that once and now it was completely forbidden.

'Take great care of yourself and see you soon,' she said as she hugged Michael and kissed each cheek, trying not to notice that involuntary little flinch. He's a teenager, she told herself, it's natural. Plus, he loved the school.

Then it was time to hug Petrov, her younger child. It was always hard to keep her face as cheerful as required because he was her baby. He still enjoyed the cuddles and the kisses, still met her eye-to-eye and she could see the trace of anxiety and sadness in his face.

'*Au revoir*, my darling,' she said as she put her arms round him, because this was their code word for 'I love you, I'll miss you so much and I know you'd like to be at school in London, but if you didn't go to Scotland, your father would send you to military academy and that would be much, much worse. But I will keep working on him for you.'

'*Au revoir*, Mama.' In a whisper he added, 'We'll speak every day.'

'*Ja, ja*, of course,' she agreed.

Then they were on board in their first-class seats, already talking to the other friends in the carriage, who had bunched in a knot around their table, so Svetlana had to give one last wave, which they both returned, and turn on her heel and walk back out of the station, away from those two most important people in her world, back to her waiting car.

As she reached the end of the platform, she saw a group of well-dressed men and women who she recognised as other London parents of pupils at the school. Instinctively, she drew her shoulders back, lifted her chin and prepared to acknowledge the admiring looks with a smile and friendly nod. But as she approached and then passed the group, barely a glance came her way.

Certainly no smiles, and not one of those long, lingering, admiring looks that she had been attracting from both men and women since her childhood. As she walked on, she passed a full-length glass window blanked out with black cardboard, so she caught her reflection clearly and at an unexpected angle. She took a good look and reeled at the sight. Her face looked drawn and jowly, her hair stiff and unflattering. Her once athletic legs were becoming spindly. She almost thought she could see a slight forward stoop to her usually ramrod posture. And there was no denying the widening waist, not to mention the increasingly matronly breasts. Once entirely bolstered by silicon, they now seemed to be producing unwanted amounts of padding all of their own accord.

As if this wasn't enough, she rounded the corner and found herself walking towards a lithe young woman in faded jeans, strappy sandals, and a pale Chanel-style jacket, not so different from the original Svetlana was wearing, but this girl had a vest top underneath, layers of fashionable slim gold necklaces, a row of ear cuffs and her hair tumbled all loose and bouncy and free, just as Svetlana's once had.

The pain of not being young any more, not being gorgeous any more, and not even really being *anyone* any more, washed over Svetlana. Lately, it felt as if she had lost so much and the best part of her life was now only visible in the rear-view mirror. Her triumphant beauty queen days, her glorious trophy wife days, the joy of being Mama to small children, and those magical days when she had felt the power of her glamour, her beauty and her wealth as soon as she had stepped into any room.

Where had it all gone?

Her boys didn't need her; Perfect Dress didn't take up much of her time; her investment manager took care of her money; Maria and some other staff members took care of the house; her fourth husband, Harry, was a barrister, not a billionaire gas baron, and he was currently wrapped up in a very important case.

* * *

As Svetlana walked on through the station towards her car, she couldn't help thinking about her approaching birthday. It wasn't a round number, but fifty-five still felt like a milestone, or maybe a millstone. Fifty-five... it was a big number. She had been lying about her age for so many years, she didn't think anyone else knew about this number, but maybe Harry suspected.

Now Svetlana thought of her own mother, who hadn't even made it to the age of fifty. She had been the most hard-working woman Svetlana would ever know; cooking, cleaning, planting, growing, picking, making, mending, carrying, for her daughter and for as many other families as would pay her to work for them. This was back in Svetlana's home country of Ukraine... yes, Ukraine, the country that was now war-torn and in the headlines every day. Svetlana thought of herself as Ukrainian, but her own father had been a Russian, and the father of her boys was Russian.

'*Tscha...*' she sighed to herself. Life was complicated enough, why couldn't people just try to get on with each other?

Freddy held the car door open for her and she eased herself into the comfortable back seat, noting with relief how good it felt to take the weight off her feet, but never mind, she was in no way ready to give up on high heels.

The car didn't pull off and Svetlana realised that Freddy was waiting patiently because she hadn't told him where they were going. Where was she going to go? What was she going to do with herself now that the summer holidays had well and truly ended?

As she thought of all the things she used to do and enjoy – clothes shopping, planning the new social season and the events she would attend, hostessing, taking care of the well-maintained Svetlana figure – the weeks and months stretched before her and felt empty and dull.

Even going back to the Mediterranean, which always used to make her so happy, did not appeal. She couldn't even tan like she used to. Sunshine now gave her age spots, freckles, moles and wrinkles.

She opened her handbag and pulled out a Chanel compact. In its small magnifying mirror, she scrutinised her face closely and very critically.

'We go to Berkeley Street, Freddy,' Svetlana decided.

Then she took out her phone and searched for the number of her favourite cosmetic surgeon.

5

L'Exercice – Exercise

I am not naturally sporty and I have never once been to the gym. Fortunately, I love to walk and in Paris, it is possible to walk everywhere. Daily walks allow you to get out into the world and interact with people and your surroundings. Walking up stairs and hills, walking somewhere green, and adding some simple yoga stretches to your day, will give you all the health and well-being boosts you need at no great effort and no cost.

— M.M.

* * *

'I think I'll have another Americano, please, hot milk on the side, my darlin'.' Annie lifted her sunglasses to make eye contact with the waitress and give her a smile.

If the waitress was thinking *'that will be your third large coffee'*, she didn't say it, just returned the smile, put Annie's empty cup on her tray and went off to get the fresh order.

Annie leaned back in her chair and looked out over one of her favourite shopping squares, just off the King's Road in London. From her outdoor café table vantage point, she was within a stone's throw of gorgeous clothes boutiques, plus a handful of edgy designer label stores, and she could watch the style setters walk by as she took careful note of trouser lengths, colours, clothing shapes and haircuts. There was also a stack of crisp new fashion magazines in front of her, so now and then she broke off from her careful study of people and the nearby shop windows, to leaf through the magazines, scroll her favourite sites, and try to absorb what was new and now and happening.

But somehow, despite the two coffees she'd already drunk, inspiration was not flowing. In the warm early September weather, the Chelsea shoppers were mostly clad in limp T-shirts and shorts, or summer dresses a season or two past their best, hair held up in ponytails. Plus, every third person who passed was a tourist, sweating in blue jeans, a black T-shirt and a grimy baseball cap.

Even worse, the busiest shop in the square wasn't the one selling bespoke, quilted, multi-coloured evening coats, or the Dutch designer with elegant silk clothes in every shade of neon in the window. No, the busiest shop in the square was the admittedly beautiful branch of chain store Zara, which had gone out of its way to appear classy and high-end, just as at home in this square as the labelly boutiques with the sky-high price tags.

She sighed and took a sip of the fresh coffee that had now been set down before her. This was a precious morning off, away from the twins, away from the house, and she had to focus, think, and come up with some inspirational new ideas for the TV show or... well, she didn't like to think about the 'or else'.

There was a time in Annie's life when she had had to work unrelentingly hard to support her oldest two children all by herself. It had involved a full-time job as a personal shopper in London's exclusive designer-only clothes haven, The Store, plus running around town in every spare moment on a variety of eBay-based and other side hustles.

Yes, she had been the original side-hustler. She'd been side-hustling before it was even a Thing.

Life now, with one added husband and two added twins, was still very busy, but she'd finally moved away from the desperate hustle of those former years and the ever-present fear that there would be nothing left to pay the bills, and she never, ever wanted to go back.

'*So, focus and think,*' she told herself, '*this is important... this is crucial. I need to save the series.*'

She pulled a new magazine out of her pile and opened it up. But ten minutes later, she slammed it down again in frustration. Wall-to-wall celebrities... Jennifer Aniston, Victoria Beckham, the Kardashians... what could she tell her viewers about those women?! It's easy to look amazing if you have a perfectly honed body – the product of hours of attention from your personal trainer and delightful nutritious meals from your personal chef – not to mention the five figures you can drop for every single item of clothing.

For a few brief moments, Annie allowed herself the fantasy of how she would look after months of attention from a trainer, a chef, and hundreds of thousands spent on her wardrobe. She would be able to waft around London in sparkling dresses, cashmere wraps, with envy-inducing handbags dangling from

her wrist... like a tiny, one-person, London episode of
And Just Like That.

But alas, she too was in a summer dress from,
ahem, M&S, that had seen better days. On the chair
beside her was the kind of lovely, but practical, capacious tote that held all the things a busy working
mother needed to hand and could cope with her pile
of magazines too. On her feet were sandals built for
tube journeys and all the brisk walking her day had
involved so far. And, whisper it, they were *comfort
soles... in a wide fit.*

She sighed and took another mouthful of coffee.

The last days of summer were so messy... prints,
patterns, clashing colours, bleached out, beachy hair,
raffia bags, tie-dye, trekking sandals (shudder...). It
made her long for an austere palette of plain colours...
simple clothes in restrained shades... cream knitwear,
pale caramel satin, pearl-grey... charcoal flannel, navy
canvas... crisp blue and white stripes.

Oh, now... could this be the beginning of an idea?
Navy silk blouses over pale, narrow woollen trousers.
Didn't everyone want narrow trousers again after all
that flapping about in baggy linen pants all summer?
After the riot of summer colours and styles, didn't
everyone long for the classics... tan handbags, black
leather heels, starchy white blouses?

And now inspiration was definitely coming as her ideas began to multiply. Chunky pearls, stiff trench coats, loafers with proper metal snaffles. There was something about the back-to-school mood of September that stoked the desire for classy, grown-up clothes.

She picked up her phone and began a deep search for:

classic clothes, classic dressers, classy looks,

and the internet consistently provided one heroine – actress Robin Wright in her *House of Cards* role as Claire Underwood. To be fair, the outfits from the later seasons got too grand and presidential for everyday wear, but the early season looks – her short, sharp hair, bracing white and blue shirts, perfect dark trousers, heels, trench coats, plus that incredible working woman's handbag. Wow... Annie could feel her heart beat a little faster.

This was definitely an idea... this could even be a whole episode. Right, she had to get her hands on some of these items right now. So, settling her coffee bill, Annie packed her magazines into her tote, slung it over her shoulder and hurried on her comfort-fit soles to the flagship branch of Zara.

* * *

As she flicked through the rails with a practised eye, her phone began to ring and seeing that it was her sister, Dinah, she answered.

'Hello, babes, you're catching me on a rare morning away from home,' Annie explained. 'How are you doing?'

'Oh... let me guess, are you in a lovely clothes shop planning a delightful little segment for the new series of the TV show?' Dinah teased.

'Close, but it's not quite like that. We've got to come up with box-fresh ideas for two knock-it-out-of-the-park new episodes in just a few weeks, so I'm rummaging through Zara with more than a hint of desperation. If I don't come up with something... we'll be toast.'

'Don't say that, Annie. You'll come up with something brilliant. I know you,' Dinah assured her. 'And don't stress yourself out. No one can be creative when they're frazzled. You should probably go home and lie in the bath surrounded by candles, breathing in aromatherapy oils, then it will all become clear.'

Annie snorted at the idea of this. 'Have you been to my home lately? It is not an oasis of calm, babes. With one teenage boy and two toddlers, we have tears, tantrums or vomiting just about every five minutes. And don't even mention the food shopping or the laundry! And there is no Ed now, Dinah! No Ed! He's only been away for four days and I already think I can't cope,' Annie admitted, half thinking, *surely, I'll get used to this, won't I?* But also thinking – *I don't want to get used to it... it's so much work.* And immediately the counter-thought: *I have to get used to it. I have to hold it all together, or we will completely come apart. Come on, I can do this. Maybe Dinah is right, maybe an aromatherapy bath will solve everything. Ha!*

'Oh... yes... I'd forgotten he was off already... is he having fun?' Dinah asked.

'Oh, I'm sure he's having such a good time, he probably can't even risk telling me how nice it is in case I die of jealousy. Anyway, first things first, how is Mum doing?'

Annie's mother, Fern, lived just outside London and was well looked after by her two daughters and two part-time carers, but she was on a gentle decline. Dementia was beginning to affect her more noticeably and arthritis was slowing her down.

'We had a lovely visit,' Dinah said. 'We went to the garden centre. We planted up a new window box for her. I made her some of her favourite things and stocked up the freezer. She really enjoyed having us around, especially Billie. You know how she spoils her and all the grandchildren.'

'And Billie does especially deserve to be spoiled,' Annie added fondly. Her nine-year-old niece had a special place in her heart.

'So, it was lovely and Mum is looking as well as you could hope. So, you'll go up next weekend?'

'Yes, that's the plan... now, what about you, any news on the new bathroom?'

'Due to start next week...' was Dinah's answer. 'It's going to be hell, isn't it?'

'Well...' Annie, veteran of many a home renovation, gave an encouraging, 'as long as it's over quickly.'

'But it's going to be so messy. There's some wall knocking down happening, not to mention re-siting of sewage pipes... I really don't want to think about re-siting sewage pipes.'

'No, best not, babes, best not. And remember, you can come and stay with us if it gets too intense.'

'I know and it's very nice of you, but you have quite enough going on.'

'Honestly, you can come, anytime. Just call me. I know what life-wrecking hell building work can be. Right...' Annie's eyes had homed in on exactly the kind of blouse she was looking for, straight and all business at the front, but with wide sleeves and an extravagant cuff over the wrists. Yes, that was the kind of classic she was talking about: classic but re-invented, re-imagined.

'OK, Annie, going to leave you to it, speak soon. Kiss, kiss,' and with that Dinah was off.

Annie's obsession with Marie Kondo had gradually faded, and she no longer tried to fold every one of the twins' 899 items of clothing into little envelopes, but she still couldn't help thinking of things 'sparking joy' when they were exactly right. And this blouse definitely sparked joy.

Annie took it from the rail, along with slim, cropped navy chinos, plus an oversized trench, plus the kind of narrow brown mock-croc belt that her mother might have in the wardrobe, along with a few other choice items and was just about to head to the changing room when her phone rang again.

'Oh, now what?' she hissed, juggling all the hangers so she could reply.

'Mum, there is nothing in the fridge. Nothing!' her seventeen-year-old constantly starving son, Owen, declared dramatically.

'Owen, there is bread in the usual place, there is ham in the Tupperware box, there are three kinds of cheese slices, there are pickles, tomatoes, carrots... there is even a tub of soup and a tub of crab pâté. I will be home in about forty-five minutes, so try to survive.'

Glancing at the time on the phone, she saw it was later than she'd thought. Damn, now the twins risked being brought back from their playdate ahead of her.

'Stay in the house,' she instructed Owen. 'Louise is bringing the twins home and if she arrives before me, you have to be there.'

'Muuuum!' Owen complained.

'Look, I'm leaving right now.' She walked towards the paying area and dumped her items untried into the clever holder which scanned all the barcodes for you. 'If the twins get there before me, you will be holding the fort for ten minutes max... you can do that for me, can't you?'

'S'pose,' came back the grudging mumble.

'Thank you. OK, go and make your lunch. You're probably just hangry.'

'S'pose,' came back again.

How had she managed to let the time run away like this? Work, Owen, the twins, running the house... Ed had only been away for four days and she already felt like the plates were spinning too fast.

* * *

Annie realised the long afternoon would not go down in the history of best hours of parenting, ever. The twins, worn out by their busy playdate, had refused all the lovely food concoctions that Annie had suggested from the fridge. In fact, one fromage frais was thrown against the kitchen wall by a vociferous Max because he had been expecting peach flavour and wanted to let her know how disgusted he was to get raspberry.

Throughout the fractious hours, Annie had to endure not just the whinging of the tired twins – sadly too old for an afternoon nap now – but also Owen insisting he had to put in 'some' xylophone practice ahead of meeting up with his friends. This meant Annie's afternoon was accompanied by two and a half hours of irritating plinking sounds as Owen muddled his way through various hits from *The Sound of Music*.

It was all very well having a musical husband and a musical son, but some days, *some* days, she would just like disco music to be blasting through the house and not hear one peep from the classical or school musical repertoire. OK, that wasn't entirely fair. Owen, as well as the guitar, violin and xylophone, also played electric guitar 'for lols' and was even in the first inklings of a band with friends from school. So there was some rock 'n' roll to be heard, but not a shred of disco.

When she finally had Minette and Max calmly settled on the glide path to bedtime with milk in sippy cups and a soporific episode of *Peppa Pig* playing in front of them, she nestled into the sofa beside them with her laptop, another coffee, and the idea of doing further research into:

fashion classics reinvented.

But that was when Owen bounded in and said, 'You haven't forgotten you're giving me a lift, have you?'

Annie looked back at him, part-incredulous, part-murderous. Owen's head with its mop of voluminous hair was only a few inches from reaching the top of the door these days. Every time she looked at him, she thought his legs and arms had grown another half inch and his shoulders had broadened further. Obviously, she was biased, but to her, he was growing heart-throb handsome. She saw some of her own features and colouring in his face and hair, but she also saw the elegant mouth and nose of her late husband, Roddy.

And for all these loving, maternal reasons, she couldn't even be cross with him, so just set her coffee down – half-caff with milk, in a bid to improve her sleep – and smiled.

'Yes,' she said, 'I did forget. But never mind, we'll

load M&M into the car and we'll get you over there. Unless there's any chance you could get there by—'

'There's no train near Dan's house,' Owen reminded her. 'I'd need to do two buses, which will take forever and I'm taking a cab home, so *we* agreed you'd give me a lift there.'

'Oh yes...'

Remnants of that conversation were vaguely coming back to her.

Looking at the twins, she knew she would have to employ some next-level Mummying to get them through this ordeal.

'OK, buddies...' she roused them from their sofa torpor, 'right... we're going on an adventure tonight. So, we're going to brush teeth, get you into pyjamas and then we're going in the car.'

Max perked up straight away at this suggestion. 'In the car, in the dark?' he asked.

'Yes, but only if you both brush your teeth and get into jammies.'

A twenty-five-minute hustle followed as the twins were brushed, changed, and strapped into their car seats. This was followed by the Owen leaving-the-house checklist:

'Phone?'

'Yup.'

'Wallet?'

'Yup.'

'With cards?'

He rolled his eyes. 'Yup.'

'Keys?'

'Yup.'

'Bag with all the musical/gaming essentials you want to take to your friends?'

'Yup.'

'Top-up phone charger?'

'Yup.'

'Are you sure, can you just show that to me?' she asked, weary of all the evenings she'd fretted herself almost to death because Owen had a dead phone and was completely unreachable.

Amazingly, Owen pulled the charger from the depths of his rucksack. 'Ta-dah!' he announced.

'Water bottle?'

'Mum! This is north London not the Sahara Desert. I do not need a water bottle!' he protested. 'I'll have a drink when I'm thirsty, like a normal person.'

'OK,' she conceded, and to be fair, carrying a topped-up water bottle was a level of organisation she struggled with, so probably a bit much to ask of Owen.

Of course, she sincerely hoped that there was a day in the future when she would not have to do all this thinking and remembering for him. Meanwhile, as she tried to wait patiently for that day, she would carry on with all her reminders and the checklist in a bid to avoid repeats of all those: 'I don't have my keys'; 'I didn't take my wallet'; 'I took my wallet, but then my card wasn't in it'; mini-disasters.

Just as she was about to throw her phone into her handbag, it buzzed with a message... oh, from Ed. She couldn't help herself from opening it straight away, happy that he was thinking of her.

Never eating onion soup again... the gas!

The phone dropped into her handbag. Not the kind of message she was hoping for.

Right, time to turn the ignition on the big people carrier and head through the busy roads to Owen's friend's home.

Every now and then, Annie glanced at the twins in the rear-view mirror. They weren't asleep but they were both relaxed and looking out of the windows, lulled by the warmth and the soothing motion of the car. Oh yes, she would transfer them straight to bed when she got home and then sink back into the sofa, this time with a large glass of the rosé currently chilling in the fridge. Perfect.

'Wow, Dad's been posting on Insta,' Owen said, eyes on the screen, thumb hovering to scroll onwards.

'Has he? What's he posted?' This was just so unusual. A post from Ed usually came around five times a year – either a child's birthday cake or 'Happy holidays' photo of the Christmas tree.

Owen flicked his practised thumb over the screen. 'Paris street, Paris street, Paris river, Eiffel Tower from very far away, Paris street, Paris café...' his tone was bored, clearly none of these photos were of any interest to him, but then he added, 'Hot French babe, Paris street, hot French babe.'

'What?! Are you joking?' Annie demanded.

'No, look,' Owen said and turned the phone towards his mother. 'Who do you think she is? Someone from the school he's at?'

Annie glanced over, catching only one of those dark, chic French bobs, smooth young cheeks and a red-lipsticked smile.

'Yes, of course, someone from the school... probably showing him the sights,' was her reply, delivered completely nonchalantly.

But really, she had no idea why she was feeling a slight bubble of panic. This was Ed, she reminded herself. Ed who absolutely loved her, and his family, and his home life and his job. Ed was relaxed, contented, immune surely to the charms of any foxy French babe? And why shouldn't he enjoy a night out in Paris with a lovely colleague? No doubt he'd phone later and tell her all about it.

'Just show me again,' Annie said, spotting the light ahead turning amber, so she knew she'd have a moment or two at the red light to look a little longer.

'Here we go.' Owen turned his phone again.

Chic bob, luscious lips, warm brown eyes, she *was* lovely... late twenties, early thirties maybe... but why on earth was this photo taken so close up? Just how close had her husband got to this gorgeous French girl?

'Muuuum!' Owen exclaimed.

Annie snapped her eyes back to the road, just in time to see the bumper of the car in front rush into view. She jammed on the brakes.

6

Un Certain Âge – Middle Age

In France, it is absolutely acceptable, even expected, to continue to be beautiful, fashionable and well-groomed through middle age and into old age. Older French women do not become invisible. Perhaps, the opposite. Their lipstick is a little brighter, their accessories a little bolder. What is the reason? Positive self-esteem, boosted by the compliments and charming flirtations that are a part of life here. Do we have more lovers? We are not telling.

— M.M.

* * *

Mr Phillippe Fournier, consultant plastic surgeon, sat directly in front of Svetlana in the grand drawing room of her house in Mayfair. It turned out, even if you were one of his favourite clients, you couldn't just glide into his Berkeley Street office any more because his schedule was far too packed.

So, instead, Mr Phillippe had offered to come to Svetlana's home as soon as they could find a convenient time. So now, he was seated just a foot or so away from her as the Anglepoise light he'd set up on an occasional table beside them glared harshly onto her face. He was silent as he made his long and thorough professional assessment.

'The jaw line and the neck are the areas where we could make small but significant improvements...' he said. 'Do you mind if I use my pen to explain? The marks will come off very easily with cleanser.'

'Of course,' Svetlana agreed.

Mr Phillippe drew a curved line to show where he would create an opening along her jaw, then explained how the loose skin would be removed and where the minute stitching would be hidden.

'The mid-section lift we did all those years ago is holding up beautifully and I know the little-and-often

Botox on your forehead and round your eyes has kept all the deep wrinkling at bay.' As he said this, he drew two small lines between her eyebrows and a semi-circle on the side of each eye. 'And we've used regular doses of filler for the chin and nasolabial lines.' These words were accompanied by pen strokes down the offending lines and a semi-circle under her lip.

'It's all looking very good,' he said, admiring his own handiwork. 'You're a wonderful advert for my art. A mini jaw and neck lift will work even further wonders. You're such a very beautiful woman, Ms Wisnetski, I understand absolutely that you would like to maintain that beauty through the years ahead.'

'*Ja...*' Svetlana said gently. Mr Phillippe was always so empathetic. She was not a woman who liked to show her vulnerabilities, but she believed that Mr Phillippe understood perfectly that Svetlana's face had been her fortune for decade after decade, and she wasn't going to give in to looking old and haggard anytime soon.

Plus, she hoped that maybe if she looked 'fresher', she would also feel better and some of this mental dreariness would lift.

'And while you're under anaesthetic, are there any other areas you would like us to work on?' Mr Phillippe asked lightly. 'And please understand, there's nothing to my eye that needs work, but I know how exacting you are. So if there was anything else you wanted to discuss...'

'I need a breast reduction,' she said matter-of-factly, 'and after all this time spent building the breasts up...'

As she looked down at her increasingly ample cleavage, Mr Phillippe turned a professional eye to the area.

'They are growing,' she added. 'I'm laying down fat like a goose before Christmas.'

'Most likely hormonal,' was the surgeon's explanation. 'Do you take HRT?'

At this Svetlana gave an audible gasp.

Mr Phillippe was asking if she took HRT... Mr Phillippe was suggesting that she might be *menopausal*. As a woman who was used to passing for ten years younger than her biological age, this came as something of a shock. But, of course, she reminded herself, Mr Phillippe knew her real age, so maybe she was wrong to be so surprised.

But she didn't want to take HRT because this would be admitting that she *was* menopausal and that would be close to admitting that she was becoming old.

'No,' she said firmly.

'Something to discuss with your physician,' Mr Phillippe said, 'but some women find when their hormonal balance is restored, their fat distribution stabilises once again. Let's book in a pre-surgical appointment at the clinic. We can compare the size you are now with sizes you've been in the past and decide what will be the most proportional look for you, Ms Wisnetski. Now,' his eye moved downwards to her tanned and muscular legs, elegantly crossed at the ankles, 'we've been doing some wonderful things with sagging knee skin, but absolutely no need for that kind of work here. Amazing muscle tone. Am I allowed to know what kind of workouts you're doing?'

'Of course,' Svetlana smiled at the compliment, 'kickboxing, trampolining, parallel bars and when I am lazy, I do wall Pilates. I think I could still squeeze someone to death with my thighs,' she added darkly, happy to leave Mr Phillippe guessing as to whether or not she'd ever had to resort to this.

'Very well,' she continued, 'we do a full appointment at your clinic and make a decision there about the breasts. How soon you can do this work? And how long will recovery time be?' she asked because she already felt impatient to be there, out on the other side of Mr Phillippe working his wonders.

The plastic surgeon took his phone from the inner pocket of his suit jacket and consulted his schedule.

'Nothing for a few weeks,' he said, 'but if you can be available at short notice, I can put you on my priority list.'

Svetlana gave him her most winning smile. 'This is perfect. I will speak to your office tomorrow to book in the pre-surgical appointment. Then we will do the surgery as soon as possible.'

'Marvellous,' Mr Phillippe enthused, 'I so look forward to working on your beautiful face once again. It really is a masterpiece of nature meets art.'

'Thank you,' Svetlana said, but now she found herself thinking of the surgery and the anaesthetic, and the bandaging, and the special creams and massages for scar recovery, then the dark glasses and scarves until it was all fully healed. It all felt much less exciting than usual. In fact, it felt like quite a bother.

Pull yourself together, she told herself.

* * *

Svetlana's long-standing and long-suffering housekeeper, Maria, had only just shown Mr Phillippe out of the room to guide him down the long, curved staircase to the front door when Svetlana saw a troubling message on her phone.

> New dress material here. Not what we ordered.
> Supplier refuses to help!! What now? Any advice? I don't want to bring Bradley into this. E

E was Elena, Svetlana's adult daughter, who along with Bradley, the new CEO, ran their fashion business Perfect Dress from a pocket-sized office in New York. Elena was fearsomely competent for a young woman still in her twenties, but every now and then, when a major headache problem cropped up, she often turned to Svetlana first, so as not to lose face in front of Bradley.

Svetlana typed quickly:

> Give me details and I make follow-up call to supplier. If this does not work, we bring in just one, low-key, but effective NY lawyer. Saul who did our business paperwork will be best.

Not long afterwards, Svetlana had the details and was at her burr walnut desk, facing out onto the Mayfair residents' garden that her townhouse overlooked, as she made the call.

As she had suspected, it was quite straightforward to make the supplier see sense. 'Why would you want to irritate us?' she asked calmly. They were going to be customers for years, she assured him. Plus, they had a much wider social media presence than his company and far more publicity connections – it would only cause trouble if Perfect Dress complained publicly that he had let them down and his company's service was terrible. There was nothing to gain from this. But if he sent the correct fabric, as had been agreed, there were only win-wins ahead.

'Is no big deal,' Svetlana said, 'you bring the new fabric in your truck, you take back the other material and sell it to someone else. No problem.'

'But it's been cut to order,' was the last defence offered.

'Pah, it's been cut into a 100-metre piece. You sell this piece to someone else.'

'I'll have to sell it at a discount,' he protested.

'Hmmm... wait one moment, Mr Jones.' Now Svetlana quickly fired a message over to Elena:

If you get material you want, would you also like this other material at discount? What would be good price?

It took just a few seconds for the reply to arrive:

Anything under $1,000 could work. I mean, I don't love it... but for that price, we could do something with it.

'So, Mr Jones,' Svetlana went back to the supplier, 'how about you send the material that was requested. And we keep this other material also and pay you $600 for it.'

There was a silence as Mr Jones assessed the new offer.

'$750,' he countered.

For a moment, Svetlana considered haggling, but this was a good offer. If she offered $50 less, it might just annoy him and make him change his mind.

'Done,' she said, just as she heard the front door opening below her window and Maria hurrying to greet Harry, Svetlana's husband, as he came home from work. 'Good to do business with you,' she said.

'Likewise,' he replied, 'and hopefully, we won't have a mix-up like this again.'

'No,' she agreed and then added, exaggerating her Eastern European accent, 'or I squeeze you to death with my thighs.'

There was a pause.

'Just my little joke,' Svetlana said lightly.

Her simple message to Elena was:

All done. You keep that fabric for $750. The new fabric you wanted is coming in two days. Speak later.

'Harry,' she called out from her desk, 'come upstairs and see me.'

Svetlana and her barrister husband, Harry, had been married for four years now. They had met when she was fighting her divorce battle with the father of her children and one of the most powerful men in the Eastern European oil and gas business, Igor Wisnetski. Barrister Harry, one of London's most sought-after legal minds, especially when it came to multi-million-pound divorce cases, had first of all landed Svetlana an enormous divorce settlement that included an enormous lump sum, plus her house in Mayfair and a holiday property in the south of France. Then after several attempts by Igor to seize control of the boys and their education, Harry had negotiated a ceasefire by pointing out how much wiser it was to remain on excellent terms with the mother of your children, than to begin a lifelong campaign of battles, war games and attack.

As a result, both sides had agreed they would regularly discuss custody, holiday and educational
arrangements for their boys in a civilised and grown-
up way. And whenever they couldn't decide, they
would bring in an agreed mediator. So, in the years
since their divorce, Svetlana and Igor had become
much better parents and friends than they had ever
been during their tumultuous marriage. In fact, Igor
had even offered to remarry Svetlana, but by then, she
had fallen in love.

It hadn't been Harry's intention to bowl Svetlana
over, but his sensible, grown-up approach to everything, his restrained English gentleman charm, his
tall, fit, late-fifties physique, honed on the tennis court
and cricket pitch, his exquisite tailoring, his love of the
countryside, his care and kindness for her when it felt
as if everything she knew was collapsing and everyone
she'd relied on was abandoning her, were the reasons
she had been bowled over and had decided he was
going to be her final husband. She had all the money
she would ever need and Harry would be the man
who would look after her, make sure no one ever
tricked or took advantage of her again, and be the husband who would finally make her properly English.

What Svetlana wanted, Svetlana almost always got.
So, once she turned her full-beam attention on the

pinstriped, bowler-hatted, legal Batman Harry, the lacklustre marriage he'd been in for years didn't stand a chance. But, in line with his lifelong philosophy, Harry's own divorce was as low-key, civilised and grown-up as he could possibly have hoped for. His marriage to Svetlana had happened soon afterwards.

Now, Svetlana stood up, smiled and walked towards the drawing room door, expecting Harry to come in and take her into his arms with the words, 'Hello, my darling wife,' just as he usually did whenever he came home.

Instead, he stepped into the room, took one look at her and gasped. 'Svetlana, what's happened to your beautiful face?'

Svetlana glanced at the ornate, gold-framed mirror on the drawing room wall and saw all the black pen lines left by Mr Phillippe, which she had completely forgotten to remove.

Knowing exactly what Harry would think about her having another round of plastic surgery, Svetlana said quickly, 'Oh this? This is nothing, my darling. I go and wash it off now.'

But he came up close and understood the significance of the markings straight away.

'I adore your face,' he said, putting his fingers under her chin and kissing her gently on the lips. 'I know your true age and I love you. I don't want you to let anyone carve you up any more than you've already been carved up.'

'Oh, Harry...' she felt caught off guard by those words: *I know your true age and I love you.* Svetlana had spent the past thirty years fighting the ageing process and paying a heavy price for the inevitable failure to remain twenty-five forever. So those words meant a great deal.

Still, she wasn't ready to throw in the towel just yet. 'Thank you, Harry, but it is my face, my money, my decision!'

7

LA DIFFÉRENCE – DIFFERENCE

Never be afraid to wear a successful item or outfit over and over again, maybe with a twist. Try it with a different hairstyle, lipstick, jewellery, handbag or scarf. Vive les accessories!

— M.M.

* * *

Annie collapsed in a heap onto her sofa and wondered if it was too early to make another cup of coffee. Yup, she checked her phone, 9.42 a.m., a third coffee now would cause that panicky anxious feeling that would in turn have to be quelled with the rest of that packet of jammy dodger biscuits that she had bought yesterday thinking, *these are strictly for Owen and the twins, not one single jammy dodger will pass my lips.* But so far, seven jammy dodgers had disappeared, and neither Owen nor the twins had been involved.

The twins had gone to their childminder at eight this morning and although this was precious, child-free time when Annie was supposed to be working, she'd fallen so behind on her household chores that she'd done a lightning supermarket run on her way back from dropping the twins off, and then dashed around the house, sweeping a floor here, swiping at a toilet there, putting clothes back into cupboards, toys back into toy boxes, screaming in horror at the size of Owen's laundry pile, so had put one wash on and lined up another three.

Now, she had exactly three hours to focus on the TV programme and all the exciting new ideas she was supposed to come up with. Instead, she was lying in a heap in some dodgy old sweatpants and a worn-out T-shirt scrolling through Ed's sparse Instagram account and clocking the appearance, once again, of his gorgeous, young, raven-haired, French teaching colleague. Yes, there she was, this time rocking a blue and

white, cotton, nautical top with a jaunty little red neck-
erchief. And lo and behold, did the red of said necker-
chief not exactly match her lipstick? And look at that
slight off-the-shoulder tilt to her oversized raincoat.
And the cut of her jeans so perfect, she may actually
have had them tailored. Truly, this woman was a
styling genius.

'Oh... Sylvie MontClaire?' Ed had said breezily
when Annie had asked him on their call last night
about this vision of French style personified. 'Yeah...
she's one of the other music teachers. She's so sweet.
She doesn't live far from where I am, so she's showed
me round. Told me where to score the best baguettes
and, oh, the cheese shop! I'm going to have to put in a
lot of cycling time to work off all the Camembert and
Reblochon.'

'And what instruments does *she* play?' had been
Annie's follow-up question, because Ed wasn't going to
distract her so easily with tales of his latest cheese
ecstasy.

'Instruments? Who... oh, Sylvie... she's strictly
strings, so guitar, viola and best of all the cello. When
she plays that, it's very special. She's completely im-
mersed. She and her cello... they make astonishing
music together.'

Annie could hear the admiration in Ed's voice as

she pictured Mademoiselle Sylvie creating the captivating music to lure her husband away with one beautiful French thigh on either side of an antique cello. Good grief, this was much worse than she could ever have imagined.

'And does Sylvie have a boyfriend, partner... significant other?' Annie had asked hopefully.

'Oh... I don't know,' had been Ed's disarmingly innocent reply. Oh bless Ed. He still seemed blissfully unaware that he could be attractive to anyone other than her.

Then he had ruined it slightly by adding, 'I'm sure someone like her won't be single for long.'

So now Annie was trawling the internet for Sylvie MontClaire and had found her Instagram account, private, her LinkedIn account, very professional, plus many, many photographs of her taken at concerts, school events, and one particularly pretty picture taken at what looked like a school picnic out in the countryside.

No 'significant other' appeared in any of the images Annie could find, just beautiful, beautiful friends and this was something of a worry. Because she did detect something just a little lit-up about the way Sylvie looked in the recent photos Ed had taken. Yes, this gorgeous, musically gifted young woman had definitely been just a little too happy when she was smiling at Annie's husband.

Annie looked down at herself in her T-shirt and sweatpants ensemble. She remembered that upstairs in her bedroom was the bag of Zara clothes, still untried. Really, she needed to take her own best advice and get out of these comfy, worn-out house clothes and into something much more morale boosting.

* * *

So, Annie took herself upstairs, stripped to her underwear and tipped her haul of Zara 'classics' out of the bag. One smart white shirt-blouse, one pair of tailored navy trousers, a beige trench coat, a pale-blue shirt, a boxy navy-blue cardigan, plus the slim belt and small hooped earrings that were gold-coloured and much more restrained in size than she would usually wear.

On went the white shirt, the trousers, the cardigan, coat, earrings and she scoured her wardrobe for a 'classics' type shoe. At the back she found the kind of low-heeled black pump that she must have worn on days when her feet were killing her at the end of a long shift at The Store.

She looked down at herself. This looked promising. Everything fitted, in fact, everything, bar the trouser waistband, was quite voluminous. Plus, she did feel pulled together and calm and grown-up. This could definitely work. This could be the new image, no more skirts and dresses in bright and garish colours, no more crazy heels, no more worrying about which shade of tights would match the vibrant dress. This could be her from now on, pulled-together, calm, grown-up, in charge. The kind of woman who didn't try to do absolutely everything all at once to an impossible deadline. No, the wearer of this smart and sensible look delegated things to her nanny, or even her PA.

Annie walked towards the generous, full-length mirror on the last door of the bedroom's fitted cupboards for her big reveal. She was quite excited and already planning the kind of sober and sensible handbag that should accompany this look. Something black maybe. Good grief, when had she last owned a black handbag? Black?! Black was city stockbroker, serious lawyer, headmistress kind of territory. Was she really ready to go there?

Right, here was the mirror. Time for the moment of truth. Her eyes fixed on her own reflection and she looked... and looked again.

The woman in front of her was not any kind of embodiment of sophisticated Claire Underwood. The woman in the mirror looked like the very sensible type who shops at M&S and works in accounts. Maybe it was the shoes... Annie went back to her cupboard and tried on a range of different heels. It improved matters slightly, but not enough to convince her this was any kind of new look for her. She looked dull and completely square – her waist had disappeared and the trousers did nothing for the shapely legs that were one of her favourite features.

She pushed the raincoat off one shoulder slightly, as Sylvie had done in that charming photo. But now Annie just looked like she'd left the house in too much of a hurry to put her own coat on properly.

Oh God... now what?

She sat down on the bed.

She couldn't do a whole episode on the classics if this was going to be the result. She imagined creating a whole line of ladies who looked like they worked in accounts. No offence to anyone who worked in accounts, of course. Where would she be without the long-suffering Mr Leyton, whose job it was to organise her box of assorted receipts and invoice chaos every year, about two days before the very final Inland Revenue deadline.

Annie picked up her phone and scrolled through

Ed's photos again. Just how exactly did Sylvie do it? How did she, and every other French female Annie had ever encountered, take perfectly ordinary items – black slash-neck top, raincoat, pair of jeans – and transform them into this whole 'I'm-sexy-and-I-know-it, but I'm-really-not-trying' thing?

She typed French style into the search menu and up came images of endlessly chic women doing such clever things with blue blazers, white shirts, ballet pumps and grey cardigans.

Meanwhile she, in her blue trousers, white shirt and blue cardigan, looked like a complete frump.

She took in the French icons on her screen: Audrey Tatou, Brigitte Bardot, Carine Roitfeld, Charlotte Gainsbourg, Coco Chanel, of course. Ah, Coco Chanel, surely she was worthy of one entire episode of *How To Be Fabulous* devoted just to her and her alone?

How To Be Fabulous goes French... French style, French designers, French women. And now Annie could feel the creative rush coming over her again... pulse quickening, a smile beginning to spread across her face. True French style... *How to be Fabulously French*... what about two entire episodes set, where else, but in Paris? Interviewing the important style icons, of course, visiting those legendary boutiques and designers, speaking to everyday fabulously put-together women on the street, tracking down the insider addresses. That could be completely wonderful, beautiful.

They could unearth all those French beauty secrets and find those French make-up staples. Who wouldn't want to find out about all those strange anti-cellulite massages and electrode-enhanced facials that Parisians were supposed to swear by. And they could visit tiny Paris scarf shops, offbeat jewellers, poke about flea markets for vintage Hermès clutches... it would be glorious, inspirational.

And really, not so much of a budget stretch for the TV company, surely?

If she did all the legwork first, lined up exactly where to go, who to speak to, even got in some little offbeat phone video interviews in first that could be cut in with the official filming. They would only need to send over a small crew to get the footage done within a few days. Surely HTBF could stretch to that? Especially once all the funding was put in place because this was such a great idea.

French style, Paris style was huge – always had been, would always be. Wasn't *Emily in Paris* the entire world's guilty viewing pleasure. Even the latest UK prime minister had admitted that when fighting inflation and trying to make Brexit better all got a bit much, he liked to put his feet up and watch Emily stroll through Le Marais in a puffy couture minidress and impossible heels, mispronouncing everything.

And Emily's chef love interest was, *naturellement*, dreamy.

But anyway.

Vive la France!

Now, OK, first things first, how on earth was she going to be able to make this happen? Owen would obviously have to stay here in London while she went on a big French style fact-finding mission, because of school and the all-important final year. But maybe Dinah and her family, what with all the bathroom trouble, might like to move in for a couple of weeks, just to make sure Owen was OK and regularly fed.

The twins would have to come with her. So, could she perhaps find a French nanny to look after them during her working hours? And that would be so exciting for the twins... going to those adorable little play parks in Paris, learning some French words, eating baguette and proper fromage frais. Within moments, her fingers were at the keyboard, tapping in:

French nanny

And:

Nannies in Paris.

After some dubious images appeared that weren't what she was after at all, up popped a promising-sounding website which offered to match you with nannies all over the world, according to your:

global needs.

Amazing! Yes, she definitely had global needs.

So, now, she just needed to get Tamsin on the phone and convince her what an awesome idea this was going to be. And then she would be all set for a wonderful, full-fashion adventure in one of the best cities in the world.

Well, of course... there was just the one other hurdle.

And then all those phrases Ed had used before he'd gone away came into her mind:

'I'm a bit desperate to do something just for myself.'

'A reset, a refresh.'

'A chance to really focus on what I do and get even better at it.'

'Distraction-free time.'

'Grown-up time.'

'I think it's really important to do this for me... and for us as a couple too.'

'We should be pleased that we've got this chance to be apart for a while, so we can really appreciate one another when we get back together.'

Yes, Ed had very much wanted to be in Paris by himself, on his own terms, so that he could focus on the job he loved and the music he loved.

It was going to be hard to convince him that what he really needed in his wonderful grace and favour apartment, right in the heart of La Rive Gauche, was his wife and their two young twin children... even for a few weeks. Especially as he'd only just arrived.

Yes, it was going to be extremely difficult to convince him. But the more she thought about the possibilities for *How To Be Fabulously French*, the more convinced she became that she would have to give it her very best shot. And she hardly wanted to admit it to herself, but maybe she would quite like to be around and check up on him, especially when she considered the multiple charms of Mademoiselle lit-up Sylvie.

8

LES HÉROS – HEROES

What are the five hardest-working items in my wardrobe? My trench coat because it can be worn in almost every circumstance. My white cotton shirt, for the same reason. My black silk blouse, which dresses everything up. My pale grey trousers, which suit me, not the fashion of the moment. And my navy polo shirt in a fine knitted fabric. What are your wardrobe heroes?

— M.M.

* * *

'Annie! Well done. I really like this idea. I love Paris! I love Paris style, beauty, French icons,' Tamsin said down the line once she'd heard Annie's animated pitch to set the new two episodes in the city, 'but we will have to be very focused, very structured about what we do there. The only way to bring that within budget is to have a strict timetable for the film crew. Everything will have to be lined up, the filming destinations planned to be close together, so no time is wasted in between shoots.'

'OK, I am all ears,' Annie replied. 'I can go over for research, do the prep work, the initial interviews, plenty of off-the-cuff phone videos, then work with the production team to set up the filming in October.'

'Ideally, we need at least one interview with a big-name actress, maybe, and one with a fashion icon. We need people who the audience will recognise or at least quickly appreciate, once they're introduced. I mean, someone like Carine Roitfeld would be amazing. She's not a household name, but people will quickly understand she's a former French *Vogue* editor and a total fashion legend. But, Annie, we do need someone famous... and that won't be easy.'

'Right...' Annie's mental wheels were already turning, 'two big-name interviews... then...'

Tamsin went on. 'I love the idea of visiting those

legendary stores – the Chanel boutique, the Karl Lagerfeld store – but again, it is not easy to get film access there. And I love your small, "secret" addresses idea, that should be a lot less challenging to arrange. I also love the plan to do interviews with *Parisiennes* on the street. They can talk us through their outfit, their favourite lipsticks... all that kind of detail that I know you and the viewers love.'

'Agreed,' Annie said, 'I'm so looking forward to that.'

'We need the beauty angle, too, some insider info from those beauty spa addresses where women get pummelled with needles and special masques, massages and whatnot. You probably need to be our guinea pig for all that.'

'I can't wait,' Annie said, a little bit of microneedling and spa massaging sounded like absolute bliss.

'So, basically, you need to go over there, ASAP, and you said you had somewhere to stay that won't cost the production budget anything?' Tamsin asked, sounding very relieved at this.

'Correct...' *-ish*, Annie added under her breath, as this wasn't going to be an entirely straightforward arrangement. She hadn't discussed it with Ed yet, as there didn't seem to be any point in raising the whole controversial topic with him until she'd known if Tamsin was going to go for the idea or not.

'Well, free accommodation for you in Paris is an amazing help to us,' Tamsin added. 'I don't need to tell you that. So, the next step is for you to go over there, do all this research and get everything set up – my assistant, the film crew, whoever else you need to talk to or need to make calls and arrangements for you, will be available to you, of course. Then when filming proper starts in October, we need to go back to Paris, arrangements all in place, with you and the crew, and get everything wrapped up in as few days of shooting as we can possibly get away with. And I'm warning you, there will be no frills on our side – you may be travelling back to Paris in the film crew's van.'

'Oh, the glamour of being on TV. If only people knew!' But Annie said this with a smile because, really, she loved all of it – from stepping into addresses you'd never otherwise be invited to, talking to people who would never otherwise talk to you, to slumming it with the film crew in 'cost efficient' hotels and bonding over pints in the bar after a long day's filming. And, as far as she could see, it was always a long day filming. When she was *on*, she was very *on* – fourteen, sixteen, even eighteen-hour days were the norm – when she was *off*, she was only *off* for a bit before coming up with new ideas for the next season began to take over. Still, she loved it and there was no other job she'd rather do.

So, the plan for these episodes in Paris had to be fantastic, had to blow the mind of the bigger bosses higher up the chain and ensure the funding for the new series was put in place, securing this season and, hopefully, paving the way for the next one too.

'I will talk to everyone who needs to be in the loop,' Tamsin added, already sounding like the brisk and totally focused producer Annie knew she was. 'We'll come back to you with a skeleton plan. Meanwhile, Annie, you need to get over there and start researching. Good luck, keep me totally updated!'

'Right! Thanks! It's going to be amazing!' Annie said, and she really did believe this, despite the family obstacles and very hard work that she knew it would involve.

* * *

As Annie ended the call, she looked around the kitchen. The room was somehow not the welcoming haven of deliciousness that it was when Ed was at home. The sink area was cluttered with items, washed and unwashed, that she'd not yet had time to deal with. Ed's windowsill herb garden was looking a little worse for wear, as she just couldn't remember to water things with so much else going on... or maybe she had overwatered? Herbs were so unreasonably sensitive! The twins' toys were all over the counter and the floor, plus there was a breadboard, loaf of bread, scattering of crumbs and un-lidded mayonnaise jar out, clear evidence that Owen had drifted in to make a vast sandwich and had drifted out again.

She sincerely hoped he hadn't eaten any of the quiche that she was planning to serve them all for supper – an easy, but possibly not extremely popular, choice.

Right, she needed to go and prise her babies from the TV so they could do a bracing walk and park playtime to make sure to burn off all excess energy that might otherwise convert into squabbles, standoffs and other dramas. Although, it was always a fine, fine line between pleasantly tired-out children and exhausted, tantrumy wrecks, who had to be coaxed with all the skills of a hostage negotiator from buggy to supper to bath and then bed.

OK... to the park... she urged herself on, *buy coffee on way to park. Then home, then feed children, then bath the minis and put in bed, then tackle Ed. This is the plan.*

Ed... she felt a flicker of anxiety. He wasn't going to like it, but he would have to be persuaded.

* * *

Except much later, when she was parked on the sofa with a second glass of rosé for courage, she couldn't get a reply from Ed. Not on WhatsApp or on text and he wouldn't pick up.

Never mind, she put the TV on to soften the din of Owen's music practice, and several refresher episodes of *Emily in Paris* later, 'for research purposes', she tried Ed again.

Still no reply.

It was 10 p.m., 11 p.m. in Paris and On A School Night... talking of which, she went out into the corridor and shouted up the stairs: 'Owen, it's bedtime and please tell me you've done all your homework?'

'Yes, Muuuum,' came the reply.

'Owen?'

After a moment or two, Owen's head appeared from behind his bedroom door.

'If I took the twins to Paris for a couple of weeks—'

'And left me here?' A grin began to spread across Owen's face.

'And asked Auntie Dinah, Uncle Bryan and your cousin Billie to move in,' Annie added quickly.

'Oh...' the face fell.

'Owen... you're seventeen! I'm not going to leave

you home alone for two, possibly three weeks. I wasn't born yesterday.'

'Yeah... well, I was just thinking how much band practice we could do without having to keep the noise down.'

'We do have neighbours,' Annie reminded him. 'And they do not seem to be huge fans of the drums, the electric guitar, or even the xylophone.'

'True...'

'So, could you handle Dinah and family living here with you?'

'S'pose...' Owen shrugged. 'Couldn't I come to Paris?'

'School... important exam year,' Annie reminded him, 'plus big decision about what to do after school – imminent.'

'S'pose... what about I get one weekend of pure, unlimited band practice before Dinah and Bryan arrive? With no nagging about homework, bedtime and keeping the noise down? That seems fair, Mum, if you and the twins are off to Paris.'

Once again, the skills of a hostage negotiator were going to be required.

'I will think about it, OK? Now off to bed and you know the rules, phone outside, charging in the hall.'

'Yes, ma'am.'

Annie went back to the sofa and searched for Ed's phone's whereabouts to come up on the family phone locator. Oh, there it was! He was on the move in a street not far from his flat. So, she watched and waited as the phone dot made its way back to Ed's base.

She gave him a few minutes to settle in and then she pressed redial.

When he answered, she paused for a moment before saying in her warmest, huskiest tone, 'Hello, handsome.'

His immediate response was a suspicious, 'Uh-oh... what have you done? Or, what are you about to do?'

'Ed!' she complained, but she was already thinking, *drat! He knows me too well.* 'Tell me about your evening. What have you been up to?' she asked instead.

A glowing description of an evening of bar-hopping from jazz club to jazz club with 'colleagues' followed.

'So, who were you out with?' she couldn't help herself from asking.

'Pretty much the whole music staff – Bertrand, Sylvie, Martin and Rosalie – they're all really good fun...'

Out with Sylvie and friends again, Annie noticed, of course.

'Fortunately, they speak much better English than I do French,' Ed went on, 'but I'm trying... I'm learning. *Bonsoir monsieur, je voudrais un voulez-vous cocktail,*' he told her with a laugh.

'Very good.'

'Strongest cocktail I've ever drunk,' he added, 'even if you did want to *voulez-vous*, you wouldn't be able to after two of those. Anyway, what's happening with you? Are Owen and the twins surviving your cooking?'

'Ha, ha!' she said, although she knew this was one of Ed's biggest concerns. 'We've been enjoying some lovely children's menu classics – fish fingers and peas, fried egg and chips, scrambled egg and toast... it's been going totally fine.'

Ed didn't need to know about tonight's Great Quiche Rebellion, which had ended with Max claiming he'd eaten the offending item, only for Annie to later find it crammed into both pockets of his shorts. How he'd managed to do that without Minette noticing and ratting him out, Annie still did not know.

She'd had to give him a sobering little chat about how she would rather have kept the piece of quiche in the fridge for Owen to eat later and how difficult it was to wash oily cheese stains out of shorts.

'Good to hear,' Ed said. 'I do miss you all. I really do,' he added and there was a wistful note to his voice, which sounded promising enough for Annie to take heart and begin with, 'So Tamsin and I have been brainstorming ideas for the new series. And it's pretty serious, Ed. We've got to come up with something brilliant. There is so much competition out there, so many great TV programmes competing for the funding and the viewers. So, we've come up with something really fresh...'

'You say "we", but I bet it's you,' Ed added, and she couldn't help smiling because he was always rooting for her, her number one fan.

'Yes, it was mainly me,' she admitted, then decided maybe it would be best to just come on out with it, get it over with, so she blurted, 'And we think it would be incredible to film some episodes in Paris. So, she wants me to go over... well, as soon as possible... and get the research and the prep work done.'

There was a momentary silence as Ed, no doubt, tried to digest this news.

'Come to Paris?' he asked. 'As soon as possible?'

She tried to read the emotion in his voice. Was he pleased? Excited? Annoyed? Surprised? She couldn't tell... well, OK, she could certainly hear that he wasn't exactly jumping up and down with joy.

'Yes... so, what do you think about that?' she ventured. 'I mean, I would be coming to stay with you, obviously. I would bring the twins. And that would mean a part-time nanny... Owen would need to stay behind for school, but Dinah and Bryan might be able to move in with him because they have a messy bathroom remodel going on...'

'You've already given this quite a lot of thought...'

To Annie's ears those words sounded a little bit frosty.

'Oh no, not really,' she insisted. 'You know how my mind works, always racing ahead, making twenty different plans in case the current one crashes and burns.'

'But what's happened to *my* Paris adventure?' Ed asked. '*My* chance to really dive deep into music and music teaching, *my* experience of a new school and a new city. This was about me taking some time out from family life, so we could both appreciate each other when I come back.'

'I know, my darlin',' she sympathised, 'but remember, you are there for a whole term and this is just... well, let's say ten days... two weeks tops? Surely that won't spoil things so much for you, will it?'

'I might not even be around. There's a residential trip coming up, when the staff take a group of thirty kids off to some château in the Dordogne to live, breathe, sleep music and at the end there's a big concert at the school.'

'The music staff go off to the Dordogne...?'

'For ten days... I mean it's going to be a really epic, immersive experience.'

Annie did not like the sound of this one little bit. Ed and Sylvie in a château, living, breathing, sleeping music... and perhaps many other intense emotions too. She knew how Ed could get completely carried away by music and everything that it made him feel.

'Ed, two weeks out of your three and a half months there, and you might even be away for some of it. Surely that's not so bad? We would hardly be raining on your parade. And imagine Maxy and Minette in Paris... eating *pain au chocolats*, wearing cute little French outfits... calling you Papa.'

'Oh, just a sec... I've got a call on the other line.'

'Really... a call? At this time?'

'I'll be right back,' Ed said and put Annie on hold.

Annie looked at her phone screen... 10.35 p.m., 11.35 p.m. in Paris. Call it woman's intuition, but she just knew who was calling Ed, and wondered what excuse would be given.

'So, who was that?' she asked her husband after he had reconnected her again.

'Poor Sylvie,' Ed began. 'She just got home to her apartment and she can't find her keys. So, she's calling us all to see if we picked them up.'

'And did you just happen to pick up Sylvie's keys?' It was Annie's turn to be extremely frosty now.

'No.'

'So, what's *la petite* Sylvie going to do?' Her heart was sinking rapidly.

'She's trying to get hold of a friend who has a spare,' Ed explained. 'And meanwhile, I said she could wait here, because she's only a few streets away.'

'Ed! Some foxy French music teacher cannot come and wait in your apartment after a night of listening to jazz music together... that's just...' she went for the phrase designed to strike fear into the heart of every teacher: 'Not Appropriate!'

And before he could make any reply, her mind was made up. She was definitely heading over there to make sure nothing suspicious was going on. 'We're coming to Paris, Ed,' she said firmly. 'So, you'll just have to get used to the idea.'

9

DEHORS — OUTSIDE

It takes mere moments to dress up a little for the world outside. Before I step out of the door, I like to at least brush my hair, add a pair of eye-catching earrings, a touch of lipstick, and tie on my favourite scarf du jour. *Smile!*

— M.M.

* * *

Usually, breakfast in Svetlana and Harry's Mayfair home was extremely civilised. Usually, Maria had the table all laid out for her employers well before their arrival, then she wordlessly glided in and out of the smaller dining room, as required.

Svetlana's breakfast tended to be warm water with fresh lemon juice and strong black tea, followed by a freshly made fruit salad with a daub of home-made yogurt (for the beneficial bacteria) and several hand-fuls of vitamin pills and supplements, from vitamin D (for the terrible weather) to seaweed (for the hair and nails) to calcium and magnesium (bones and nerves) to all the other good things in between.

Although Svetlana's day began in the epitome of good health, it often spiralled into too many glasses of Champagne, too much fatty food and even a cigarette or two. But at least every morning, she reset the inten-tion to look after herself as much as possible.

Usually, Svetlana quietly checked messages, emails and the news headlines on her phone, while across the ironed linen tablecloth was Harry, who usu-ally read peacefully through his freshly delivered copy of the *Financial Times*, drinking a coffee and chewing meditatively through a thin piece of buttered toast and as much of an English breakfast as Svetlana would allow, for the good of his health – one slice of organic bacon, one large tomato, some mushrooms and a small poached egg. She had suggested adding slivers of avocado to this ensemble. But he had shuddered with horror at the thought of this green interloper at breakfast and told her he had put up with as much breakfast interference as could possibly be tolerated.

Today, however, the usual breakfast harmony had been completely disturbed. Maria could tell all was not well as soon as she entered the room with the fresh toast and top up of hot coffee for Harry. So once these items had been served, she disappeared again as quickly as possible.

The truth was, Svetlana and Harry had gone to bed with the facelift argument unresolved and here they were again this morning, still in dispute.

After a long ten-minute silence, Harry put the paper down and looked at his wife. Clearly, there was more he wanted to say before he left the house for the day.

'Svetlana, doesn't your medication make surgery more risky?'

'Pah!' Svetlana said and swigged down three pills at once with a mouthful of her black tea. 'I just stop taking those pills for seven days before.'

She hated, *hated* to be reminded that she was on medication for her heart. It was yet another thing that made her feel too old.

'But that will increase your risk of a stroke,' Harry pointed out.

'Pah!'

'You are already seven years older than your mother,' he added.

Now she wanted to throw her cup of hot lemon water at his head.

'And may I remind you that your last brush with the plastic surgeon brought an infected scar which took months to heal and left you with a permanent red lump behind your beautiful ear. Svetlana, my love, you look perfect to me in every way. I don't want you to do this. I don't want anyone to carve your face or stretch your skin or change in any way the beauty you have right now.'

He reached over, took her hand in his and told her warmly, 'I know no one likes to think about getting older, but all that matters is health, happiness and having people who love you. You have all of these. And you look truly stunning. If a few more wrinkles come, let them. Laugh in the face of your wrinkles, my darling.'

Svetlana took her hand away and replied, 'It's different for you, Harry. You are a man. Provided they stay fit, men always age well. A thicker epidermis,' she added as explanation, 'and slower hormonal decline.'

'Will you at least think it over for a few weeks? That's all I ask.'

'But I'm on his priority list...'

'As one of Mayfair's most famous faces, of course you are,' Harry protested.

'I will go, get the work done, and rest, fully recover at his hospital before I come back. You won't even need to think about me.'

'How could I not think about you?' Harry protested. 'All I ask is that you don't rush into this. I know, now that Petrov has gone away to school, that this is a time of change for you. You need to consider carefully what you would like to do next. This is an important time... a big turning point for you.'

Svetlana looked deep into Harry's kind eyes and felt a little comforted because there was real understanding there.

'Just think it over... That's all I ask of you,' he said, finally.

Then he drained the last of his coffee, folded his newspaper, and took the heavy linen napkin from his lap to pat at the corners of his mouth.

She knew this meant he was about to leave, so she accepted a parting kiss.

'Busy day for you?' she asked.

'As always. Would you like to come out with me

tonight?' he suggested. 'Let's go and have dinner some-where delicious.'

'Maybe...' she shrugged, 'I let you know later.'

* * *

Once Harry had left, she sat at the dining table stewing it all over as Maria cleared away the dishes and tactfully didn't say anything.

Then Svetlana felt as if she must go out, couldn't bear to be in the house any longer. It was too warm inside and she felt bored, frustrated and stifled. That was the word – stifled.

In the lobby, she donned a fresh coat of lipstick, large sunglasses and a light jacket, then went out, slamming the shiny black, painted and polished to perfection, wooden door behind her. But when she was outside, sunlight winking off her heavy dark glasses... well, then she didn't know where to go or what to do with herself.

What is the matter with me? she couldn't help asking herself. *I was never like this. There has never been a single minute in my life when I didn't know where I was going and what I was going to do when I got there.*

She wanted to scream.

Where did she want to go?

What did she want to do? Today?

This week?

This month?

This year?

These all felt like impossible-to-answer questions.

She couldn't go straight back inside again. She couldn't bear it. But she didn't want to walk anywhere either. She looked at the high railings and dense green shrubbery on the other side of the road before her. Just for a little while, she decided, she would go and hide in the residents' garden, until she had pulled herself together again.

* * *

Inside the garden, Svetlana chose a bench that was tucked away from view behind a clump of thick rhododendron bushes. She didn't sit down immediately, first of all she opened her handbag and found a paper handkerchief to brush away the dust and debris. Then she smoothed out her skirt and sat down.

It was still early, hours before her usual curfew, but nevertheless, she opened her handbag again and from its creamy calfskin interior, brought out a packet of cigarettes and selected one. This she lit with her small gold lighter.

In the past, when she had been beset with difficult feelings and sadness, she had powered energetically through them, always determined to make her life better, brighter, bolder. And, so far, this approach had always worked. Whenever she'd faced setbacks before, she had tried harder – more exercise, more surgery, tighter clothing, wealthier husband, more important connections, bigger business aspirations. She felt as if she had always won though – no matter what the setback had been.

So, these feelings of uncertainty, hopelessness, defeat even, they were entirely new to her. And although she knew the best approach was to power on through them and come out triumphant on the other side, the problem was that, for once in her life, she didn't know what was next. She didn't know what to power towards.

She had two wonderful sons, who she had to allow to grow up and move away from her; a daughter, who helped to run her company; a beautiful home; a kind, loving and worthily successful husband; enough money to last many, many lifetimes... Svetlana exhaled smoke with a deep sigh. Her whole life had been about hunting things down and achieving them, growing more ambitious, growing more important, achieving more illustrious connections and power. But now, she seemed to have stalled. Now, she seemed to spend much more time looking backwards than forwards.

She found herself thinking about when the boys were small and how much more time she could have spent with them if she'd realised how short those precious childhood years were going to be. Then there was her daughter, Elena, with whom she had only been reconciled once Elena was an adult. She had missed all of Elena's childhood. Her daughter had been brought up with relatives in Svetlana's home country of Ukraine.

Oh... and Ukraine. She could only think of it with sadness. Before, when she'd told people she was from Ukraine, they had looked at her with only the vaguest idea of where the country was. Now, the word invoked only expressions of sadness and regret.

She didn't know what she wanted next. She didn't know what was going to drive her forward over the coming months and years.

'Get more involved in your dress business,' Harry had urged her. But the truth was, although Perfect Dress had some outlets and customers in the UK and Europe, it was the US that loved the dresses most. And Bradley and Elena were best placed to run it from New York. Much as Svetlana loved a trip to New York, or even better California, she had no intention of spending months at a time over there for work. Plus, her daughter had told her often enough that, now with Bradley, Svetlana's current level of involvement from the UK was enough and no more was required of her.

Svetlana blew smoke out once again and looked with closer attention around this garden. She had hardly been in here since the boys were small. The long, dry summer had left the grass completely parched and worn out. The shrubs looked tired, dusty and undernourished. On many of the bushes, she saw the yellow-tinged leaves that she still remembered from her rural childhood as a sign of the soil needing more nutrients.

Some well-rotted manure was required all around this garden she realised as she looked in more detail. Even the plane trees looked thirsty and dusty, while the hedge running round the perimeter had been brutally cut into squared-off neatness, but it was thin and straggly.

Thinking of the plants and what they needed to thrive made Svetlana think of her mother, who had worked back-breakingly hard on the scrap of land she had owned to provide for herself and her daughter in the years after Svetlana's father had absconded.

As soon as Svetlana had turned sixteen, she had

left, with her mother's blessing, for the city to start her journey towards a glorious, dazzling new life, hardly ever returning to visit.

It was twelve years later, when Svetlana was a seasoned beauty queen, married to husband number two, that her mother had died of a sudden heart attack and somewhere, deep inside her, Svetlana knew she still felt deep grief about this injustice, this unexpected snatching away of the woman she had longed to repay for all her love and care.

But to open that boxed-up grief felt far too dangerous. Instead, she had channelled her emotions into anger and ambition and let them propel her on her journey towards the life she had dreamed of as a little girl sitting by a fire, rereading the small pile of well-worn fashion magazines she'd been able to get her hands on.

Her mother had raised a handful of animals, for their meat, milk, eggs and manure. She had grown all the vegetables they could ever eat, plus a surplus to sell. She'd grown fruit and berries, then used these to make jam, cakes and tarts to stock her weekend market stall.

In the evenings, with Svetlana's help, she'd plaited stalks and grasses into mats and ornaments. Even pine cones were collected in the woods to decorate wreaths and garlands and they'd made sellable hair accessories out of scraps of spare material. Her mother had worked creatively and tirelessly to keep as much money coming in as she possibly could. And in every way, when she was not at school, Svetlana had helped.

She had loved this woman and they had worked together as a joyful team. Laughing and enjoying their successes, weeping together when things had gone wrong – heavy rain washing away precious new seedlings, the pig escaping to eat an entire basket of apples.

Yes, here she was, a girl who'd once cried over a lost basket of apples, now the owner of a house in Mayfair.

What could she and her mother have done with a patch of land like this Mayfair garden? Svetlana imagined raised beds of soft earth filled with vegetables and fruit bushes. Then there would be more fruit trees, even nut trees that could be harvested and enjoyed by the residents. Ground this hard and dry could have lavender plants... she remembered her mother's lavender full of bees and the harvest of the seeds to make the plump bags, the thick scent drifting around you as you fell asleep, as you opened drawers and unfolded precious woollen garments.

She looked once again in her handbag, this time

for her phone. She thought maybe it would lift her gloomy mood to speak to someone else. Right there, almost at the top of her contacts list was Annie's name and number.

They hadn't spoken since that unfortunate phone conversation in May and now it was September. Svetlana felt a fresh burst of annoyance at how unreasonable Annie had been. It was purely a business decision, there was no need to take it so personally. Yes, it was unfortunate about Lauren, but Lauren was a bright young girl, who had probably been snapped up by another employer already.

As Svetlana scrolled through the jaunty messages and photos that Annie had left her previously, she realised that even if she wanted to reconcile with Annie, she couldn't face her right now. Svetlana was gloomy, uninspired, not herself and the thought of all the cheerful optimism and energy that Annie could radiate... it was almost too much. Svetlana didn't want anyone to help her.

10

LES ENFANTS — CHILDREN

Shopping for children's clothes is an irresistible temptation, but children grow so quickly that you soon find yourself giving clothes away almost as fast as you acquire them. Comfortable, washable items, with room for play and growth work best. Robust denim dungarees, trousers and skirts are perfect for every day, alongside soft cotton tops and sweatshirts. There is still room for the special occasion outfit that you want to see your darlings wear, despite their protests!

— M.M.

* * *

Travelling any significant distance with small children was an all-round nightmare. Annie knew there were few ways to circumnavigate this ordeal. But as soon as Ed had phoned back the day after their bad-tempered evening call to say that, of course, she and the twins would be welcome and it would be lovely to have them for two, three – or even beyond – weeks, Annie had been deep in travel prep.

First, there had been the in-depth conversations with Tamsin and her assistant – already a shortlist of potential interview candidates had been drawn up, and agents and PRs were being contacted. French fashion and the love of trench coats, nautical tops, ballet pumps and knockout handbags had been dis-cussed to death. A list of 'secret' and 'top' Paris shop-ping addresses was being created.

Then there was home organisation prep – Owen had been issued with an endless array of lists and in-structions. Dinah and Bryan had to be coaxed over with their daughter to escape the builders and keep an eye on Owen. Annie's occasional childminder and the new nursery had to be placated that this was only a temporary absence and the twins would be back very soon. Both the fridge and freezer had to be fully stocked for Owen and Dinah's family.

Then Annie had gone with the twins to see her mother, Fern, on both Saturday and Sunday, to keep her company, to get her fill of her Mum, and to make sure that everything was running as smoothly as it could with her.

'We will keep in regular touch,' Annie had promised her as she prepared to drive away. 'You can come with me on some FaceTime walking tours of Paris, my darling.'

Finally, when the journey was only two days away, Annie could begin to concentrate on what she and the twins would need for a two- to three-week trip to Paris in the extremely fashionable month of September.

She kept messaging Ed and checking her weather app every five minutes.

What's the weather like?

His replies were vague:

Sunny-ish, warm-ish... a bit of cloud and rain.

What shoes are people wearing? And what about coats... is it raincoat weather, or still summer jackets, or has the transition to wool coats begun?

The replies to this were even more vague:

What shoes are people wearing?! Shoes! People are definitely wearing shoes.

So, no sandals then?

Well... I don't know... I might have seen some sandals.

The result of all this indecisiveness about weather and sandals, jackets and/or coats was that Annie needed two suitcases worth of outfits – one for warmer weather clothes, and a larger one for cooler weather outfits. Plus, a third suitcase was required for the twins. A quick tour of the twins' wardrobes revealed that they had outgrown almost all of their cooler weather clothes, so she was going to have to dash into town, even though there was hardly any time, and rush-purchase some essentials for them.

* * *

Svetlana's favourite bistro in Kensington was quietly busy, but she chose her table carefully. It was still warm enough to sit outside, so she picked a chair where the terrace met the bistro's interior. This allowed her to watch the café's glossy clientele on her left-hand side, but also gave a good view of the pavement passers-by on the other. As soon as she was settled, she realised how much she liked this spot. From here, she could truly see and be seen. Suddenly, she felt her back straighten and her spirits revive in a way that they hadn't done for weeks. She was here, in London's beating heart, in September. Her time was her own and she could do anything she wanted to do... yes, just as soon as she had worked out what that was.

'A glass of Champagne,' she told the waiter. Champagne... she would celebrate and raise a glass to herself.

'*Svetlana Wisnetski*,' she told herself under her breath, when her glass arrived, '*a climber, a fighter, and a survivor.*'

But somehow, as soon as she'd swallowed a mouthful of the crisp bubbles, her gloom instantly returned. Was this what she was now? A woman who sat and drank in the afternoon... all alone? She pushed the glass away.

Looking up and along the street, her attention was

caught by a woman walking down the pavement, still some distance away. This woman was hurrying along at speed, her skirt billowing out behind her in the breeze. Her arms were bent at the elbow, powering her forward through the busy throng. Big sunglasses, sandals that were on the high side for this purposeful walking, a big red handbag... as the woman drew closer Svetlana was swept with a feeling of recognition, but through her dark Chanel sunglasses, she couldn't be sure.

She knew she should look away, otherwise the woman would see she was being watched, but the feeling of recognition held her. Now, the woman was coming clearly into focus and Svetlana's cloud of confusion instantly cleared. '*Annah*?!'

In the same moment Svetlana had formed the thought, Annie, powering along on her shopping mission for the twins, realised with surprise that the elegant woman, sitting in one of the loveliest spots in London with a glass of Champagne on the table before her, was her friend, her business partner and the person she was still in an unresolved argument with.

It was too late for Annie to pretend she hadn't seen her... and anyway, she could never be the kind of person who would walk past anyone she knew and pretend not to see them.

So, despite all the complicated emotions that this unexpected reunion might throw up, she stopped in her tracks and exclaimed, 'Svetlana!'

And then there was this odd, breathless pause, as Svetlana remained seated and Annie felt herself freeze, not sure whether to keep on advancing or not.

Into Annie's mind rushed all those choice phrases she had uttered during their last, heated conversation: *'Could you be more lady of the manor?'* and *'What Svetlana wants, Svetlana gets.'*

Annie felt suspended in mid-air, one foot poised to move forward, unsure about what she could say exactly, and would Svetlana even want her to say anything?

But she reminded herself, this was Svetlana – once her treasured personal shopping client but who, many years ago now, had become a friend. Yes, a friend. What else do you call someone who has been through so many things with you? Even if her wealth happened to be equivalent to the GDP of certain small countries.

The women looked at one another for a long moment. Neither of them moved. It just seemed so important to know what the next move was going to be and who was going to make it. Just one small gesture and this argument could all be over, or it could stoke up once again into an enormous, and perhaps unforgivable, bonfire.

The moment extended, as the women looked at one another, both frozen.

And Annie saw Svetlana, really saw her, and somehow, although she couldn't put her finger on what it was exactly, she caught a glimpse of vulnerability. Maybe it was the fussy skirt suit, which she remembered helping Svetlana buy years ago, maybe it was those huge sunglasses, shielding her face even though she was sitting in the shade, maybe it was the fact that she was alone, this woman, who usually came with some sort of entourage. Maybe it was that solitary glass of Champagne, which didn't look as if it had been touched.

Life really was too short, Annie thought. So, she was going to do it. She was going to smile big, swoop on over there and show that she was absolutely ready to forgive, forget and move on from that ugly disagreement. If she was rebuffed, well, too bad. She was a big girl. She could handle it. She would just have to find someone else to fill the Svetlana-shaped hole in her TV show and her life.

* * *

11

LUNETTES DE SOLEIL – SUNGLASSES

A beautiful pair of sunglasses that suits your face shape is a wonderful addition. Dark glasses protect your eyes and the delicate skin around them from bright light and ageing rays. They also add a dash of chic and an air of mystery. What other accessory goes with every outfit, from your winter coat to your swimsuit?

— M.M.

* * *

Annie's face broke into a grin, then opening her arms wide, she exclaimed, 'Svetlana, sweetheart! It's so nice to see you!' With that, she headed straight towards the table.

For one sweat-inducing, blood-freezing moment, the expression on Svetlana's face didn't seem to change. *She has had a lot of work done... not to mention Botox,* Annie reminded herself as she continued to approach, her big smile in place. *Maybe she wants to smile or look pleased to see me but she can't...*

Then, just as Annie was almost at the table, the glacial expression finally cracked. The glasses were removed, the corners of Svetlana's mouth tweaked just a little bit upwards. Her eyes widened and seemed to soften. And now, she was pushing back her chair and beginning to stand up.

Annie came right round to Svetlana's side and hoped her body language made it clear she wanted to hug, kiss, make up, forgive, forget and be friends again. Good friends. Maybe even the better for this fallout.

Conflict is an opportunity for growth... hadn't she read that? Or heard it somewhere? Or maybe it was on a tea towel, or an Instagram meme... Anyway, maybe this messy conflict could, if they gave it a chance, prove an opportunity to become even better friends than before.

She put her arms around Svetlana and felt the impact of that firm cleavage against her much squashier one, felt taut, toned arms grip her tightly. Her face was briefly enveloped by a gust of classic Chanel No. 5, the brush of a crisply hair-sprayed tendril, and the gentle thwack of a heavy dangling diamond. Svetlana had dressed up for this café visit.

'Annah! How good to see you. Come and sit with me,' Svetlana said, 'tell me all about your summer, tell me why you are rushing around Kensington.'

For a moment, Annie hesitated. She was on a very tight schedule, those mini dungarees and little cotton tops for the twins were not going to buy themselves. Plus, although asking her to come and sit down was, of course, a reconciliation of sorts, after that huge row, after such a long time of not speaking, surely, they were going to have to talk about a bit more than their summer holidays?

But, then again, sitting down to talk to Svetlana was the first step, so never mind, she would shop for the twins in Paris, this was more important.

'Darlin', I would love to sit with you,' Annie said, settling herself down into the other chair at Svetlana's table. 'But I have exactly forty-five minutes, so I'm going to set the timer on my phone, and when it goes off, I need to rush back and take over with the twins.'

'And how are your twins?' Svetlana asked, which was unusual, as in Annie's previous experience, Svetlana's interest in her children was fairly passing.

A waiter appeared, poised to take Annie's order. For a moment, she considered joining Svetlana on the Champagne, maybe it would make this conversation a little easier.

But no: 'I'll need a large filter coffee please, no milk,' was Annie's decision. This conversation would need to be caffeinated. There was a lot of ground to cover in not very much time.

'So how are you?' Annie asked. 'Did you have a lovely summer with the boys?'

'Beautiful,' Svetlana said, then she turned to her Champagne flute, picked it up and took a sip with an unusually thoughtful look.

Maybe Svetlana was tired, maybe Svetlana was even a little sad. Whatever it was, this was not the brusque, determined, energetic woman who had called her a *woman without any vision* in the heat of the moment.

'And are the boys back at school already?' was Annie's next question.

There was only a nod in response to this. So, Annie ventured into the tricky territory with, 'And how is it going with the new CEO at Perfect Dress? Is he working out well?'

'Ja... it's going very well. He and Elena are a good team. I have very little work with the company now.' This came with a little shrug and there was a lack of energy to the response that gave Annie the definite feeling that everything was maybe not going so well with Svetlana.

'And what about you?' Annie ventured. 'What's new with you?'

'I'm having a new facelift,' Svetlana announced.

'Really?' this caught Annie completely by surprise. Svetlana felt she needed another facelift?! *Svetlana*? Annie looked much more closely now at the face only a few feet away from her own. Because she knew, or thought she knew, Svetlana's real age, Annie considered this face incredible. The skin was creamy and taut. Her jawline was straight as a ruler. Her neck was firm with only the faintest of lines, even the skin visible at the top of her chest was ivory-coloured and looked soft as velvet. There was nothing crêpey, or saggy, or droopy to see here. A host of expert hands had worked on this face with lifts, tucks, injections, tweaks, fillers, and no forgetting the massages, creams and weird facial exercises that Svetlana adhered to religiously, so nothing looked fake, tight, stretched, or wooden. There was just an overall calmness to Svetlana's face. A slowness to make any expression was the *only* giveaway that you weren't looking at a younger, woman.

Annie couldn't help thinking of all the pearls of skincare wisdom she'd had from Svetlana over the years: *massage, massage, massage, every night with cleanser, use a facecloth, vigorously, move the blood and lymphatic fluid around. Eat full fat – essential fatty acids are wonderful for the skin. But don't get fat, then thin, then fat again as this stretches everything. Eat fish and vegetables and vitamins, drink water, water, water. But sometimes you need Champagne and a Sobrani cigarette for stress because stress is terrible for the complexion.*

Annie struggled to see where there was any slack along those angled planes for the surgeon to lift.

'What are you planning to have done?' she asked.

With some signs of enthusiasm now, Svetlana pointed out where the incisions would go and where the millimetre-perfect adjustments would be made.

'But I think you look completely jaw-droppingly amazing right now... are you *sure* that's what you want to do?' Annie couldn't help herself from asking.

'Ah,' Svetlana sighed, 'you are like Harry, always questioning why I am trying so hard. I think it is because you are both British. All my friends from...' she waved her hand expansively, 'east of Berlin, they understand.'

This landed a little badly with Annie because although she knew Svetlana moved in various social circles that she was not part of, she'd never really thought of her as someone with many other friends. Svetlana had always struck Annie as a woman with many, many acquaintances, but who kept a very tight inner circle of husband, children, household staff and financial advisers. Before their argument, Annie had felt honoured to have broken through to the rank of friend. And now, here was Svetlana telling her she had lots of friends... and maybe she no longer thought of Annie as one of them.

'And what about you, Annah?' Svetlana asked now. 'When does filming start for the new series?'

So Annie launched in to explain about the new episodes that had to be planned, the Paris idea and the fact that Ed was on exchange in the city, and that she was going there with the twins tomorrow.

'*Ja,* I like this,' Svetlana said. 'I will think of a French theme to my money segment for these episodes... maybe French property investment... or how Coco Chanel went from penniless orphan to multi-millionaire.'

Before Annie could even show how delighted she

was to hear that Svetlana wanted to come back to the programme, Svetlana was telling her, 'You must film at the House of Chanel. You cannot cover Paris style without Chanel. Chanel is Paris. Paris is Chanel.'

'Ah, I don't think we'll be doing Chanel,' Annie told her sadly. 'Believe me, I've already been on the phone to Chanel and offered both a kidney and a child to their press office and I am getting nowhere. Apparently *How To Be Fabulous* is not "on brand" for Chanel.'

'Pah!' Svetlana said so forcefully that it made Annie smile. Now, this was more like it. This was the kind of determination, the kind of disdain for mere mortals, that made life around Svetlana stressful on occasion, but also highly interesting.

'I am a Chanel customer,' she said in her deep and, despite all these years in London, heavily accented voice, 'I will talk to them.'

Annie couldn't repress her smile. When Svetlana said, 'I will talk to them,' she sounded like a mafia boss. And she meant it. She would talk to them. So, Annie could leave the Chanel situation alone now Svetlana was on it.

'Babes, I have missed you,' she told Svetlana, and even took the risk of putting her hand gently on Svetlana's arm.

Svetlana looked at her carefully.

'Yes, Annah, I have missed you too,' she said. 'I've spent all summer with the boys and now they have both gone to the very north of Scotland to school.'

This was delivered calmly, almost neutrally. But Annie thought she understood. Svetlana had been too wrapped up in the imminent departure of both of her boys to boarding school to give much thought to the unresolved argument.

'So, Petrov has gone up north too now?' she asked. When Svetlana nodded in reply, Annie added, 'Goodness, the house must feel so quiet without them.'

And she thought she saw some expression pass across Svetlana's face that was rarely seen – a mournful, wistful look. Maybe this explained something else too... maybe this explained the worry about getting older, getting left behind, and the feeling that only facial surgery could help her to slow the inevitable progress of time.

'When is your surgery?' Annie asked, feeling the first inkling of an idea.

'I don't have a date, but I'm on the priority list,' came the reply.

'Of course you are! And what if I could make you look even better, even younger without surgery, would you consider cancelling it?'

Svetlana gave a little laugh. 'You cannot and I will not,' she said sternly.

But Annie had known her for too long to be put off by any kind of sternness.

'But you would let me try, wouldn't you?'

'Why do you care if I have a facelift or not?'

'Darlin',' Annie began gently, 'aren't you on heart medication?'

'Yes, but I just stop them for some days before and after... there is a small risk,' she admitted, 'but, worth it, I think.'

'And haven't you had a few lifts before?'

A mere raised eyebrow and tiny nod in reply to this.

'So don't the risks go up... scar tissue, muscle damage... that kind of thing...'

'No, no, Mr Phillippe is one of the most skilled surgeons in the world.'

'I would have expected nothing less. But if you could avoid it?'

'I'm not scared,' Svetlana retorted. 'I always take risks. Taking risks makes life sweeter.'

'But if I could help you?' Annie offered, knowing just how many ways there might be to bring back the energy, enthusiasm and maybe even fun back into

Svetlana's life without resorting to another showdown with the surgeon.

The timer on Annie's phone began to beep. She had to go, speed back home, relieve the childminder and start the packing task.

'OK, Annah...' Svetlana raised both hands in a gesture of mock defeat, 'if you want to try some things, is fine. We try some things. And then I go for my surgery looking very good. When I come out, I look even better.' Svetlana smiled at her.

'Will you promise me, that if you like what I do, you'll seriously consider not taking the knife option?'

'OK, I promise you.' Svetlana's smiled widened and Annie smiled back.

The agreement between them felt warm and conspiratorial.

'Well, what we need to do, my darlin',' Annie began, her mind flooding with ideas now, 'is book the film crew and have you in Paris for a truly Parisian, "woman of a certain age" makeover. That is going to be... incredible! You can get to Paris in a day or two, can't you?'

For a moment, Svetlana was silent.

C'mon, Annie couldn't help thinking, *agree! This is going to be fantastic.* Because what Svetlana really needed, Annie thought as she took in the yellow-blonde lacquered updo and the slightly fussy ladies-who-lunch jacket, skirt and pussy bow blouse, was not a facelift, but an image update – not just clothes, the whole thing, top to bottom.

In Annie's long experience of helping women dress, she knew that there were these pivotal moments in life, the crucial transitionary times – a divorce, the big-zero birthdays, menopausal rumblings, children leaving home, redundancies – when you were faced with choices.

You could try to stay as you were, clinging to your view of yourself, hoping to hold back time, and looking back longingly to those good times in the past, or you could be brave, bold and move forward. But this involved updating, reinventing and letting others help you see yourself in a whole new light, so you could be reinvigorated for the new and even daring things that still lay ahead for you.

Both of Svetlana's boys heading off to boarding school just as she hit that tricky mid-fifties age, must be a pivotal moment for her. She was no doubt wondering how she would spend her time and what her focus would be. Clearly, the dress business wasn't enough for this very capable and ambitious woman, and maybe her famously robust self-esteem had taken a knock. Annie knew she could help to give her the reset she needed, and it would make for wonderful viewing, if she would just agree to come to Paris.

In a coaxing whisper, Annie added, 'The sexiest women in their prime are in Paris. You need to come and join them.'

Finally, Svetlana uttered the words, 'I like this idea. Maybe I will contact Igor and see if it is possible for me to stay in his Paris home. I will let you know.'

'Amazing!' Annie exclaimed. 'I can't wait... and I can't wait to tell Tamsin.'

Then she jumped up, knowing that she had to get home.

'And if you love what we do to you in Paris, you'll cancel the surgery?' was Annie's parting request.

Svetlana laughed. 'We will see, Annah, but I don't think I will change my mind.'

'Then the challenge is on!'

12

L'Eau – Water

One of the best and cheapest secrets to health and soft, pillowy skin is water. A glass of water every waking hour and replacing some of my daily cups of tea and coffee with herbal teas makes a big difference. Mineral waters and herbal teas also bring healthy micro-nutrients into the body.

— M.M.

* * *

The journey began with hauling bags, buggy and twins into the taxi, followed by hauling bags, buggy and twins out at the entrance to the station. Then came something of a tussle with a fellow passenger to secure what appeared to be the one baggage trolley in the entire railway station forecourt. Once the trolley was loaded, Annie pushed ahead, holding Max by the hand and ordering Minette to not let go of Max's hand on Pain Of Death. She had to start half-jogging to the right platform, with trolley, bags, buggy and twins, when she saw to her horror that there were only six minutes left to get on the train.

She trotted a little faster and the twins' jogging sped up too. They made it through the gates and trot-jogged to their carriage, where she hauled bags, buggy and twins once again. Not long after they'd boarded, the doors slid closed and before she had even stacked the luggage in the rack, the train began to move.

Cue wild excitement from the twins: 'Is this the train to Paris?'; 'Are we going to Paris now?'; 'Are we going to see Daddy?'; 'When are we in the tunnel?'; 'How long are we in the tunnel for?'; 'Is Daddy going to be at the station?'

'OK, buddies... let's just get into our seats and get all comfy, OK?' she tried to calm them.

Once all three were installed in their chairs, Annie

brought out the drinks and snacks that would buy her a few moments to scan for any urgent messages on her phone.

First up, a message from Ed wondering:

Did you remember my foot cream? And nose hair trimmer?

He wasn't going to win Most Romantic Message of the Year anytime soon.

Next in the queue were another handful of temporary nanny CVs. Annie glanced over at her precious Max and Minette, one drinking thoughtfully from a water bottle, the other prising a raisin from its little cardboard box, and then back at the girls who were offering to look after them during their Paris stay.

These girls looked so young. She couldn't help feeling that her twins would have sweet-looking Marta outfoxed in about five minutes. She needed someone sussed. Someone with siblings, who understood just how tricky and manipulative the under-fives could be. Well, not really Max, Annie couldn't help thinking, as she turned her eyes to Ed's mini-me, with his big blue eyes and fat, bouncy curls. He was a sensitive little boy, but he adored his sister and would do anything she asked. And Minette, who had a poker-straight blonde bob, eyes of hazel and the kind of rosebud lips and creamy complexion that made her look innocent, well, Minette was Annie's girl through and through. Always scheming or sensing an injustice and angling how to get more. Annie adored this little hustler's attitude and never paid any attention to the busybodies who told her Minette would have to be curbed... or else.

Ha! Or else... or else what? She might actually get what she wants from life, instead of settling for just pleasing everyone else all the time.

Both Annie and Ed knew they had to be one step ahead of Minette, so she had to find a nanny who could work that out too.

Now... who was this?

Annie looked at the photo that had accompanied one of the latest CVs. This girl with that knowing expression on her tanned face and in her olive-green eyes, she looked like the kind of person who could understand what was needed to keep Minette and her little hero-worshipper, Max, on side.

Samia, twenty-two, was a *Parisienne* studying Philosophy and Economics, who was available on Monday, Wednesday and Friday afternoons, and for some weekend babysitting. She provided several pages of previous experience, including summer camps in the States (*quelle horreur!*) and two references.

Annie messaged her back to ask if she was available for an interview and then put her phone down and concentrated on the little people sitting across from her. Sensing that they now had their mother's attention, a stream of excited questions broke out once again.

'Will we be able to eat baguette every single day?' Max was first to ask.

'With butter AND Nutella?' was Minette's follow up. 'Because that's how Daddy makes it and it is the best.'

'We will be eating baguette and beautiful French jam every single breakfast,' was as much as Annie wanted to promise. Nutella aside, Ed had pretty strict rules about what was appropriate for the children to eat. Annie and the twins did their best to follow them.

'Mumma?' Minette's next question began. 'You know you put our blankies in the hallway so we wouldn't forget them. Which bag did you put them into?'

Annie could feel the colour draining from her face, the sensation of sweat prickling in her armpits. She knew. She just knew. There was no need to go rummaging through any bags.

As a way of stalling for time, she told Minette and Max, whose face was also turned to her now, 'Oh, we don't need the blankies on the train. It's so hot! We need to look out of the window and see if we can see the tunnel yet... and we can play "I spy".'

Oh no, how had she done this? How had she forgotten to pack the blinking blankies?! She felt completely tripped up and worse, it felt sobering, like bad luck almost. This seemed like a warning that maybe this trip to Paris with the twins wasn't going to be quite as straightforward or as successful as she'd been trying to convince herself.

What if these Paris episodes didn't come off? Or if Svetlana didn't come? Or, even worse, there was a serious reason that Ed still wasn't totally enthusiastic about their arrival?

13

La Robe d'Été – Summer Dress

In the summer, you do not need to wear a flowery dress if it is not really you. I like to go monochrome – a white outfit, or all black, or maybe all light-blue chambray. Lovely accompaniments to summer outfits are espadrilles, Greek leather sandals, bead jewellery you bought at the beach, a straw basket, and two items you steal from menswear – the straw trilby and the oversized linen suit jacket.

— M.M.

* * *

Ed was not coming to meet them at the station. Annie was trying not to read too much into that. He'd told her he had a school music rehearsal he could not miss and had suggested she take a taxi, even though it would be expensive.

After a long wait at the rank, the taxi was warm and stuffy and although the boulevards, buildings and bridges all looked stunningly beautiful in the bright sunlight, the traffic was slow and snarly. Max began to get that pale and slightly sweaty look of potential vomiting ahead.

'We're nearly there, Max,' Annie assured him, although according to her phone map, there were still a solid twelve minutes to go. 'Let's open the window and get you some fresh air.'

Just when she thought she was going to have to halt the cab and release Max from his seat to go and make a tactical upchuck on the pavement, the blessed words in stilted English, 'This is the address,' came from the grumpy driver.

Annie popped open the door and made sure Max was out first to inhale some lungfuls of cooler air and steady his stomach. Then she unbuckled Minette and they were all on the pavement looking up at a truly Parisian dream of an apartment block. Ed had warned them it was lovely, "much lovelier than I need", but

Annie hadn't pictured a sandstone 19th century building with tall, elegant windows and wrought-iron balconies spilling over with plants, or this beautiful street with its pavement café and immaculate little fruit stall, bicycles and mopeds parked haphazardly against the walls and railings.

'It's the heart of the left bank, baby,' Ed had told her. 'I can't pretend that you aren't going to love it. Think the Kensington of Paris.'

'Oh my God,' Annie couldn't help herself from exclaiming aloud, 'this is gorgeous, perfect! Oh, babies, look at this place!'

The taxi driver helped her to get her bags to the big wooden apartment door before she paid him with crisp new euro notes.

She rang the bell marked 'concierge' as Ed had instructed and after a delay, a small man appeared. He seemed to know all about her arrival and helped her drag her cases towards a lift that made her immediately anxious. It was the kind of lift with manually closing metal grille doors that you only see in old black-and-white movies.

He handed her the apartment key with the words: *'Quatrièm étage, a droit.'*

Four, she thought, fourth floor and... which way had his hand pointed? Right. They followed their cases and buggy nervously into the tiny lift and the concierge pulled the grille shut.

'Mummy,' Max said, taking her hand, 'I don't like it.'

No, Annie thought, she didn't like it either... but surely it would be fine, perfectly fine.

'I'm glad you're both holding my hands because I feel a bit nervous too. OK...' the lift jolted into action, 'let's count how long it takes to get to floor four.'

'One... banana... two... banana... three... banana...' she began, the addition of the word banana between every number lightening the mood.

* * *

It turned out to be eleven bananas to the top. There, bags, babies and buggy were all hauled out again and as she put the key into what she hoped was the right lock, she felt as if she'd completed a marathon obstacle course and if there wasn't a decent coffee maker and enormous bag of coffee at the end of this journey, she would weep out loud.

She opened the door carefully, a little worried about what the apartment would be like inside. She already knew that's Ed's idea of 'luxurious' was very different to her own. This was a man who considered an air mattress inside a tent as a bit too much.

OK, the hallway was very promising, with vintage black and white floor tiling and an ornate console table styled with two large glass vases and a woven basket for mail. The twins ahead of her, she passed two doors on the right but was drawn forward to the bright, white sitting room ahead of them. Oh yes, the old wooden floor, the squishy cream sofa, the plants, lamps and vintage coffee table were all beautiful and it was so neat and tidy – bonus points, Ed – but those tall windows and the view out over this street and beyond, oh wow, that stole the show, that truly took the breath away.

'Where will we sleep, Mumma?' Minnie asked.

'Maybe this room...' Annie said, heading back into the hallway and pushing open a door. She'd guessed correctly, there was an adorable little room with two single beds made up for the twins. There were two brand-new children's books in French, which would hopefully distract from the continued no-show of the blankies. Should she tell Ed about that? Was there any chance he could somehow find replacements before the end of the day?

It was at this point that Annie had to go into the stylish white kitchen and, Hallelujah, there it was, the coffee machine! And it was all set up and ready to go, with a note from Ed saying:

Just click the small round button my darling xx

When her small, strong cup of coffee was in her hand, she went to investigate the main bedroom. Oh, so tidy and so white, with beautiful muslin curtains framing the windows and their view. The bed was freshly made and smelled of clean laundry. There was even a bunch of flowers on one of the bedside tables.

'What does that say?' Max, who had come into the room behind her, pointed to the A4 piece of paper taped to the iron bedstead.

'It says – hello darling, can't wait to see you. Good times ahead, kiss, kiss. That's very nice of Daddy, isn't it?'

Annie was impressed. Maybe the drought of bedroom good times was finally going to end. Maybe she'd completely imagined that Ed wasn't overjoyed about their visit. Annie decided that as soon as the coffee was downed, she would unpack all the bags to make sure the bedrooms were just as tidy when Ed came back, as he'd left them.

So, she slid open the big white door on the double wardrobe to see how much room there was in here for her things. In front of her were Ed's things, hung in a neat row and at the sight of his favourite green tweedy jacket, she leaned forward and put her face against the fabric to snuggle up and breathe him in. How could she have had suspicious thoughts? This was her darling, lovely Ed.

The jacket made a crackling sound and she saw there was a corner of paper sticking out of the pocket. Curiosity made her pull it out and now she had a note in her hands, handwritten in black ink. It gave a Paris address, a phone number and underneath, a series of Xs and doodled love hearts.

Wait. What on earth?!!

14

LES BIJOUX – JEWELLERY

I love signature jewellery. The piece that is so me, that gives me such a boost, I wear it almost every day. I have a classic gold wedding band and on the same wrist, I wear a gold bangle in a bamboo design. These two items go everywhere with me and go with everything. Instead of a jewellery box crammed with ho hum items, consider hunting down the one or two treasures that matter to you.

— M.M.

* * *

One day behind Annie, Svetlana also travelled to Paris. Svetlana always preferred to fly whenever possible. But even she could see that taking the train to Paris would save hours of time and trouble. Plus, St Pancras had charm and beautiful cafés and stores to at least walk past and admire.

There was a time in her life when Svetlana had lived to shop, but lately, she found that with shopping, as with so many other things, she just could not be bothered. All that trying on and deciding and having things altered to fit her as perfectly as she demanded, then all the making room for the new items and storing away the older things. One entire floor of her house was devoted to her previous wardrobe items and really, the bother of remembering what she had and then having to ask Maria to take it out of storage again, meant she existed quite happily on her packed dressing room full of clothes next door to the master bedroom.

Nowadays, she enjoyed walking past the beautiful stores or going in briefly to cast an appreciative eye over all the lovely new items, but then, she would just walk on. So, her outfits were usually assembled from clothes bought years and years ago, but all so little worn and of such beautiful quality that really, what did it matter?

Although, she had to admit, that moment of walking past the young woman in the Chanel-style jacket... that still mattered, because sometimes it felt as if she was out of touch after so many years of being so very in touch.

Freddy, her driver, unloaded her bags from the back of the Bentley and onto a trolley he had located. Then he accompanied her right onto the first-class carriage, stowing her luggage in the rack and making sure before he left that she was settled in her seat with the cool bag of food Maria had prepared for her journey on the table in front of her.

Soon enough, the train began to move. Svetlana ordered a glass of Champagne and after a little while, her lunch arrived and it was perfectly acceptable, although she enjoyed some of Maria's exquisite blinis with slivers of smoked salmon beforehand. Afterwards, Svetlana leaned back, rested her head, and realised she was quite looking forward to this little adventure.

* * *

When the train arrived at the Gare du Nord, there was no question of Svetlana queuing for a taxi with the other mortals. Igor had invited her to use his apartment in the beautiful Saint Germain des Préts quarter and with the apartment came Igor's Paris staff, so she was to be collected from the station.

She recognised the driver straight away because he was wearing the understated 'uniform' of Igor's staff: black chinos ironed but not with a crease, black polished shoes, a teal-blue polo shirt with short sleeves and a small, embroidered logo based on Igor's initials, then an official Swiss railway watch on his wrist. Igor insisted staff always run early and the watch was there to keep them to time, remind them how important time was to their boss, and serve as an added badge of recognition for moments like this.

As soon as Svetlana made eye contact with him, he stepped forward and greeted her.

'Good afternoon, madame, which language would you prefer? English, French or Russian?'

'English is good, thank you,' she told him.

Then he commandeered her trolley and led her out into the street where one of Igor's fleet of black BMW SUVs was waiting, number plates always with some permutation of the letters 'GAS'.

The driver opened the rear door on the pavement side for Svetlana, then loaded her luggage into the boot. She noticed he took a soft cloth from his pocket and ran it over the side of the gleaming car as he made his way to the driver's seat, to remove any slight speckle of dust.

'How is the traffic?' she asked, as he pressed the starter button and the engine thrummed to life.

'Steady,' he replied, 'we'll be there in around twenty minutes.'

'Very good.'

Then he turned his attention to the steering wheel and Svetlana took out her phone and checked messages and emails. There was not much to see here. And once again, she felt the pang of no longer being so important in the lives of any of the people who mattered to her. Michael and Petrov were at school, busy with their timetable and their friends, Bradley and Elena were running Perfect Dress beautifully so her input was rarely required, and Harry was buried in his latest case.

She sent Harry the message that she had arrived, but she wondered who else was to care that she was here and now on her way to Igor's? She hated, *hated* herself for it, but she felt a wave of self-pity. All those sad and lonely thoughts that had plagued her since the end of the summer came flooding back.

I don't matter enough.

What am I doing with my life?

What is my purpose?

Who really needs me now?

She caught a glimpse of herself in the driver's rear-view mirror and reminded herself that Annie was here and there was even going to be a film crew to capture some of their exploits. Maybe working on the TV programme would help her to feel better again. Putting her phone back in her handbag, Svetlana turned to look out of the window and took in the Paris street scene, noticing all the ways it differed from London. The elegant balconies, the flower stalls and ranks of parked mopeds, the windows of bakeries and pastry shops, and yes, the famous French chic of the passers-by.

Paris had always been just a little too tasteful for Svetlana; she had never quite understood Igor's obsession with the place. Svetlana loved cities that were properly hot in the summer, properly cold in the winter. Brasher cities where you could wear boob tubes or furs, where there couldn't be too much gold or bling, where being tanned and showing off the work of an excellent plastic surgeon were *de riguer*. For these reasons, she loved New York, Monaco, Vienna and Moscow.

* * *

Soon, the BMW pulled up in front of the ornate *Belle Époque* building which was Igor's home in Paris. Svetlana looked up with some wistfulness at the carved stone, the elaborate balconies and the windows, retrofitted with bulletproof glass. Yes, she was very happily married to a man she truly loved and who loved her in return. She could imagine being with Harry until 'death do us part', but those years with Igor had been sensational, had given her the kind of life only a tiny percentage of people in the world would ever enjoy. If Igor hadn't divorced her, she would still be the *chatelaine* of this incredible address, among many others.

Igor enjoyed the kind of wealth that royalty has. He owned some of the finest houses in the world, then there were the luxury cars, yachts, planes, and hundreds of members of staff. She had relished the sense of importance that was everywhere he went. There were always businesspeople and government people around, important deals being closed with last-minute deadlines and enormous amounts of money at stake. Being so close to that truly high-powered world had been very exciting.

His request for a divorce had come as a complete shock, like a surprise notice of redundancy or eviction, and then, her marriage and her place in his world had ended alarmingly quickly. Igor had literally *messaged her* to say he'd decided to be with another woman, so could Svetlana please contact his lawyer to discuss a settlement and custody of their sons.

She had been an excellent wife to Igor, she knew that. Her only crime had been to become an older woman, despite the vigorous exercise and regular rounds of plastic surgery, than he was prepared to be with.

Their acrimonious divorce had been extremely hurtful to her and the boys. First, she'd had to fight a legal battle with Harry's help to get a fair settlement. Then, the custody battle had come to a head when Igor had taken her sons without consent and tried to enrol them in some Eastern European military academy.

But Harry had brokered the truce between Igor and Svetlana. In fact, everything had become so civilised that just before her wedding to Harry, Igor had proposed a remarriage. But, by then, it was too late, she'd decided to give 'true love' a try.

That one day the Igor empire would belong to her sons and any potential children Igor's new wife may produce, was something Svetlana didn't like to think about. She already had enough money to make her children wealthy when they were adults. But Igor had a vast fortune and ran an empire so huge that she knew Petrov and Michael would be put under huge pressure in the future. Svetlana didn't need to watch TV to understand how it usually turned out for wealthy dynasties. She had seen friends of Igor and their families torn apart by their empires.

Still, here she was – someone who had grown up on a smallholding, proud but very poor – arriving by chauffeur-driven car at one of the finest addresses in this beautiful city. Already, one of Igor's uniformed maids was standing by the front door, as the driver got out to open the car door for Svetlana. He would, of course, bring her luggage into the house.

'Welcome, Mrs Wisnetski-Roscoff, I'm Yasmina. Let me show you to your room,' were the maid's opening words.

Igor's maids, all dressed in the same polo shirt, chinos and Swiss watch uniform, were never young and pretty, they were always older, almost matronly. Igor wanted his staff to be serious and to serve well. He was not interested in any kind of friskiness going on behind the scenes.

Svetlana hadn't been in this house since her divorce and she was struck by how familiar it felt. The maid showed her up to the guest suite of rooms, talked Svetlana through the selection of pillows, asked how Svetlana would like her clothes unpacked, and wanted to know if madame would like to come to the dining room for afternoon tea. Yes, the selection of menus Svetlana had emailed over had been received, and would madame wish to dine in or out tonight?

'Who is in the house apart from me?' Svetlana asked.

'Me, madame, the driver, the housekeeper and the handyman-gardener are all in the house or garden during the day.'

'No other guests?'

'No, madame.'

'And I don't expect to meet Igor during my stay as I believe he is in Brazil?'

'Yes, madame, we don't expect him here until November.'

This was all good news to Svetlana.

'I think, no afternoon tea for me,' Svetlana told her. 'I will go out for a few hours. I'll be back at...' she glanced at her watch, disconcerted by the hour-forward time change, 'maybe seven or eight o'clock and I will have dinner then.'

'Very well, madame. Is that everything for now?'

'Yes, thank you.'

'I'll give you my mobile number,' Yasmina added, 'if you want to make any requests, or changes, just let me know.'

* * *

When the maid had left, Svetlana went into the huge bathroom, decorated with cream-coloured fresh flowers, a bank of scented candles and luxury toiletries, to freshen up before she ventured out onto the streets of Paris. It was another wistful moment when she looked at the polished limestone floor and remembered sitting with the designer and picking out those very tiles – it must have been about seventeen years ago now when this house was stripped out and fully refurbished. Back when she was a young woman in her thirties, not that she would have appreciated her youth. Even then, she was Botox-ing, nipping, tucking and in a panic about hitting her fortieth birthday milestone. That was when she had decided to become much more 'economical with the truth' when it came to her age.

Under the flattering lights of the bathroom mirror, she looked her face over carefully and critically. She poured out a glass of water from the chilled bottle of mineral water, touched up her foundation, smoothed on some of the gleaming bronze eyeshadow she liked so much, then added fresh mascara and a new coat of lipstick.

With her sunglasses on and handbag over her

shoulder, she stepped out onto the sunny pavement. She had this afternoon and the whole of tomorrow to herself before her filming with Annie began. So, what to do with herself? Ah, it was no good! No matter that she was in one of the most beautiful parts of Paris, with that question, back with a vengeance, came all the nagging feelings of uncertainty and pointlessness.

15

Pâtisserie – Pastry

Paris is famous for its pâtisseries. The most wonderful gateaux, brioches, millefeuilles and pain au chocolats are available on every street corner. But I can promise you that women who wish to keep wearing the beautiful pieces they bought five years ago will only indulge in these delights at le weekend. *A small slice of* tart au chocolat *on Saturday and a buttery croissant on Sunday, perhaps. A lifetime of slimness involves daily discipline,* naturellement, *but the occasional indulgences must be enjoyed to the full.*

— M.M.

* * *

The first night in Paris with the twins had been eventful, or maybe traumatic would be a better word. Ed had not been able to source new blankies on his way home from work at 6 p.m. The twins had appeared to accept the missing blankets at first. But late into the evening, Max had become upset, then Minette, too, and it had taken two phone calls to Owen at home to assure them the blankies were there and he would look after them, followed by making room for the twins in the not exactly spacious bed of Mum and Dad.

Then, just as Annie had finally fallen asleep, Lauren had called from New York to offload about some weird noise she was hearing in her new room that was making it impossible to sleep.

'You're the one making it impossible for me to sleep!' Annie had complained.

With all that going on, she and Ed had barely had time for a rushed hello, let alone any kind of romantic reunion, or any chance for Annie to ask about the mysterious note in his pocket.

Now, 10 a.m. the following day, she was jittery with the coffee she'd already drunk, but the twins were playing in their room, as instructed, while she waited to interview Samia, the potential nanny.

When the door buzzed right on time, she opened it and was a little taken aback by her first glimpse of prospective nanny, Samia. The beautiful student, deeply tanned with corkscrew liquorice curls, was leaning against the doorframe looking not so much like a nanny, but a pouty model, in her white cami top, mid-thigh denim shorts and suede cowboy boots. Over this was a pink suede jacket with fringing along the sleeves. But her expression quickly changed to a welcoming smile.

'Annie Valentine?' she asked.

'Samia?' Annie began hesitantly. 'Am I pronouncing that the right way?'

'Yes,' Samia confirmed. 'It's Algerian, my parents are French-Algerian.'

'It's beautiful, like you,' Annie said, making Samia laugh. 'Thank you so much for coming to see us. Would you like some coffee?'

'No, water is good,' Samia told her.

The interview felt straightforward enough. Samia had done plenty of childminding before, plus she had grown up with a much younger brother and sister. And as her uni classes didn't start for a few weeks, she would be available whenever required and could also do some weekend babysitting.

Annie liked the idea of spending the mornings with the twins and then having the afternoons free to work, research and explore Paris for film crew and interview destinations.

After a satisfactory half hour in which Samia seemed to answer every question well, the twins were allowed to come out of their room to meet her.

'*Ah bonjour!*' Samia's face brightened at the sight of them. 'You must be Minette and you must be Max? Wow, you both look much older than four!' A compliment designed to flatter every small person.

'Do you know any French words?' was her next question. And the twins decided not to waste time being shy, but to get straight on board with this friendly girl.

'Baguette,' Minette offered.

'Taxi!' Max said and laughed because he knew this word was the same in French and English.

'*Metro,*' was Minette's next word, 'and *merci.*'

'*Pantalons,*' Max offered the French word for trousers and for some reason this set both children off into raucous laughter.

'Do you want to show Samia your room?' Annie

offered, and the twins jumped at the chance to take her away to their space.

After ten minutes or so of listening to the chatter between Samia and the twins, Annie offered her a week's trial, 'to make sure we all get on', followed by another two or three weeks of work if everything went well.

'I'm so happy,' the new nanny gushed. 'Would you like me to start tomorrow?'

'That sounds perfect,' Annie agreed. 'Would you like to do a longer day? Maybe 11 till 6 p.m.? Because, I have filming... oh my goodness,' she realised with a start, realising how much she still needed to organise today.

'I'm off this afternoon,' Samia said, perhaps picking up on the harassed expression on Annie's face. 'Would you like me to come back later and take the twins out for a few hours. It's a beautiful day, we can go visit some play parks.'

Max and Minette jumped up and down at the prospect: 'Please, Mumma!'

So that was settled.

* * *

Luckily, Samia's references came up shining and in time, so when she arrived back at the flat, in pristine jeans and sneakers this time, Annie helped the twins into their shoes and gave each one a tender kiss before seeing them out of the door.

There was still that anxious moment though, when she looked at them all and said, 'Have a good time,' but had to check, 'You've got my number in your phone, Samia? And the twins have our numbers written inside all their shoes just in case of, you know, the unexpected.'

'We are going to some lovely parks. It will be very safe and fun!' Samia assured her. 'But numbers in their shoes is a good idea. I love it!'

An hour later, Annie was hard at work in the sitting room. She'd rechecked all the arrangements for filming tomorrow and the day after. She'd messaged Svetlana to confirm and was now trying to make some new friends and contacts in Paris, but this wasn't going so well.

'Yes... I'm on television in the UK,' she was trying to explain to the next very important fashion PR on her list.

'No, it's not the BBC... but we have about 1 million viewers, so it's a really well watched show.'

'What is this programme called?' came the unin-terested voice at the other end of the line.

'*How To Be Fabulous*... and we're doing two episodes set in Paris, all about French fashion, so, of course, we want to feature you.'

'Who else in Paris has agreed to be on this show?'

This was currently the difficult question. She was putting out her first feelers, but so far, everyone had asked 'who else has agreed?' and as soon as she admit-ted, with total honesty, that her list was still 'wide open', well, the shutters went down.

So, time to try a new approach: 'This is my first day of contacting people and I've come to you first, of course,' Annie gushed. 'If we can't do something really creative and interesting involving the Karl Lagerfeld brand then why come to Paris?'

'*Exactement!*'

Was it Annie's imagination or was there just a little more interest in the PR's voice now.

'Would you be interested in a feature with Choupette?' was the next question.

'Choupette?' she repeated. The name rang a bell and she didn't want to admit to not knowing who Choupette was... a new designer? A new model? Or muse?

'Yes, the late Monsieur Lagerfeld's cat, Choupette.

The cat was a very important inspiration, even a mentor for the label. She has her own fashion line and her own representation. I can give you their number and see if they will let her be featured on your show.'

'I see... well...' Annie did not like the way this was going. She was about to be brushed off by her fifth fashion house in a row and left to interview a cat... and even if the cat did have her own fashion line and representation, it was not what she was looking for.

A cat!

'Yes, please give me the contact details for Choupette's representation,' Annie went on as cheerfully as she could. 'How clever of you to think of this. Do you think we could possibly get permission to film in your store? Maybe one morning, before opening time? Maybe one of the assistants could show us round some items from the latest collection? We love details,' she went on, 'we want to see what sets these amazing clothes apart from the kind of clothes you can buy anywhere.'

'Especially in the UK,' the PR sniffed, 'your clothes are truly cheap and horrible.'

'Right... yes...' *And thanks for that.*

'Give me your contact details, I can make a request, but I think the answer will be no,' the woman told her.

'Look, why don't I call you again in a few days,

once I've spoken to Choupette's PR, and see how that request is going?'

'Yes, if you would like to do this, but I am not optimistic... your television show is not "on brand" for us. We only want to associate with luxury lifestyles, premium products. So, I do not think this will be a fit for us.'

Annie drew the call to a close as positively as she could, but as with the calls before, she felt no great surge of optimism. In fact, she felt dismissed and looked down on. All the calls she'd made so far to the big fashion names had not gone well. She had no great hope that any of them would come back with a positive answer to her requests. Interviews with important fashion-house people were looking extremely unlikely. Even her requests for permission to have little thirty-minute filming slots inside the hallowed stores were not being met with any enthusiasm.

And everyone's most important question for her was: 'who else has agreed to this?'

Short of lying and telling everyone she was calling them first, or pretending that Chanel had already said yes... what could she do?

For goodness' sake, she told herself, *it was far too early to get downhearted about this.* She pulled her shoulders back, decided a fresh cup of coffee was in order, and gave herself a bracing talking to.

This was Paris! It was full of fashion snobs. No one said this was going to be easy. And if everyone gave up at the first sign of a no, where would we be?!

Right...

She switched the coffee maker on and flipped thoughtfully through the French magazine that Samia had brought her when she'd arrived to begin her first shift with the twins.

'My favourite fashion magazine,' she'd announced, handing it to Annie. 'I thought you might like to look at it, because of your job.'

Just the fumes of coffee coming from the little machine were already starting to revive her. She flicked through the pages and liked what she saw. Outfits with style and edge, prices that were affordable. She held the magazine up to get a better look at the designers that were credited. New French names, and names that sounded Moroccan, or Algerian in origin.

This was promising.

She was sipping at her coffee now and thinking hard.

Maybe she was going about this all the wrong way. She had thought she would work from the very biggest 'must have' names down, but maybe it would make much more sense to work her way up. If she had a list of small and then mid-sized exciting and fashionable designers that had agreed to speak to her, maybe she could work her way to the very top of the pile.

Maybe the sniffy girls at Lagerfeld and Yves Saint Laurent would be much more receptive if she told them some edgy new designers were already in the bag.

Start small, she thought. *That's what I have to do.* So, she began to look even more carefully through the magazine, noting names of clothing, handbag and jewellery designers and looking them up online. If they were a favourite of an up-and-coming fashion or film person, so much the better.

She sent out messages, tweets and emails. For those where she could find a phone number, she decided it would be worth trying to have a call.

'Hello?'

'Allo?'

'Do you speak any English?'

'Ah... are you speak the French?'

'Not really...' So she decided to put it as plainly as possible: 'I want to put your shoes on television in London.'

There was a pause followed by hysterical laughter

and a volley of French she couldn't possibly follow. Then the line went dead.

Oh good grief!

Did they not want to be on television? Were they too high fashion? Or did they think this was an elaborate practical joke. She didn't know.

What she did know was that almost an entire afternoon had gone by and she had nothing else to fill those episodes with yet, except Svetlana.

* * *

Annie glanced around the apartment searching for where she had last placed Samia's magazine and spotted one of Ed's jackets lying carelessly over the back of a chair. She went over, picked it up, brushed it down and carried it through to the bedroom, intending to hang it up properly.

After what she'd found the day before, she couldn't help herself from making a sweep of the pockets and to her astonishment, she pulled out another note.

This one was decorated with hearts, kisses, plus the words:

Je suis obsédée par toi.

She thought she knew what that meant, but she typed it into Google translate to check. Yes, as she'd feared:

I am obsessed with you.

Ed... Ed? And surely that gorgeous Sylvie? That was what immediately sprang into her mind. And she felt so shocked, so overwhelmed... so completely wounded that she had to sit down.

Ed? He'd never in their years together made her feel that there was any risk. Her late husband, Roddy, oh yes, charming, handsome actor, Roddy, who used to go abroad for long stints of filming with beautiful actresses. He had made her just about insane with jealousy, although there had never been any hard evidence or any admission of an affair. Actors... what happened on the film set almost always stayed on the film set.

But Ed? Her loyal and loving husband, who went to school, who parented, who stayed home most evenings and most weekends, unless he had a musical event to go to. Well, maybe that was the problem, maybe life had become far too predictable and this was how he was reacting to his first taste of freedom.

Two notes... and those lit-up Insta photos... and,

now that she thought of it, she never did hear about whether Sylvie got her keys back that night. Could something much more serious than she was even suspecting be going on?

And... now what?

She had to meet him... before the twins came back. She had to ask Ed straight out about this.

16

LES LÈVRES – LIPS

Red lipstick is the ultimate morale boost – there is a shade out there that is for you, keep on trying until you find it. Buy a palette and mix if need be. I recommend applying with your finger so it blurs and sinks in well. It should feel just like lip balm.

— M.M.

* * *

While she was still holding the note in her hand, while she was still wondering what Ed would offer as an explanation, Annie's phone began to ring. She saw it was a French number, so answered immediately.

'Hello?'

'Hello, is this... Madame Valentine?' the woman at the other end asked.

'Yes...'

'Ah, excellent! I have been given your number by Blanche at Lagerfeld.'

Oh, good grief, Annie couldn't help thinking, surely this must be about the cat.

But no, this woman, Geraldine, proceeded to explain that she ran a huge bookshop, close to the home of the late Karl Lagerfeld. Once or twice a week, Karl used to sweep in with his entourage and buy stacks and stacks of books.

'Art books, philosophy books, history books, photography books, Karl loved them all. He wanted knowledge and he wanted to be inspired all the time, every day. He used to give everyone gifts of books that he thought they would enjoy. Imagine, he gave models lavish copies of Ludwig Wittgenstein's work. Our bookshop is beautiful with thousands of volumes on the shelves. I was contacted by the Lagerfeld press office and we thought maybe this would be a nice feature for your television programme.'

Although Annie's knowledge of Wittgenstein was

extremely sketchy, to say the least, this still sounded promising. And it proved that at least one important PR was taking her seriously.

'Do you have a good selection of fashion books?' Annie asked.

'Of course, there is a wonderful fashion selection. What do you think of coming to visit us?'

'I think it sounds fantastic. Let me consult the schedule and we'll make an appointment to come and tour your bookshop.'

'Perfect... Monsieur Lagerfeld always told me that fashion comes from both the heart and the head. You have to look and to feel, *naturellement*, but you also have to think, to study and to learn from the ideas of all the brilliant minds the world has already created. This is why he loved books and our bookshop so much.'

Annie took Geraldine's details, they made an arrangement, and before Geraldine rang off, Annie asked her the question she was now asking everyone she spoke to in Paris: 'So who else do you think it would be good for me to contact? Are there any special fashion shops or fashion people that you think we should feature? Anyone you know?'

Geraldine thought for a moment, then replied, 'My

cousin owns the basket shop where Inès de la Fressange shops.'

'Really!' This was exactly the kind of insider information that Annie was looking for. 'Can I get in touch with her, tell her you suggested it?'

'But, of course,' Geraldine enthused and immediately offered the contact details and promised that she would think of some others. 'Paris is full of fascinating fashion people and places,' she added. 'How lucky to be making this programme.'

Buoyed by this success, Annie fired off her next round of requests with much more confidence Then, setting aside thoughts of the conversation she needed to have with Ed, she decided to go out, wander around, rub shoulders with this city and hopefully spur on some fresh ideas.

* * *

Getting ready to go out in Paris did require some proper thought. She looked over her 'at home' outfit of slouchy, favourite shirt dress in coral-pink and decided that it would not do at all. No... maybe she could give her Paris minimal basics another go?

So, into the crisp white shirt she went. Then she pulled on the navy-blue trousers followed by a pair of navy ballet pumps for that Parisian touch and, on top, the obligatory raincoat.

She sighed at her reflection. That sensible, dressed-for-the-weather, woman from accounts was still looking back at her. She mussed a squirt of hair product through her short blonde bob, so the fine hair looked bouncier, then she took her favourite red lipstick and applied, pressing her lips together to set it. That was definitely better.

From the wardrobe, she pulled out one of her classiest handbags. It was small but chunky and a bright, pillar-box red. Yes... this was all looking much more fashion-forward now. But she wavered, was it Parisian enough to carry a bright red handbag with a designer label? Maybe she should have a unique raffia creation or an heirloom crocodile Yves St Laurent tucked under her arm?

For crying out loud, she told herself off, *you are fine! Completely fine! If you don't leave the house now, you'll never get out!*

Oh, sunglasses! That was the first thought to hit her as she emerged through the antique wooden door of the building out onto the bright street. Everyone in Paris wore sunglasses all the time. Even when it was cloudy. It added to their indefinable allure. But, no, she wasn't about to risk another trip in the rickety lift, let alone walk up four flights of stairs, to go and search the bedroom for her sunnies. She would just walk on the shady side of the street.

So, she set off in the direction of the beautiful café she'd passed when she was out with the twins earlier, planning to stop at all the interesting shops with filming potential on the way. Then it occurred to her that school would be finished by now and maybe Ed could meet her at the café and then they could get to the bottom of those strange and confusing notes.

She messaged him and to her surprise, the reply came almost immediately:

Be there as soon as I can xx

But now what? Was she really going to put everything on the table, come straight out and ask him?

* * *

Annie was installed at a table just inside the café, but with a view of the street outside, when she spotted Ed striding down the street. The first thing that struck her was how handsome he looked, much better than back home in London. His well-cut jacket was open, he was wearing a good belt around his slim waist, there was a smile on his tanned face and his hair was different... how had she not noticed before that it had been recently cut and appeared to even be smoothed down with... could that be some kind of *hair product*? On Ed?! The next, almost simultaneous, realisation was that her husband was not alone. *Oh no...*

That girl... Sylvie, the cello-playing, red-lipstick wearing music teacher, with the thick dark locks and wide smile, the possible writer of notes with love hearts and talk of being obsessed, was walking closely beside him and they were laughing together. Annie felt shaken by the sight of the two of them. Then shaken even more when this good-looking, much more groomed version of Ed slowed down to turn into the café and they *kissed* goodbye... on both cheeks!

She even saw the girl reach one hand around her husband's waist as the cheek kiss was in progress. Annie leaned right out of her chair to try and make a proper assessment of this kiss. OK, it was not the kind of lingering snog that lovers would make before they parted, no it wasn't that. But it was not a casual, we're just colleagues, see-you-in-class-tomorrow kind of thing either. It was definitely in between. It was straying into the grey area. This was a kind of '*aren't you so fascinating?*' kiss that she did not like the look of one little bit.

The girl was definitely interested in him. Far too interested. Maybe even *obsédée*. And judging by the lingering smile and general glow that Annie could see on Ed's face as he approached the café, he was not oblivious to this interest. Maybe he was interested too. Annie already knew she was in Paris not just because of her TV programme, but because she had some serious marriage resuscitation work to do.

She and Ed had been together for many years now and everyone knew relationships didn't just carry on being wonderful without some dedicated effort on both sides. Anyway, here he was, approaching the table, so she stood up and greeted him with a big smile, hug and kiss of her own.

'Oh dear, I've left a smudge of lipstick on your cheek...' she began but followed this up with a pointed, 'Or maybe it wasn't me, maybe it was Sylvie?'

'Oh... did you see that?' Ed rubbed at his cheek and had the decency to look a little embarrassed as he took the seat opposite hers. 'It's a French thing, honestly kisses are like handshakes over here. People are kissing all the time. The teachers kiss each other, the kids kiss hello and goodbye in the playground. To be honest...' he caught her eye and gave her a smile, 'it makes me feel a bit British and awkward. But you know... I'm trying to get used to it.'

'Hmmmm... I see,' was Annie's unconvinced reply. The notes... was she going to just come out straight away and ask about them?

But then Ed put his hands over hers and told her how nice it was to be just the two of them.

'We never do this,' he added, 'go out as the two of us, just for coffee, or drinks... we're always working, or childminding, or you're rushing off somewhere. This is good.'

'Well... there was that dinner, remember? But you turned up unbelievably late, looking like a mess and then Max threw up.'

'Exactly! Even on a dinner out, we never have any time.'

'Yeah...' she agreed, but there were still a lot of questions she needed to ask. 'So... do you want a coffee? Or have you had one already? Maybe you were out with your "colleague" Sylvie discussing... your latest orchestral manoeuvres.'

Ed smiled and shook his head. 'No, nothing like that. We were just heading out of school in the same direction. She lives literally around the corner from this café.' Ed pointed out the street. 'Over there, number 31, she said. In fact, she offered to give me a coffee at hers, but then I got your message.'

This was another jolt for Annie – was her husband

having an affair? Or was he about to have an affair? Did he *want* to have an affair? She felt as if she was no longer at all sure about the answers to these questions. And she didn't know where to begin with her questions.

'Ed, please don't go to Sylvie's for coffee, ever,' she blurted out.

'Why not?' he protested, looking offended. 'There is absolutely nothing for you to worry about – if that's what you're getting at.'

'Isn't there? I know you think that... I *hope* you think that. But I saw the two of you just now. She looks interested. She is flashing all the signals. And... she's gorgeous, Ed! Most men would be very flattered. And a flattered man is... well, not what I want you to be, babes... unless I'm the one doing the flattering.'

Ed leaned back in his chair and rolled his eyes.

So... was Annie going to ask about the notes? Did she want to let him know she had been searching his pockets like a suspicious person? Would that make him angry? Or even damage the trust they had built up over the years?

They locked eyes again and smiled at one another. He really did look well. He was lightly tanned, had that glow of a person who exercises. He even smelled particularly fresh and ferny.

'Paris suits you,' she told him. 'Or maybe having lots of lovely Parisian women fawning over you is suiting you. Have you done something to your hair?'

'Just a haircut,' he insisted. 'And, ha ha... you've only been here two days. Wait until the Parisian men start fawning over you. How am I going to compete with the likes of him over there, for example?' Ed gave a sidelong glance to indicate who he was looking at.

'And, oh boy, he's getting up and heading this way,' he added. 'Probably coming over to ask for your phone number and how you take your *café* in the *matin*.'

'Very funny,' Annie replied, but it was true that the extremely dapper gentleman in a three-piece pale-lemon suit with a sky-blue handkerchief emerging from the pocket, was approaching their table, a friendly smile on his dark and handsome face. Annie looked up at him, wondering what on earth he was going to say.

He said some words in French which Annie thought sounded as if he was sorry to interrupt.

Ed replied in French along the lines of, not at all, and then the man switched to English.

'I hope you don't mind for me to ask this question,' he began, looking a little embarrassed.

'We are married,' Ed added, 'just to explain. Have been together for years.'

'Oh, congratulations...' the man said, looking a little confused.

Annie looked up at him wondering what was going to come next. Was he going to fawn over her, as Ed had suggested? Or maybe he was going to ask her where her handbag was from? Or her totally Parisian trench coat... maybe he was a stylist, or an influencer? And he had spotted her. Maybe she didn't look quite as much the lady from accounts as she had thought.

'I would like to ask monsieur where his tweed jacket is from? I have been looking for exactly this jacket for years. This weight, this colour, it is perfect,' he added, practically gushing at Ed.

'Oh!' Ed looked both astonished and as if he was trying to suppress a burst of laughter. He was avoiding Annie's eye, as if a glance in her direction would definitely set him off.

'This old thing?' Ed said, glancing down at the green tweed. 'Umm, I suppose it is quite nice. I have no idea... Annie, do you remember where it's from?'

'This old thing!' she repeated in mock outrage and gave Ed's latest admirer the name and address of the modest gentleman's outfitters on Jermyn Street in London. 'Their clothes are old-fashioned British style, but the prices aren't crazy. They have a website,' she added, 'and they will probably deliver to

Paris, but you might have to pay extra. You know...
Brexit.'

The man was standing right behind Ed now and
looking at Annie.

'This is very helpful, very kind of you. Now, one
more question...' and to Annie's total amusement, he
seemed to lean down and sniff at Ed's shoulders, fan-
ning the air upwards with his hand.

'This cologne... again, it is gorgeous, exactly what I
have been searching for.'

'Annie?' Ed asked, still trying not to laugh and
clearly unable to remember what it was he had
sprayed onto himself not even that long ago.

'Penhaligon's *Quercus*,' Annie said without having
to think about it. 'It's Latin for oak tree. Basil, lemon
and jasmine with a woody, mossy depth,' she went on,
recalling the sales assistant's pitch as she had dithered
between three different choices for her husband's
birthday. She had loved the idea of Ed smelling like an
oak tree and that had made the decision for her.

'I don't know if they can send that in the post,' she
added. 'You might have to make a trip to London... or
maybe they have a shop in Paris?'

'Thank you so much for this information. This has
been fascinating.' Turning to Ed, he added, 'Your wife

obviously takes very good care of you. I hope you care very much for her too.'

'Oh yes, of course...' and Ed did his slightly British and awkward thing at the prospect of a public declaration of his love.

With a flourish, the man produced a little embossed card and handed it to Ed, who passed it to Annie. 'My name is Emmanuel,' he said. 'Please take my details. If there is some question I can answer for you in turn, maybe you will be in touch. I am so sorry to disturb...' he added.

'No, no,' Annie insisted, then picking up her handbag, she added, 'Please take my card too. I'm in Paris on a research trip for my TV programme. You never know, you might have some good ideas for me.'

Emmanuel took the card graciously then floated off, out of the café on noiseless, perhaps even suede soles.

Annie was left staring at a practically speechless Ed.

'I know you're going to find this hard to believe, my love,' she began, 'but in Paris, you seem to have morphed into some kind of style icon... in fact, some kind of love magnet, fashion god... an inspirer of obsession even,' she added.

Ed laughed heartily. 'This is ridiculous. You're the one who is all about fashion. You are the guru.'

'Yeah... well... maybe over here, not so much,' she admitted. 'There are a lot of extremely stylish women in Paris.'

* * *

Their coffees arrived and as the waiter left the table, Annie took a breath and thought she would now say something about the notes. Really, she had to just blurt it out and find out what was really happening.

But Ed spoke first, to ask, 'Have you spoken to Owen, lately? Is he making any progress on deciding what to do when he leaves school. We should be talking to him about it.'

'Well, I've messaged a lot,' she began. 'But it's like messaging a guy who really isn't that into you. No reply ever. I did speak to Dinah yesterday and everything sounded under control. My new thing is to regularly check Instagram. If it tells me Owen or Lauren have been online in the last few hours, at least I know they're alive.'

And now, within just a few sentences, Ed was somehow talking about Sylvie again, even though Annie couldn't see what the connection was and how she had come up in the conversation. Annie couldn't help thinking that this was just like when teenagers had a crush, when they couldn't resist mentioning their crush's name at every opportunity.

So, Sylvie lived at number 31. Annie glanced down the street Ed had pointed out, as he talked about her astonishing cello skills and how she had been a professional musician for a few years. Maybe Annie would have to wander up and down there and do a little sleuthing. Maybe she could bump into the foxy Miss Sylvie and find out how to put her off the scent... of Penhaligon's *Quercus*.

Annie turned Emmanuel's card over in her hand and glanced down at the words. Her knowledge of French was pretty shaky, but even she didn't need a translator to understand the words:

Emmanuel Adongo, director, Talent Paris.

'Oh good grief, Ed!' she began. 'Looks like Emmanuel works with one of the big talent agencies... you know actors, film people, models...'

'Really?'

'I should call him... tell him about the show. Tell him what we're looking for... see if he has anyone.'

Annie's mobile began to ring and to her surprise, it was a new French number.

'Ooooh, could be interesting,' she said, hitting answer.

'*Salut*, is this Annie Valentine? We have just met. I gave you my card.'

The voice at the other end was Emmanuel's.

'Oh my goodness, hello, I've just realised who you are!' she told him. 'You might have people who would be amazing for our TV show.'

'Would you like to interview Katie Rock-Thomson? We are doing press for her new production later this week?'

All worries about Ed and Sylvie and the mystery notes took a back seat as Annie tried to keep the squeak of excitement from her voice: 'Katie Rock-Thomson, the English superstar actress who lives in Paris? Oh... we would love that! We would kill for that.'

'I will see what I can do,' Emmanuel told her. 'But I must warn you, her press handler is fierce!'

17

Le Foulard – Scarf

A scarf in the colours you love – cashmere or lambswool on colder days, printed silk or cotton when it is warmer – is a beautiful way to add colour and personality to a basic outfit. A gorgeous new scarf can refresh faithful old coats and jackets. There are so many ways to tie, drape, fold or tuck your scarves – enjoy experimenting.

— M.M.

* * *

For a few minutes, Annie had some respite in the softly lit reception area of the beauty salon where soothing spa music was playing and a vaporiser was squirting lavenderish wafts into the air. She was parked on a spindly white and gold chair designed for the teeny tiny *derrières* of Left Bank ladies, but fortunately, it did seem to be holding up under her much more substantial English behind.

She and Svetlana had already spent two hours at the salon this morning, along with a gruff French cameraman, Pierre. He had set up his lights and camera in the treatment room, giving them all the impression that he thought this was a ridiculous job and he'd much rather be off shooting a nature documentary or possibly covering a war. But undaunted, Annie had filmed her interview with senior beautician, Imane, who by one of those small-world coincidences, turned out to be her nanny Samia's auntie. Now, Imane was ministering to Svetlana's precious face, neck and shoulders, while Pierre filmed and Annie took a few minutes to go over the arrangements for the next part of the day.

Her long experience of bringing her clients out of their ruts or their difficult transitional times had developed into something of a four-step process. It didn't always work, of course, but it usually helped and sometimes to dramatic effect. The steps were, number one, a deeply relaxing salon session with a massage, a pampering facial and, when required, eyebrow shaping, new make-up and a manicure. Then came a sharp new haircut, preferably with a different hairdresser and the bigger the change, the better. This was then followed by a wardrobe overhaul.

Once these three steps had been taken, the much bigger changes – the moving to a new job, or career, or partner, or country even, the dramatic shifts that made the real difference – all seemed to happen much more easily as people were able to see themselves in the new light that a brand-new look could bring.

Annie liked to think of it as her 'rut-buster' programme. And the excitement she wanted to bring to the show was that if a woman like Svetlana, who had everything anyone could possibly wish for, could get into a slump and not be at all sure of who she was or what she was going to do next, then anyone could. Annie just had to hope that her steps would be as effective on Svetlana as they usually were for, well, more ordinary beings.

She already suspected that hair was going to be a sticking point. She'd known Svetlana for almost a decade, she'd also seen many photos of her as a much younger woman and she didn't think she'd ever seen her without the big, blonde updo, which Annie suspected contained a generous amount of clip-in hair extensions. Getting Svetlana to move on from that look was going to be difficult.

As she sat in the reception area, she thought about the other big problem on her mind. What with all the arranging filming details, food shopping, blankie shopping, feeding and entertaining the twins, calling the older children, choosing an outfit for today and so on, last night had been a blizzard of busyness which had left her and Ed collapsing into bed, still without her having made any mention of The Notes. But for now, she would have to push that situation out of her mind and concentrate on her working day.

She glanced at her phone and all was quiet. This was a full day for the twins with Samia and at the back of her mind was that worry – would everything go smoothly? She reminded herself how careful and capable Samia seemed to be and tried to put that to the back of her mind, too, especially as a door was opening and a flushed and distinctly more relaxed-looking Svetlana was emerging. Blood did seem to be flowing more vigorously into the usually ivory and extremely composed face.

Annie jumped up from her chair and had to ask: 'So, how was it? Oooh, you do have an amazing glow.'

'It was very, very good...' Svetlana confirmed, looking almost slightly dazed, 'very good. Imane has wonderful fingers that seek out all the knots, uncover the tension... and she has a needling machine and a wand with electrical currents. Yes, there is some pain,' Svetlana admitted, 'but it is good pain. Tension is leaving. The toxins are going. I need to drink more water!'

The woman behind the reception desk quickly obliged by filling a glass from the cooler and handing it to Svetlana.

Imane, who looked surprisingly like her niece, followed close behind.

'Once again, thank you so much,' Svetlana told her. 'My neck and my shoulders feel free. Blood is flowing to my head again!'

The beautician smiled. 'This is very good,' she said, 'good for the face, good for the brain, good for the happy feeling. Come and visit me again. It will be my pleasure.'

To Annie she said, 'I am so happy that Samia can help you with your children. My sister hopes it will stop her thinking so much all the time about her new boyfriend. She is... I think you say "obsess" with him.'

Although this word gave Annie a shudder inside, she still had to smile knowingly at this information. 'Boyfriends!' she sympathised, with a shake of the head. 'Ohmigod, I don't know how I survive all my daughter's drama! He loves me... he loves me not!'

This made Imane laugh.

'It has been lovely to meet you, Imane. But it's time for me to take Svetlana to my next address. Come on, darlin', the taxi awaits.' Annie pointed to the cab visible through the window. 'Pierre knows the address and is following us.'

* * *

Once they were in the taxi, Svetlana naturally wanted to know where they were heading next. She really did look much more relaxed, Annie couldn't help thinking. The shoulders were lower, her rather upright rigid posture was looser, there was even a softer expression on her face.

And this was all good, because Annie knew that it might be a struggle to get Svetlana to this next address, but it was definitely where Svetlana needed to go. Even if there were going to be tears, or a rekindling of That Argument. But this was step two and it was important.

'So where are we going now?' Svetlana asked again, turning to look at Annie.

'Darlin', we're going to the hairdresser's and before you—' but Svetlana was already jumping in to interrupt with a sharp gasp, a shake of the lacquered updo and the words, 'Oh no, Annah! Carlos cuts my hair. He has been cutting and colouring my hair for almost fifteen years.'

Annie suspected it was longer and that Svetlana, as usual, was shaving at least seven or eight years from the truth. When were straw-coloured beehive updos last all the rage?

She suspected Svetlana had seen a Brigitte Bardot film at a young and impressionable age and had decided that was her hair, that was how she looked best and had stuck with it ever since, aided in this *conspiracy* by Carlos. What other word was there for it? Good hairdressers nudged their clients along. They made tweaks and trims and adjustments, suggested different tones, treatments, styles and shades. They did not let clients get away with requests for 'exactly the same as last time and not one tiny difference'.

Because everything changed, everything had to change, even hairstyles, and even subtle changes made slowly over time eventually took you to a different place.

'Carlos can cut and colour your hair for the next fifteen years, too, but today... today, we're going to do something different. And it will be fine, my darlin'.' Annie tried to reassure her. 'It's just hair. If you don't like it, grow it right back to where you are now. No problem. But surely, it's good to try something a little new, right?'

'I am not sure you understand...' Svetlana began.

'Of course I understand. I've been through all of this and much more with many, many other clients before.'

'No... but...'

Svetlana put her hands up to her hair and held on, as if there was a danger Annie might somehow tear the tresses from her very head.

'It's a good ten minutes' drive to the hair genius, so you've got time to talk to me and explain.'

Svetlana sank bank in her seat and gave a long sigh.

'Can I smoke in the car?'

'Ermmm... no,' Annie decided. 'I'm not sure that's a great idea... health and safety of your colleagues, the driver, etc.'

Svetlana gave another longer, deeper sigh.

'It's OK, you can tell me,' Annie assured her. 'You can cough it all out to me.'

For a long moment, Svetlana was silent. Then, haltingly, she began to explain.

'I love my long, blonde hair. And it's long, halfway down my back. But...' Svetlana twisted the handle of her handbag in her hands. 'You know, Annah... you know some of my story... my mother did not want me to have a life like hers – an honest life, but full of work and no chances.'

'Yes, I know,' Annie said gently, 'but one haircut won't—'

Svetlana broke in. 'She used to tell me about Ivana Zelníčková, who became the first Mrs Trump. We followed her life story, her transformation from humble beginnings in Eastern Europe. And my mother, once I turned fifteen, would put my hair up, just like hers, and sew me dresses copied from hers. She sent me to Kiev and then out into the world to meet the most important people I could find.

'I did beauty competitions, I got invitations for glamorous parties,' Svetlana went on. 'And don't forget, I did national service for ten months...'

Svetlana stared defiantly ahead, then declared, 'This hairstyle, this is mine. This is me. This is the hair that made me who I am today.'

Annie listened. She completely sympathised and she understood.

The hair had become fundamental.

That rock solid blonde hair, Svetlana had so much identity invested in it. Too much.

'No one is saying you can't have an updo, darlin','

Annie began. 'You can have one every single day if that's what you want. But what about you cut the hair just a little shorter? With a few softer layers around the face, maybe. And deep, deep condition it and then, just once in a while, at home all alone if you like, you can wear it down? You can let it fall, let it be soft and natural and frame your gorgeous face.'

Svetlana's expression didn't seem to change. She was not going to be convinced easily.

'Two-inches below the shoulder, even shoulder-length hair is still easy to put up,' Annie went on. 'You might even find it easier to do.'

'This takes me less than one minute,' was Svetlana's counterargument.

The car was pulling up outside a gorgeous hair salon with glamorous gold lettering above the door, and a caramel and cream coloured interior.

Annie could see Svetlana looking out of the window with an expression close to fear.

'You're booked in with Stephan... and look, darlin', you can go in there and just get a wash, condition and blow dry, if that's all you feel ready for. Honestly, no pressure from me. No stress. This is about us taking care of you.'

'He will just wash and style if that is what I want?'

'Yes, of course...' And that was absolutely the truth.

'Why do you want me to cut my hair?' Svetlana demanded. 'Just to make a television moment?'

'It will make a good television moment,' Annie admitted, 'but it's also about letting you see yourself in a different way. Usually, interesting things happen when people see themselves in a different way.'

Svetlana only sighed in response to this. Then Annie found herself remembering a time in their past when Svetlana had cut into a woman's hair so drastically with a pair of dressmaking scissors – to supposedly free her locks from a button – that a radical haircut had been the only solution. That particular incident had turned out just fine... but no, her cutting into Svetlana's beehive with the mini chainsaw that would probably be required was not going to be any kind of good idea right now.

The softly, softly approach was going to be the best one to adopt here. Maybe trust would have to be built with Stephan over several washes and styles before any kind of trimming could begin.

Fifteen years with the same hairdresser, cutting the same hairstyle! That was like a marriage and here she was trying to persuade Svetlana to have her first affair.

And maybe she would have succeeded, maybe she would have persuaded Svetlana to exit the taxi and step through the doors of the salon that had come highly recommended by her new Parisian best friend, Emmanuel. But just then, Pierre, the cameraman arrived and began to carry his equipment towards the salon, shooting an extremely huffy glare in their direction.

At this, Svetlana folded her arms and looking straight ahead, declared to Annie's dismay, 'No, Annah, I will not do this. Tell Pierre to leave. And tell this taxi to take me back to Igor's. I will not change my hair!'

18

LES ÉVÉNEMENTS – EVENTS

Dressing for important events is guaranteed to make even the most careful dressers nervous. Above all, I like to be comfortable in my 'special occasion' clothes. Items that crease, or show stains too easily, are out. If I've chosen something new, I make sure to wear it at home for an evening to ensure it fits well and is comfortable. If not, I have time for alterations or a re-think.

— M.M.

* * *

So, unfortunately, yesterday had turned into a fiasco.

There had been no coaxing Svetlana out of the taxi. Annie had tried every kind of persuasion she could think of, but finally, she'd had to get out of the taxi and let Svetlana go. Then she'd had to send Pierre away after assuring him he would still be paid for the work he'd been contracted to do. Next, she'd had to go into the salon and make a grovelling apology and, even worse, she'd then had to call Tamsin in London to explain what had happened.

'But where does this leave us?' Tamsin had demanded. 'Apart from out of pocket on an expensive cameraman booking? Is Svetlana still going to film her fashion makeover with us? Is this whole idea even going to work any more?'

'I hope so... I mean, I think so,' Annie had tried to reassure her. Before disappearing back to her gilded apartment, Svetlana had appeared to agree that she would still turn up for their clothes-shopping session, which was booked for the tomorrow, again with cameraman Pierre.

'But not the high street,' had been Svetlana's parting words. 'I shop with you at the boutique, fine, but not the high street. That would be a lie. Is all horrible fabrics and slave wages, Annah. I will not support it.'

Annie had decided to gloss over this latest infuriating decision of Svetlana's in her call to Tamsin. Her hope was that the boutique clothes makeover would be such a success that she would either cajole Svetlana into a chain store afterwards or convince Tamsin that Annie could go and do the second lower-budget round-up without her high-maintenance "friend" in tow.

Am I even friends with her? Annie wondered as she tried to gather her thoughts for the very busy schedule ahead of her today. Svetlana was every bit as irritating as ever and still nothing had been said to repair any of the damage done by that argument earlier in the year.

Never mind, never mind... today, she needed to park Svetlana and concentrate on the big-name interview she'd landed at very short notice, thanks to Emmanuel. This was the day that the Paris-based English actress, Katie Rock-Thomson, was doing interviews to promote her new play, and Katie's fearsome PR, Elodie, had grudgingly agreed to give Annie twenty-five minutes of Katie's precious time at 4.25 p.m. precisely. As this had only been agreed at the last minute, Annie had devised her plans for today with military precision because there were so many moving parts.

One major headache was that Ed was going to be unavailable in the late afternoon and early evening because it was a school concert day. This meant rehearsals with different groups throughout the school day, followed by a quick break at school between the end of lessons and the start of the concert for food, plus nerve-, tantrum- and tear-calming.

'My pupils, not me...' he'd told her. 'Well, maybe a little bit me.'

Then he would be straight into welcoming the parent audience and drinking a glass of fizz with them.

'Actual fizz! Not tea and coffee – can you imagine?' he'd said. 'Mr Ketteringham-Smith of St Vincent's would have a nervous breakdown. But welcome to Paris!'

Then it would be on with the show.

'Will you be able to come for at least some of it, Annie?' he'd asked. 'It would mean a lot.'

But there was no way Annie could come for any of the show. 'Absolutely no childcare,' she'd informed him. 'I'm completely stretching it with Samia covering my KRT interview. She has a new boyfriend and said boyfriend is leaving Paris about one hour after my interview to fly to Mexico for three months and she has to see him off at the airport, or— well, she *has* to. So, she has to leave work at 5 p.m. prompt. Has to! She has made that very clear.'

'But isn't your interview in Saint-Georges from 4.25 p.m. to 4.45 p.m.?'

Ed had spotted the exact problem in her plans.

'And didn't you say Katie's "people" were very precise and very strict,' he'd added, as if she was likely to forget. 'In fact, I think you've told me this about 30 times.'

'*Exactement!*' she'd replied.

'Good to see you are getting into this French thing.'

She had explained her careful plan to Ed – she would rush out of the interview at 4.50 p.m. and meet Samia and the twins at a play park, very close to both the interview location and a Metro station that would start Samia on her journey to the airport.

'So, we are all organised,' she'd told Ed. 'Totally sorted.'

'And what if your interview runs late? Have you thought of that?'

'But there's no way it will,' she'd insisted. 'You've heard how strict that woman, Elodie, is. If you aren't there early and ready to go for your interview slot, you're dropped. Those are the rules. In fact, she stipulates you have to be twenty minutes early, so she can bring interviews forward should anyone be late. The park is just moments away from where I'll be, so honestly, everything is going to be totally fine. But unfortunately, I can't come and marvel at the wonders of the brass section.'

'No French horn for you.'

'Ha! Once again...'

'So, until the interview... how will you be keeping yourself busy?' Ed asked.

'A morning of twins, then when Samia takes over, I spend a couple of hours doing deep KRT research, then I'm going to walk slowly to the venue, giving myself loads of time and looking out for some of those very special little boutiques and designers that I want to get queued up for my new episodes. Busy day, but I am prepped and pumped... as the young people say.'

* * *

So, it was now 2 p.m. on KRT day and she was putting her plans into action. Her children had been handed over to the nanny, her research had all been done and now she was all set to leave the house in the carefully considered outfit she, Minette, and even slightly Max, had spent quite some time putting together.

What on earth did you wear to meet an absolute style icon? Everyone in the fashion world would have frozen in fear and reverted to a default head-to-toe black outfit. But Annie didn't do black. Well, almost hardly ever. So, the pile of clothes heaped up on the bed were evidence of how much trial and error had taken place this morning.

At first, she'd thought a top and a flowing skirt with heels, à la Carrie Bradshaw. But several versions of this outfit later and she'd realised her almond-croissant-enhanced waistline, if it was going to fit into any of these skirts, would require iron-clad corseting, and, realistically, high heels just wouldn't work for crossing Paris in a forty-five-minute walk. No surprise that Carrie Bradshaw only ever tripped down a flight of brownstone steps straight into the back of a taxi.

Annie tried on every single day dress that she had brought to Paris, but this one was 'too clingy', that one was 'too droopy', and so on, until there was only one that made her stop before the mirror with a, 'well... that's not too bad, maybe this could be...OK?'

This dress was made of grass-green 'vegan' leather. Yes, that was *technically* plastic, but it had gold buttons, a bulge-smoothing structure and the kind of high collar which made you lift your neck and hold up your head. The bright-green worked nicely with her blonde hair and pale skin tone. There was a matching belt which tied at the waist to disguise offending areas. Then she had pale suede ankle boots, elegant but very wearable, which went well with the dress, but still made the pavements of Paris manoeuvrable.

'What do you think?' she'd asked Minette, who was still showing some signs of interest. Max had long retreated to playing games on her phone.

'It's very shiny,' was Minette's verdict, 'and a nice colour. You look like a big shiny apple.'

Not exactly the look Annie had in mind. But she turned this way and that in front of the mirror and decided it was better than all the other options. And as there was no time to start browsing through internet sites and ordering one-hour special delivery panic buys, this would Have To Do.

'Big gold earrings?' Minette suggested. 'And which handbag? A scarf... or would that be too much?'

'That's my girl!' Annie said proudly. 'We know what Coco Chanel always said...' together mother and daughter chanted: 'Before you leave the house, look in the mirror and take one thing off.'

'It's always better to be undressed,' Minette added seriously.

'No! Underdressed, Min, underdressed.'

'Does that mean in your underwear?'

'No, darling, it means not too fancy, not too fussy,

not too many bits and bobs – rings, bracelets, necklaces, scarves, hats...'

Minette gave her mother another serious look. 'But you do dress fancy, Mumma. And I love it.'

At this Annie had to kneel down and scoop Minette in for a hug. 'I love you,' she said, covering that gorgeous little face in kisses.

'Your dress squeaks when you move!' Minette said with a giggle.

This was true and it was not exactly ideal, especially for filming. It also chaffed just a little underneath the armpits, and if Annie got too warm on her walk to the venue, it did not exactly provide much ventilation.

Never mind, never mind, she told herself. If I get far too hot, I'll hail a cab. Anyway, wasn't it the French who came up with the idea of having to suffer if you wanted to be beautiful? Well, today, she would just have to suffer a slightly squeaky, chafing, too-warm dress, because quite frankly, once she had the boots, earrings, eye make-up, right handbag and lipstick in place – this dress was going to *slay*. She could even imagine KRT leaning over to her at the end of the interview to ask quietly, *'That dress is so good... where did you find it?'*

And she would reply, *'Oh... it's a little shop in High-*

gate. I've known the owner for years. I'll give Elodie the details and she can pass them on to you.'

Just before she exited, she saw a linen suit jacket of Ed's on a hook beside the door and she flung it over her shoulders, hoping to exude a touch of Sarah Jessica Parker style.

* * *

Annie was out in the street now, the twins safely in Samia's hands. She had strategically plotted her route on Google Maps to take her past several sandal shops, handbag shops and the place that made the little silk slip tops that all the models were wearing this season.

Oh, those sandals! She stopped to look through the window of the little boutique. Here was leather in all different shades and styles, leather soles, wooden clog-type soles, heels, flats, every kind of sandal. She went in and asked if the owner was around. Within minutes, she was deep in conversation, admiring all the latest looks and got a delighted 'yes!' to the suggestion of being featured on the show.

Just before she left, the owner told her with enthusiasm, 'Go down this street on the left and speak to Lucille with the handbags and Pernille who makes the semi-precious bracelets and... anyone else you want to speak with. This part of town is full of wonderful fashion and creative businesses. You need to tell everyone in London about it.'

Annie went and looked in the windows, assessed what she liked the look of best, then went into her chosen stores to sprinkle her business cards and mobile number around. Then, as she checked her phone, she realised two things with a slight jolt: one, she had to get a shift on, and two, Max's game-playing and all this Google Map action had severely drained her phone battery, which she'd forgotten to re-charge before she set off.

'I've got to go! Very important meeting in Saint-Georges and I have to be early,' she explained to the excited jeweller, who had brought all of his latest creations to the window to show them off in the best light.

Back out on the street, the sun had come out to create the not at all ideal temperature for a woman in a hurry in a plastic leather dress. She began to squeak even more as she walked and there was further underarm chafing, not to mention the slightly soggy feeling of sweat forming in the plastic-y, greenhouse environment the dress was creating.

The light linen jacket would have to come off and

maybe she could open another dress button to increase airflow.

Did she have any tissues to dab at her sweaty forehead before her make-up began to trickle down her face?

She pushed her hands into the pocket of Ed's jacket and felt nothing except a crinkly, foil wrapper brush against her fingers. Taking hold of it, she brought it out into the daylight. What she saw made her stand still with shock. There was no denying it, no getting away from it. She was holding an opened condom wrapper in her hand. A condom wrapper! Oh my God... no! If she had needed any proof that something was definitely going on with Ed and that French woman, well here it was. Right here in her hand. For a moment, she thought she would have to sit down on the pavement and cry.

How could he? How could this have happened? Yes, things were hardly great in the marriage bedroom, but didn't everyone with small children go through this? Surely, it was a phase and they would get over it. But this?! She scrunched the wrapper in her fist. There was no getting over this. He had cheated on her! He was most likely still cheating on her.

Ed? Ed?! She could hardly believe it.

But then, hadn't everything been staring her in the

face? His new interest in keeping his hair groomed, wearing his good clothes, smelling delicious. The shock and the pain were very quickly giving way to furious outrage at the situation. Bloody Penhaligon's bloody *Quercus*! She had bought that cologne that he and Sylvie were rolling around in!

Good bloody grief!!

And today! She could hardly jump into a taxi and turn up at his school and yell at him today, no matter how much she may want to.

Today, she had to get herself to a KRT interview to try and make up for Svetlana's refusal to get a bloody haircut.

I will deal with this later. I will really, truly deal with it on a monumental scale. She was too angry to imagine what the details of *dealing with it* would involve, but it would be furious and unforgettable.

But right now, and for this entire afternoon, she would somehow have to keep that under wraps and carry on with this interview. Otherwise, she may well blow up her career along with her marriage. She shoved the wrapper back into the pocket, took the jacket off and threw it over her arm, then undid the dress button and walked very fast to try and create the breeze she very much needed to cool herself down.

Good bloody grief... what next?!

* * *

Turning a corner at speed, Annie now recognised two things not very far in front of her. The first was the charming café where she and Ed had been sitting when Emmanuel had asked for details of bloody Ed's bloody jacket and his bloody cologne. The second, well, she couldn't believe it. Right there, walking past the café, bob swinging in the breeze, beautiful bare thigh peeking from between her denim miniskirt and her slim black knee boots, was Sylvie. The woman who Annie was sure was to blame for an empty condom wrapper in her husband's jacket pocket.

Annie checked her phone map quickly. She had a full one hour and fifty minutes before the start of the interview, and only thirty-seven minutes left of her walk. So, OK maths was never Annie's strong point, but she definitely had time to detour from her route and follow in Sylvie's footsteps just to see where her apartment was. That way, she would be able to return and stalk/haunt/take her revenge on this woman at a more suitable time.

So, despite the phone instructing her to 'make a U-turn', she began to follow Sylvie at a slight distance.

Maybe Sylvie is on her way to her flat to meet him there. Maybe I'll see her going in and then Ed arriving? Oh

God, hadn't Ed said something about having just one hour off in the day. Maybe he and Sylvie were going to spend it together at her flat making the kind of passionate love that had been sorely missing from her life lately. Oh, dear God!

This was all so terrible to think about that she didn't want to follow Sylvie, but yet she couldn't help following Sylvie.

Sylvie, who was about one third of the length of the street ahead of Annie, was slowing down now and pulling keys from her pocket. Annie reduced her pace and glanced at the building Sylvie was stopping in front of. It was another of those beautiful old Parisian apartment blocks with long windows and wrought-iron balconies. Surely, this was far too expensive for a music teacher. But maybe she had an accommodation deal from the school too. Or a wealthy parent... or boyfriend, of course.

Sylvie opened the heavy apartment outer door and let it fall closed. Annie walked towards the building, just to take a closer look, well... OK, just to be completely nosy about this person who was potentially wrecking her life. The door was close enough to the street for Annie to see that it hadn't closed properly. Maybe Sylvie hadn't locked it because she was about to dash out again, or maybe she'd just been careless. But that solid, wooden door was just slightly ajar.

For a moment, Annie stood rooted to the pavement and stared. Was Ed having an affair with Sylvie? Really? She couldn't honestly believe it. But the horribly incriminating wrapper in his jacket pocket said otherwise. She felt as if she had to find out. And here, right in front of her, was some kind of opportunity to know more.

Without even giving it too much thought, she stepped towards the door and pushed it open. She had no idea what she would say if she suddenly bumped into Sylvie... '*I was just passing/I thought I saw you go in here/I wondered if this could be a shortcut...*' none of those were really going to stack up, were they? Or maybe she would just blurt out: '*Are you sleeping with my husband?*'

She had no idea. Nevertheless, she slipped through the door and was now in a cool passageway with a worn stone slab floor that was almost certainly installed with the original building. There was an apartment door on her left and a wide stone staircase leading to the upper floors. Straight ahead was a charming wooden door with glass windowpanes that lead out into a sunlit courtyard. She tapped along the corridor in her boots, as the prospect of having a peek at a genuine Parisian courtyard, at Sylvie's genuine

Parisian courtyard, was too irresistible. And maybe from the courtyard she would be able to get some kind of glimpse into Sylvie's life.

The back door opened easily and Annie stepped out into exactly the kind of courtyard she'd expected. There were worn flagstones set into the earth, ivy running up a trellis that disguised the neat line of bins, and a selection of shrubs and well-tended plants in big terracotta pots. Two small café tables had been set up inside the generous space, with a selection of grey metal chairs. The noise and hustle of the city beyond was completely muffled by the tall buildings all around and this was a little haven for sipping a drink and chatting at the end of the day.

Startled to hear a door open, then close, followed by the sound of footsteps ringing out against the stone paving, she quickly tucked herself in behind the ivy trellis beside the bins. She did not want to be found here, definitely not. Sylvie coming across her in this courtyard was not exactly ideal. As she'd told herself just a few minutes earlier, there were hardly any convincing excuses that she could give.

The footsteps seemed to approach, but then halted. There was a faint clicking sound before they turned and went further away from her. Finally, she heard the clang of the heavy front door closing.

Obviously, Annie couldn't see what was going on from her place behind the bin trellis, but her guess was that Sylvie's flat was on the ground floor, and she had done whatever she needed to do in the apartment then headed out again. There was no obvious sign of Ed, so that was a slight relief.

As Annie returned to the back door, she saw the tall glass window on the back wall that belonged to one of the ground floor apartments, possibly Sylvie's. Just taking a little glance in there... that wouldn't exactly hurt anyone, would it?

Annie approached the window and leaned close to look inside. There she saw the distinctive leather jacket that Sylvie had been wearing earlier hanging from the back of a chair.

As she looked more carefully, Annie could see that she was peering into Sylvie's bedroom. There was an old, wooden double bed with white sheets, unmade, with the duvet tumbled about on top. Across from the bed in the plain, white-walled room was an antique wardrobe in dark mahogany wood to match the bed. One of the wardrobe doors was hanging open and inside – Annie pressed her face right against the glass to get a better look – there was a row of wooden shelves, neatly stacked with piles of clothes. The glimpse of a dress beside the shelves suggested that the rest of the closet was full of items hanging from a rail.

It occurred to Annie that right here, she could be looking at the holy grail of French style: the complete wardrobe of an effortlessly chic *Parisienne*. The whole thing, from tops, to dresses, to jeans, to blouses, to shoes, it was probably all in there. And having an antique wardrobe like that, compact, with limited shelf and rail space, automatically meant it had to be curated, regularly and carefully edited, with the new things in and the used-up, old things out. Why had it never occurred to her before that part of the secret of the *Parisienne* wardrobe was it had to be small? Everything had to be perfect and multi-tasking?

OK, so, setting aside what may or may not be going on between Sylvie and Annie's husband – and she still had to find out more about that – Annie was going to snag herself an invitation to look through that wardrobe, or one very like it.

But right now, she had to get back to her walk across the city to the KRT interview. She pulled out her phone, horrified to see she'd been here for fifteen minutes already and there was only 18 per cent battery left. Hopefully, enough to get her there if she took a screenshot of the map and turned off the directions.

She hurried across the courtyard to the back door

and turned the handle. Nothing happened, the door did not open. She turned it again and pushed against the door with her shoulder. It didn't budge.

Feeling panicky now, she turned the handle and banged heftily against the wood and glass. Absolutely no use, the bloody thing was locked! Sylvie must have walked to the end of the corridor and locked the door before she headed out again. Bloody, bloody, blinking hell. Annie went back into the courtyard and looked around. Was there another exit? Surely there must be an exit from here out onto the street. She looked around and then rushed over to the bins, calculating that the bins must go out onto the street to be emptied. Yes, there was a wood and metal gate set into the stone wall, but it was bolted and the bolt was padlocked.

Annie looked at the height of the wall... at least 10 feet or so. Even if she pushed the chairs and café tables up... no, she couldn't imagine herself being able to clamber up there and what would she do on the other side? Hope someone would offer to catch her as she threw herself off?

Oh, no, no, no... this was a nightmare. She could feel sweat forming in her armpits and then trickling down the sides of her tight pleather dress. Much more of this and she would feel exactly like a boil-in-the-bag chicken. Oh my God... *oh my God*... she told herself off.

Just look at what you've done now? The KRT interview! Complete with camera crew and lighting people, who were waiting there just for her. And she had given herself So Much Time! She had set off so early. There had been absolutely no chance of anything going wrong.

Hadn't she promised KRT's PR, Elodie, that she would be there half an hour early, at least. And now here she was, stuck in a sodding courtyard because she was obsessed with a music teacher called Sylvie who, let's face it, her husband may well be having an affair with, but this is Ed we're talking about, she reminded herself, Ed! He has never once given me any cause to be jealous. Maybe there was some completely rational explanation for him having a condom wrapper in his jacket pocket. Maybe she was cooking this all up in her head, due to her completely feverish, overactive imagination and being stressed out from having to resuscitate this series once again.

'Hello!' she shouted, a little timidly at first, but then with more gusto. 'Hello!! *Bonjour! Je suis ici! Je needs help!!*'

Didn't these buildings have caretakers? Concièrges? Wasn't there someone who might pop in, come to the rescue, arrive with a key and let her out before Elodie and KRT pulled the plug on her?

She decided her best bet, when no one replied to her calls, was to wait right beside the back door. Surely someone would come in or out of the building in the next fifteen minutes even, and then she could call out, be rescued and rush herself over to the appointment in a taxi.

She looked at her phone. Was it worth sending Elodie a message? Should she say that she might not be half an hour early, or would that result in instant cancellation?

A message bing-ed in and she felt almost tearful to see the words:

Good luck with your interview. I'm sure you'll be amazing! Ed xx

For a moment or two, her fingers hovered over the keys. What could she say? What should she say? 'Please send Sylvie home, I'm stuck in her courtyard'? That was what she should say, but it was ridiculous. Ed would be completely baffled. Well, if there was nothing going on... What on earth was she doing there, he would want to know.

And if there was something going on – what was she doing investigating it today?! What the bloody hell was she doing stuck in an enclosed courtyard, while on the other side of town Katie Rock-Thomson, no less, was getting ready to meet her.

Oh no, oh no, oh no. She began to knock on the back door of the building, rapping briskly, making as much of a sound as she could. Was there anyone in? Was there anyone around who could possibly come and help her out of this?

19

L'ATTENTION – ATTENTION

The confidence to be fully yourself in any outfit often comes down to giving a great deal of care and attention when you buy an item. Does it really fit well? Does it really suit you? Does the colour complement your colouring? If the answer to these questions is yes, then when you wear it, you can forget about it, knowing you look good.

— M.M.

* * *

After her morning spent touring some of the smaller private art galleries in the capital, followed by lunch, Svetlana was back at Igor's apartment, relaxing in her sitting room. Her back ached. There, she'd said it. She'd admitted it to herself. The small of her back was criminally sore. Sore when she stood, when she sat, even when she lay down. She walked carefully around the room, massaging the tense muscles.

Already, the relaxing effect of Imane's facial and massage had completely worn off and she felt as tense and stiff as when she'd entered the salon yesterday. Going round the galleries in high-heeled shoes had probably brought on this latest bout of back pain, but too bad. She wasn't going to give up heels anytime soon. Heels were an inextricable part of who she was, just like her hairstyle. For a horrible moment, she pictured herself being wheeled around a gallery in a wheelchair, her feet still encased in three-inch Manolos. Quickly, she shook that image off. This was just muscle tension, wasn't it? Maybe she should ask the housekeeper if she could call a masseur up to the apartment, right away.

No, maybe first of all, she should try a soak in a hot bath. Surely that would help. Plus, it would take up some time. Between now and her appointment with Annie first thing tomorrow morning, there seemed to be a yawning chasm of time that was passing extremely slowly. She felt as if she'd been out all day long, but it wasn't even 4 p.m. in the afternoon.

OK, long, hot bath, and then she would call Petrov. He finished lessons at 4 p.m. and the hour afterwards was often a good time to talk to him before he got involved in the activities of the evening at school.

She went into the beautiful bathroom and for a moment considered calling the housekeeper up to run her bath, but then decided she would take charge and do it herself. She set the hot water running in the huge tub and then used the long candle-lighting matches, stored in a glass jar with a circle of sandpaper on the base, to light up the bank of scented candles all around the marble-topped counter beside the sink.

There were fifteen candles in total, all about ten centimetres wide and she lit every single one of them. Then she dimmed the ceiling lights, pumped several generous dollops of the exquisite bath gel into the water and undressed in her room as a generous blanket of bubbles began to form.

After twenty minutes of relaxing in the hot and soothing water, Svetlana could feel the tension in her back subsiding. Thick towels and a beautiful bathrobe had been freshly set out for her this morning, so once she was out of the bath and dried, she swaddled herself in the robe. Then she went over to the large mirror above the sink and decided to redo her hair.

She took out the strategically placed hairpins and down came the heavy blonde tresses, then she unclipped the extra extensions of real hair that bolstered her chignon. Carefully brushing through her hair, she scrutinised her face in the light provided by the bathroom mirror and the bank of candles. Her hair was long, falling well below her shoulders and it took time to brush through the sections clumped together with generous applications of hairspray.

Her neck... she pulled at the skin, inwardly criticising the slight looseness and faint lines. After spending her entire adult life on guard against any sign of ageing, she wasn't ready to give in yet.

Once the hair was brushed to her satisfaction, she clipped the extensions back in and prepared to give it all a fine coating of spray before she wound her enhanced tresses back into her signature style and then set them firmly with another thorough misting.

She took her can and gave it a vigorous shake, then holding it almost at arm's length, she released the first blast towards her locks, almost immediately realising what a terrible mistake she'd made.

The hairspray vapour shot out over the bank of candle flames and instantly ignited. There was a faint whooshing sound as the ends of her hair on her right-hand side caught fire and the blaze quickly leapt up the spray-covered tresses.

Svetlana, who had done national service, been trained in first aid, and had once come under gunfire intended for Igor, did not panic, although she had a clear view of her head on fire in the mirror. As quickly as she could, she loosened her dressing gown and pulled it right over her head, pressing hard to extinguish the flames. Then she rushed to the walk-in shower and turned the cold water on. It was agonising standing under that cold water for long, long minutes as the sensation of cold gave way to acute pain. But she knew the only way to make sure her ear, scalp and face did not suffer burn damage was to stay here for at least twenty minutes.

She began to count the seconds and then the minutes to make sure she was under the water for long enough. When she'd lost count of the number but thought it must be about fifteen minutes, she hummed two interminable songs to keep herself under that freezing spray for longer. The thought of having inflicted burn damage to her face kept her in place for just another minute longer than she thought she could bear.

When it was finally time to come out, Svetlana

wrapped an enormous bath towel around herself and stood for some time looking down at the limestone tiles she'd chosen for this room all those years ago. For several moments, she shook and was almost tempted to cry.

This is just shock, she told herself firmly. She was going to be fine. Still, it was several more minutes before she felt ready to look in the mirror and assess the damage.

Finally, she walked back towards the sink and the offending candles and dared to fix her eyes on her reflection. She couldn't help it. What she saw there made her gasp in horror.

20

L'ARMOIRE – WARDROBE

Organise your wardrobe so you can plan your outfits and any additional purchases. A well-planned wardrobe will let you create endless looks from a limited range of items. The best-dressed people do not typically have as many clothes as you would imagine.

— M.M.

* * *

The longer Annie remained in the courtyard, sweat trickling and pooling in the inner recesses of the plastic emerald dress, the more she lost hope. Her phone, with its fast-fading battery, was telling her that already too much time had passed. Even if someone appeared in the next few minutes, it was most likely going to be too late. Even if she could teleport to the interview, she was not going to be thirty minutes early, so Elodie would pull the plug on her. She thought of the film crew waiting for her, and Tamsin, and all the explaining she would have to do. And she felt terrible. First Svetlana's failed haircut and now this. How would she be able to repair this damage? How could she possibly make it up to everyone again after blowing KRT?

Her phone began to trill and she almost didn't want to look, certain it would be Elodie asking where she was, or a child demanding something, or maybe even the film crew beginning to get anxious. But no, Svetlana's name was flashing up.

Almost automatically, Annie pressed reply, although she couldn't think of any way in which Svetlana could help her right now.

'Annah!! Annah!' Svetlana blurted in distress. 'I have burned off half my hair!'

'What?!'

'With the candles and the hairspray,' Svetlana went on. 'I have made a fireball and half of my hair has gone!'

It took Annie several moments to process what Svetlana was telling her.

'You've burned off your hair?!' she repeated, wanting to be sure she'd heard this right.

'*Ja*... on one side of my head. I used the bathrobe to save the rest.'

'Are you OK?' was Annie's next question. 'Are you burned? Do you need a doctor? Or to go to hospital?'

'I am fine. I am very lucky. I stand under cold water for twenty minutes...'

'Oh my God...' Annie was trying to read Svetlana's voice. She didn't sound high-pitched or frantic, but she certainly sounded very upset.

'What do I do, Annah?' was the next question. 'Oh, I want to cry. I have lost half of my hair. And the smell... the frizzling!'

After their fraught conversation in the taxi outside the hairdresser yesterday, Annie could only imagine how distressing this was.

'It's OK to have a cry,' she assured her, 'oh my God, I'd be bawling my head off. Are you sure you're OK?' she asked again. 'I think you should see someone to make sure you aren't burned.'

'The skin looks fine, but the hair...' There was a break in Svetlana's voice, but she carried on. 'I don't cry, Annah. I never cry. But what do I do?!'

It wasn't as if Annie had nothing to think about right now. She had about one million things to think about, but somehow, she made a little extra space to answer Svetlana's question with some kind of plan.

'Cover the poor burned hair in conditioner, my darlin', then wrap it in a towel. I'll see if we can get you squeezed into that hairdresser's tomorrow morning, very first thing, before we do the clothes filming. And I'm sure some magic can be worked. And please, my love, just remember, you have lovely, healthy hair, it will grow back. You can grow it all the way down to your knees if you like. And darlin', once you and your hair are all wrapped up, why not ask for a beautiful cream cake and some Champagne to be brought to your room and then sit in bed with the remote and work out if you can get Netflix on Igor's guest TV.'

This at least made Svetlana laugh.

'Where are you, Annah? Are you filming today?'

'That... well, that's a long story I can't go into now, but look, I will phone the hair salon and we'll see what we can do. I'll come back to you later, OK?'

'OK... and thank you, Annah. I phoned you first because you always give me such good advice.'

And with that, Svetlana was gone. But Annie found herself staring at the phone with a smile. That call had felt very bonding and that last remark, that was probably the closest Svetlana would ever get to an apology for their fallout.

Despite the worryingly low level of battery, she called the salon and her pleas for an early morning appointment were answered.

Then she walked towards the locked back door intending to bang on it again and try to raise someone but, to her excitement, she saw two faces coming in through the front door. She began to wave and call out frantically, even though she could now see that it was Sylvie, returning to her flat, which was going to be spectacularly awkward, along with another woman.

Annie waved frantically and there was quite the look of confusion on Sylvie's face as she opened the back door and seemed to register who she was looking at.

'I have seen your photo before. Are you Madame Leon?' she asked.

'Please, call me Annie...' Annie began. 'Do you live in this building, Sylvie?' she asked, trying to sound as surprised as possible, as she thought through her explanation for being here in Sylvie's courtyard. 'What a coincidence! Oh, thank goodness you're here! I thought I was going to be stuck in that courtyard all day. Look, I know this is going to sound bizarre, but I was in such a hurry and I thought I was taking a shortcut... I mean, my phone told me... Google Maps...'

It was lame but it was the best she could do in the circumstances.

Sylvie laughed, showing bright, white teeth against her vibrant red lipstick.

'Your phone brought you here? To the courtyard? I have never heard of this! And then you were locked in here? In our courtyard? Oh *merde*.'

'I have to make a call, try to rearrange a meeting... just give me one moment,' Annie said, looking at the time on her phone and feeling a wave of helplessness. It was too late... but she had to try.

The call didn't take long.

She opened with the words, 'Elodie, I am so, so sorry, I've been trapped in a—'

But she was immediately cut off with a screamed, 'Too late!! It is over! I send your crew away!' before Elodie hung up.

Annie was horrified with herself. How could she have let this disaster happen? How could she still be here in St Germain while Elodie, KRT and a film crew were waiting for her in Saint-Georges?

For a moment, she could feel the scratchiness of tears forming at the back of her throat. But she swallowed hard to ward them off.

'Oh dear... I can't rearrange my interview...' she told Sylvie, feeling completely deflated, 'they are very strict about time and I'm too late.'

'I am so sorry,' Sylvie commiserated, 'and because you were stuck in our courtyard, because of your phone map... this is so bizarre!'

'And now my phone is dead,' Annie confirmed. 'I've blown it. Well...' she shrugged, 'at least the film crew and my producer can't phone and shout at me right this minute.'

Then she leaned against the wall for support, realising how hot, weak and exhausted she felt after this very difficult hour.

'Are you OK?' Sylvie asked. 'Please, come into my apartment and have a drink.'

'No, no...' Annie protested.

'Yes, of course,' Sylvie insisted. 'And maybe there's a phone charger you can use. And this is Anouk,' she introduced the woman beside her, 'but her English is terrible!' she laughed again, 'so you will have to talk to her in French.'

'*Je regrette*,' Annie began, 'my French is terrible.' She and Anouk smiled apologetically at one another.

'Come on, come in and at least have some water,' Sylvie encouraged her.

Annie thanked her and despite thinking that it was

maybe weird to go into the place where Sylvie and her husband may, or may not have used the condom, she agreed. She followed the pair along the hallway and through the door into a beautiful sitting room, where she saw pale walls, old parquet flooring, a marble fireplace and high windows onto the street with filmy curtains that filtered the view. There were a few pieces of nice furniture: a tan leather sofa, an antique wooden desk and chair, plus an upright piano and a cello leaning against the wall beside a black metal stand with sheet music. A huge black and beige abstract painting, plants and a scattering of belongings gave the room a cool, lived-in vibe.

'This is a beautiful place,' Annie exclaimed, 'do you two live here together?'

Sylvie and Anouk exchanged a glance, some laughter and Sylvie just said, 'Sometimes,' before she began to hunt for a charger. But, alas, neither Sylvie nor Anouk had one that would fit Annie's phone, so, there was no solution to that problem.

'Please, sit down and I'll bring you a drink of water,' Sylvie insisted, 'you look as if you were very warm in the courtyard. This is a beautiful dress,' she added, 'but too hot in the sunshine, no?'

'Very hot... so hot...' Annie agreed, feeling a little wobbly all over again. 'In fact, could I possibly use your bathroom and I'll splash my face, cool down a little.'

'Of course.' Sylvie pointed the way.

Already, Annie was imagining the bliss of unbuttoning this dress and wiping herself down with a cool cloth. Maybe that would help her to calm down from this whole KRT/Elodie disaster. It was the one decent interview that she had secured so far. The one 'showstopper', or in this case, more like the 'showstarter'. The film crew would be furious. Tamsin would be furious. Annie had never, ever let everyone down like this before. She always tried her utmost to be the most professional, least diva-like presenter that she could be.

In the bathroom, she didn't wait a moment to strip off the dress and hang it on the back of the door, where both a filmy pink and filmy black negligee were hanging, it didn't escape her notice. Sylvie... she seemed lovely – beautiful, stylish, sexy, funny, generous, and of course, musical. Could it be possible that this woman was having an affair with her husband? Would she be so warm and welcoming to Annie if that was happening? Would she have believed the story about the phone map so readily?

It didn't seem real... it didn't seem right. Annie suspected it wasn't just the heat that was making her feel faint, it was also these overwhelming thoughts. As soon as her mind went back to the condom wrapper, well, she just could not compute. Ed, Sylvie and a condom... she couldn't think about it.

She filled the sink with cold water and plunged her hands into it. Then she dipped one corner of a nearby hand towel into the water and wiped at her flushed face, neck and chest. She held the cool towel corner against her neck for a few moments. That felt better, she could almost feel her completely frazzled thoughts gathering.

Maybe there was still a chance to make things up with Elodie and KRT? She would at least try. Maybe she could send them both a huge bunch of flowers... and something else, something very 'fashion' and special. Maybe Svetlana could help in some way.

Annie even wiped the inside of the dress down with the towel corner and when she put it back on, it felt cool and much less sticky. In her handbag, she located her new lipstick and applied it. She also gave herself a little squirt of zesty perfume. Then, feeling much more pulled together, she took a look around Sylvie's bathroom, curious to see what her favourite products were. Did all women do that in each other's bathrooms, Annie wondered? Have a little glimpse into what product choices had been made, where the brand loyalties lay.

Sylvie's glass bathroom shelf was home to a handful of French brands, sensible things – cleanser, moisturiser with sunscreen, foundation. There was also a mascara and a black eyeliner stored in a small glass, and a big bottle of perfume. That appeared to be it, as there was no cabinet fixed to the wall to have rammed full of bathroom extras. Annie glanced over to the shower above the bathtub. Again, a very restrained selection of pump-top bottles and an actual bar of soap was arranged there.

When she came out of the bathroom and went back into the sitting room, Sylvie poured her a glass of water, with ice and several slices of cucumber, and told her to sit and drink it.

'You work in television, in fashion, don't you?' Sylvie asked. 'I remember this because your husband does not seem to care about fashion at all, but he is always so beautifully dressed, so I think this must be because of you.'

Annie smiled at her. 'Well, I do what I can, but like you say, he doesn't really care or even notice much, I don't think.'

'Oh, I'm sure he does. We all like to be looked after, no? I absolutely adore fashion. My number one love is music, of course. But if I was not working in music, I would be working in fashion. Unfortunately, if you work in music, you will never have enough money for all the things you would love to buy. *Tragique, non?*' But she laughed as she said this.

'You dress beautifully,' Annie told her. 'I've looked inside so many women's wardrobes for my job, so many, you wouldn't believe it. And you would think the people with the most money would be the best dressed and, it's true, they often have the most beautiful clothes... but the people who are the best-dressed are usually the ones who love fashion but have a limited budget and have to be so creative to get the best out of every single piece.'

Sylvie was smiling again when she said, 'Now this sounds like me.'

Annie thought of that mahogany wardrobe in the bedroom and she suddenly had an idea so good that she thought maybe it would go some way to making up for the disaster that had been this afternoon.

'We would love to look inside an "everyday" Parisian wardrobe – with the film cameras. Talk about which items you have, why they are classic Paris style, how you wear them... where you bought them. How would you like to do a segment like that with us? Inside your wardrobe?'

Sylvie's eyes opened wide.

'Really?!' she asked. '*Me*?! My wardrobe?! But it's ordinary... normal! Like everyone else in Paris.'

Now it was Annie's turn to look excited. 'But that's exactly what we want – to look at a typical wardrobe, understand how ordinary people all over this city manage to look so put together, so chic every time they step out of their homes. Look at you right now...' Annie began.

She started her professional appraisal from the top: 'You have thick, shiny hair in a lovely choppy bob, but you've taken the time to blow dry it and then used tongs to create a ringlet or two. Then there's the gorgeous dark eyeliner and classic French red lips. Now, we have the denim miniskirt and you've gone with a floral long-sleeved blouse... mainly blue and white, picking up blue from the skirt but also with dashes of lemon and don't think I haven't noticed the lemon-yellow bangles to pick up on the lemon in the blouse and then long black suede boots which match your hair and finish your outfit off – top to toe, it's a triumph, Sylvie. And maybe you didn't even think it through, maybe you put it all together instinctively, which is even more interesting. Suggests you've been creating lovely outfits for years and years and maybe grew up appreciating how everyone around you was put together.'

Sylvie looked delighted with the compliments. At first, she laughed and told Annie she was the Sherlock Holmes of fashion. Then she raised her eyebrows and some sort of conspiratorial look passed between her and Anouk before she told Annie, 'I think you need to come into my bedroom and look in my *armoire*. Then I can tell you my secrets.'

'Oh yes,' Annie agreed, 'I think I do.'

Her interview was blown, her phone was dead, everyone was furious with her, and she couldn't even get in touch with them to explain and to grovel, so she might as well take the chance to set something new up and go some way to repairing the damage she had done – this was Annie's reasoning.

And as for the Sylvie and Ed connection... she was operating on pure denial. Surely, it just could not be true.

'Anouk?' Sylvie then rapid-fired French at her friend/flatmate, Annie wasn't sure what, but it may have been something to do with tea.

'You would like tea, no?' Sylvie then asked Annie. 'Ed showed me the English way to make tea... with just a "splash" of milk and I love it.'

Now several other things were passing through

Annie's mind: she wanted to see into the wardrobe, definitely. She was excited about that, but then, *Ed* had showed Sylvie how to make tea! Where? At school? Here in this apartment? And when? When he'd dropped in for a cuppa one afternoon? Or when... her imagination plunged straight ahead with... he'd woken up in her arms and they'd decided to have breakfast together. Oh, that was ridiculous?! Wasn't it?! *Condom wrapper...* She tried to put her lid of denial right back onto that thought.

And then there was some other troubling undercurrent of a thought, some feeling that there was something else she was supposed to do? But... she couldn't think what and put her general anxiety down to being so upset about Elodie and the film crew and Tamsin. And she did need to phone them as soon as she had charge again. But, right now, the opportunity to just take an initial look inside Sylvie's *armoire* was a very good one. Maybe she could at least bring the typical Parisian wardrobe to Tamsin as some kind of olive branch after today's utter disaster.

'OK,' Annie said, as Sylvie opened the door to her bedroom, 'yes to tea please and then to the wardrobe please and show me what you've got.'

* * *

The doors of the mahogany armoire parted and Annie could almost hear the 'tah-dah' in her head. Here was the treasure chest, the Holy Grail of the French Girl's Wardrobe.

She took in the neat shelves and the rail of items on hangers.

It was minimal.

It was strict.

This was extreme curation. These were clothes that had been chosen with an eagle eye and were kept, maintained, cleaned, or binned according to the discipline of their owner.

Her first scan revealed two pairs of blue jeans, one dark, one lighter. One pair of white jeans. One pair of slim black trousers, satiny fabric. One pair of what looked like navy tweed trousers.

'Wide legged or skinny?' Annie asked, pointing to the jeans.

'I don't care so much about the jeans fashion, I go with the jeans that look best on me – a long, straight leg. The white ones are shorter for summer,' Sylvie told her, adding, 'I *love* dark jeans, they go with everything. They go for work, for casual, for evening. It is hard for me not to wear jeans.'

'Did you know that Yves Saint Laurent wished he had invented blue jeans?' Annie offered.

'Yes!' Sylvie said. '*Exactement*! They are so perfect!'

There were two jackets... just two! A sleek black blazer and a soft grey tweedy number with wide lapels, a nipped in waist and just the slightest hint of puff over the shoulders.

'Where is this one from?' Annie asked, pulling the grey one slightly out from the rail.

'Ralph Lauren but vintage, and I changed the buttons. They were *de trop*... too much.'

'Gorgeous.' Annie looked at the black leather buttons which Sylvie had stitched on in place of, maybe, the gold or silver ones that had been there before.

Four shirts and two blouses, all in different shades of pale were next on the rail. Then a cotton shirt with big, billowing sleeves in navy. Then came a slinky black silk shirt. 'APC but in the sale,' Sylvie said. 'I wear these blouses all the time. To dress up with jeans. Once you have these with jeans, that's it. No need to worry about what to wear.'

She added, 'When I go shopping, I take time to find the exact, perfect item. Then I don't look when I am paying because the price is usually two times what I want to pay, even in the sale. But then I wear, wear, wear until I can't look at it! That's when I put it to rest in this part of the wardrobe,' she demonstrated, 'and I will bring it out again maybe a year later, when I am not bored with it any more.'

'I love that,' Annie said, 'everyone should do much more of that, buy exactly the right thing and keep it forever.'

There were two more jackets she saw now – a sequinned bomber and a dark, velvety number, patterned with flowers. Both were perfect for dressing up the jeans and the slim satin trousers.

'This one is Zara,' Sylvie pointed to the sequins. 'I like some cheap clothes – the T-shirts, the men's shirts sometimes, the summer dress you throw away in September and sometimes one crazy, perfect thing is in the chain stores. And that was this bomber. You say bomber?' she checked. 'Or '*Arrrrington*, no?'

'Harrington, yes,' Annie said, but she liked the way Sylvie said "Arrrrrington' better.

There was a little black dress, of course – black satin, knee-length with a square neckline.

There were also two stretchy night-out-on-the-town dresses, one in red. 'For when I'm feeling wild,' Sylvie explained, pulling it out, 'and one in navy. I always try the red one on, then I change into the blue. Always!'

There was a shelf of black vest tops and T-shirts,

neatly folded into little cubes. 'Marie Kondo changed my life, of course.'

'Me too...' Annie agreed.

Then came a shelf of white vest tops and white T-shirts.

'Is that it?' Annie asked admiringly. 'Just black and white?'

Sylvie shrugged. 'Makes life simple, no? If you want colour, you can have a necklace, earrings, lipstick, or a scarf, of course. I always add scarves as soon as summer is over.'

She pointed to a shelf of about twenty scarves, all different colours, textures and patterns, rolled up Marie Kondo style again.

Annie thought of all the jumbled wardrobes she'd been brought in to rescue, where every colour of top, skirt and dress jangled together, and had to admire the simplicity of this approach.

She knew just how many unsatisfactory items people had that they wore once or twice then stuffed back into their cupboards and still had 'nothing to wear'. So, on went the endless cycle of agonising in shops and then agonising even further in front of their wardrobe.

Sylvie's wardrobe was simple because there were rules, and a colour palette.

'What you've understood perfectly is that everyone needs a neutral, foundation colour,' Annie said. 'It doesn't have to be black or blue, it can be beige or white or... in my case, it's probably red.'

'Yes,' Sylvie agreed, 'a background, a principal colour. Like the violins in the orchestra – they are the main sound and then all the other instruments have their moment.'

The orchestra... yes. And now Annie was thinking of Ed... and Sylvie... and the denial lid had to be pushed back on again.

She admired the shelf of knitwear – mainly cardigans in blue, black and grey but with one lilac and one red jumper. Then she ran her hand over the hanging skirts, one black satin, one navy cotton, one beige cotton with deep side pockets, cargo style, one a tweedy grey check, and guessed these must be Sylvie's work outfits to match with the smart shirts, blouses and jackets.

'Culottes,' Sylvie announced, pointing to two of the skirts. 'I play the piano but also the cello. So, culottes with a nice shoe or boot is stylish but no accidental reveals to the pupils.'

Or handsome members of staff – aaargh!

There were two one-off evening dresses, one silver with a high belt, the other black and gauzy. On the far right hung one denim jacket, one trench coat, one woollen overcoat in bright-lilac. 'Winter can be so grey and depressing,' Sylvie announced as she pointed to it. There was also a selection of co-ordinating woolly hats and gloves, and a small box of black and navy-blue swimwear.

'*J'adore le* navy-blue.'

Sylvie showed her some of the more whimsical pieces tucked into the side of the cupboard... a soft maxi coat in a boho floral velvet, a mini kilt with blanket fringing, a white broderie anglaise summer dress with big puffy sleeves.

'I'm a musician. I need to have some crazy clothes, no?'

'You have an insanely good eye,' Annie told her. 'Everything in here is perfect and perfect for you. Where do you shop?'

Sylvie shrugged at this. 'Everywhere! Vintage shops, the good labels when they have a sale on, on-line of course... the indy designers who are making just a small quantity of something. And sometimes, I have an exact idea of the item I want, like blue velvet shorts. So, I just type it into the internet and see what comes up. I have bought many things like this... idea in head... Google... *et voila*! And you should know that I can sew, so when something is not fitting in the waist maybe or the sleeve length, I can make it perfect.'

'Ah, that is a big advantage. Everyone should realise what a difference these little alterations can make,' Annie agreed. 'Now, talk me through your shoes,' was her next request. Truthfully, she was lost in admiration of this stylish, wearable, infinitely variable wardrobe. It was all so thoroughly thought out from top to bottom. So many separates that almost all worked together. She needed to encourage her audience to think more carefully about their foundation colour and the joys of mixing and matching separates.

The shoes were a chic array of patent pumps and kitten heels with buckles on the front. Sylvie was big into buckles, and flat ankle boots. There were sneakers and sandals for summer, well-worn gold evening shoes, plus knee-high, over the knee, crêpe-soled and chunky boots, as well as a spindly high pair for parties.

'I see now my shoes are black, brown, gold, or white... and I've never even thought about it before,' Sylvie said. 'I might have to buy something a little colourful and crazy. Maybe Chie Mihara, one day. Have you heard of those shoes?'

'Oh yes, babes, I have heard of those shoes. So

beautiful and so high but so comfortable. The woman is a genius,' Annie enthused.

'I can only walk in flats. There are cobblestones...' she said the words uncertainly, 'everywhere in Paris. As soon as you wear high heels, you have to take a taxi, or go on your moto or you break your ankle.'

There were still handbags and jewellery to discuss. No doubt, there was a gorgeous vintage jewellery box somewhere in this room, filled with gold hooped earrings, vintage tiny diamonds, clunky amber and semi-precious stones, and rings as unusual and interesting as the three Sylvie was wearing today on her thumb, her pinkie and her middle finger.

But Annie's investigation into accessories was halted when Sylvie said conspiratorially, 'So, do you want to know the true secret?'

Annie had already noted the solid foundation of black and navy, the careful palette of other colours, the multi-tasking separates, the eye for cut and quality, Sylvie's emphasis on fit and what suited her, the blend of style, sophistication and sexiness – and now there was still a 'true' secret to reveal?

'I am all ears, babes,' she said. 'Why don't you tell me?'

'So, Anouk is a sustainability researcher and she has done so much work on this at the university. And it turns out that the secret to the perfect wardrobe is owning seventy-four items.'

'No!' Annie had never heard this before.

'Yes. I am not counting underwear and stockings, but all the clothes and coats. If you have seventy-four items, you have more than thirty outfits and you are making your clothes work hard. French people buy much less than in the UK or the US... people in the US are crazy with the shopping! In the 1960s, Anouk says the average French woman had forty items and was still beautifully dressed. If we want to be sustainable... have a planet our children can live on in the future, we can buy five new things every year. So, we have to choose very wisely, plus swap with our friends, buy used items and recycle everything.'

'That is so interesting...' Annie had to admit the sustainability of fashion was not something she liked to think about. Imagine trying to work out how many items she'd bought over the years... or how many she'd persuaded others to buy? Yes, many items would have been high-end and would stick around for years, but there was also a small landfill of polyester-based impulse purchases with her name on it.

She really liked Sylvie. If she wasn't convinced, on some level, that there was *something* between Sylvie and Ed, she could have embraced this lovely young woman as her chic new Parisian best friend.

* * *

Annie could definitely have spent hours talking to Sylvie about her wardrobe, but that was when fashion mathematician Anouk appeared and said in rapid French something along the lines of needing to get ready and go out.

'Oh, of course,' Annie said, a little flustered that she'd been so engrossed and taken up so much of Sylvie's time.

Completely at sea without her trusty phone, Annie wanted to know what the time was.

'Just after 5 p.m.,' Sylvie replied.

'Oh!' At first Annie was just surprised at how long she'd been here... had it even been 4 p.m. when she'd arrived?

In her mind, Annie ran through that Samia was with the twins until 6 p.m., so there was still time to get back to the apartment, charge her phone and spend time making grovelling phone calls to KRT's PR and the film crew. She would call Tamsin too. Might as well get the worst over with... but now at least there was Sylvie's wardrobe to offer as something of a compensation. Plus, those smaller boutiques she'd spoken to much earlier in the day. And what with Svetlana now needing a haircut tomorrow morning – maybe it wasn't going to be so bad.

But then again, compared to blowing a sit-down interview with KRT and wasting an entire afternoon of film crew time, well... It was going to take a lot to make up for that.

'I need to get back to school,' Sylvie said, folding up one of the tops that had been taken from the wardrobe and putting it back onto a shelf. 'Are you coming to the concert tonight? Ed has been working so hard with the students.'

The concert? The worry that had been niggling away at Annie, the feeling that there was something else that was supposed to happen at 5 p.m... somewhere she was supposed to be. At the mention of the concert, it all exploded into life.

'Oh. My. GOD!!!'

The twins!! Samia was supposed to be leaving early to see off her boyfriend! Annie was supposed to be collecting the twins at the park! She was already so late! And she would never make it now.

Samia couldn't call her and she couldn't call Samia. She didn't know Samia's number without her phone, so she couldn't borrow Sylvie's phone to call her.

Deperately wondering how to make contact, she asked Sylvie, 'Can you text Ed for me, please? Tell him to call Samia and apologise because I'm so late.'

'Yes, of course, but I don't know if Ed will get this message. He will be with the students, rehearsing, talking, busy...' Sylvie explained.

Oh dear God, this disaster of an afternoon was now building into even more of a catastrophe.

Annie was already on her feet and burbling apologies and 'got to rush' and 'what's the quickest way to Saint-Georges?' and 'Metro or taxi? And thank you so much, I'll call to arrange filming. Thank you, thank you so much.'

Out on the street, the traffic looked awful. And she was so far away from the park. She felt truly dreadful – what kind of mother is so distracted by the contents of a *closet* that she forgets her own *children*?!

21

Le Beret – The Beret

Only if it suits you!

— M.M.

* * *

For several fraught minutes, Annie had stood in the street cursing her dead phone and frantically tried to decide what to do.

Back to the apartment? Or on to the park? She was so late already. Would Samia still be waiting there? Or would she have given up and gone back to the apartment with the twins?

After further churning out there on the pavement as the rest of Paris bustled past her, looking as if it was the best day of their lives and no one had ever had anything to worry about, she reasoned that going back to the apartment had to make more sense because she could plug in her phone and find out very quickly what was going on.

So, she hailed the next available cab that passed and after ten agonisingly long minutes, she was running up the apartment stairs because the lift wouldn't come, wondering just how she could have let this afternoon get so out of control.

She opened the door, big smile on her face, preparing to catch the twins up in a hug and apologise profusely to Samia for ruining her airport farewell. But she could immediately sense the quiet.

'Hello?!' she called out. 'Anyone home?'

No reply.

She hurried into the kitchen, plugged in her phone and waited impatiently, walking in a circle around the little table as it powered up enough to finally switch on.

At last, the screen lit up and it buzzed with the messages received. As she looked, her eyebrows shot up in disbelief. She had never seen such a blizzard of messages and missed calls: 14 missed calls, 12 voice-mails, 38 texts, 56 WhatsApps.

She didn't know where to start and decided the best thing would be to phone Samia and just find out straight away if she and the twins were still in the park.

The ring tone buzzed in her ear... and buzzed and buzzed and buzzed. No reply.

She stared at her phone. First of all, she opened the WhatsApps from Samia – noticing in passing that there were fifteen waiting for her from Elodie, eleven from the cameraman and one, no doubt very pointed and severe, from Tamsin. Oh God, oh God, oh God.

Scanning down Samia's messages was not a happy experience.

Where are you? / You are late? / Why are you late today? You know how important this meeting is to me. It is my chance to say goodbye before he goes to the airport. / I won't see him again for three months. I can't believe you are doing this to me. / And there is no one else I can call. Your husband is not answering his phone. / I have tried an emergency nanny service, but they need two hours' notice mini-mum. / I don't know what to do. / Where are you? / I cannot believe you! I quit! I am never looking after your children for you. / It is not the children to blame they are lovely. It is you. / There is a nice Papa here with his little girls, I have asked him to look after the twins as surely you must be here in a few minutes. / I have to go. I quit. / Please pay me 40 minutes extra for today.

Nothing about this stream of messages had sparked joy for Annie, that was for sure. But the message that had run a sliver of ice down her spine was the one that read:

There is a nice Papa here with his little girls, I have asked him to look after the twins...

Annie read it again and then once again just to make sure she'd understood this. Samia had left her twins with a 'nice Papa' in the park. Left them... precious Max and Minette... in the park...

She couldn't pay attention to anything else that her phone was telling her. Not the Tamsin message, or the messages from Elodie, or whatever else might be there. She had to find the twins. That was the single most important thing.

While one part of her mind was urging her to think, think, slow down, decide what was the best thing to do next, another part of her brain was shouting and cursing at her: how could you have let this happen? How could you have hired a nanny who would do this? How could you have detoured into Sylvie's courtyard? And then have forgotten about the park pick up? And missed it for a wardrobe discussion?! How could you have gone out without a charged-up phone? This is All Your Fault!

She tried Ed's number wondering what advice he could give... but it went straight to voicemail.

With a trembling hand she clicked on her voice-mails and listened, maybe the answer would be there. The first messages were all women screaming at her, mainly in French. PR Elodie and nanny Samia seemed to take turns, first a burst of Elodie, then Samia, then they alternated. In the course of her messages, Samia seemed to get calmer. The message about the Papa was delivered almost deadpan; she was washing her hands of the whole thing and rushing to her airport farewell.

Then came a man's voice, speaking in French, deep and serious. At first, she thought it must be the nice Papa, please let it be him explaining where she could find her twins. But, no, she couldn't understand it... she played it again and again... she made out the word 'police'. She listened again one more time and thought she could work out an address... was this man telling her the address of a police station?

Had the nice Papa taken the children to the police?

Oh no, oh no, oh no... her mind reeled and really, she was all out of swear words for herself and the situation.

Oh. My. God.

OK... first things first. She messaged Ed with a simple:

There's been a snarl up. I'll explain later. On my way to get the twins.

Then she hunted quickly, efficiently around the apartment and found the portable phone charger, mercifully charged.

Then with phone, charger and handbag, she ran out of the flat even more quickly than she had run in. There was a taxi waiting in the street, thank God. She jumped in and gave the address of the police station. The taxi driver seemed to raise an eyebrow at her. Maybe wondering why she was in such a hurry to get there. But he set off. So, it must be true. There must be a police station at that address. And it sounded as if her twins were there.

Should she phone the station? How would she find the number? Would she be able to explain enough in French?

She slumped into the back of the seat, once again, she felt completely overwhelmed. She shouldn't have come to Paris with the children. She should speak better French. She shouldn't have chosen Samia and made all these complicated arrangements for today.

She had tried to please everyone – as usual – KRT's demands, Elodie's demands, Ed having to work late, the nanny having a big farewell, the twins' needs. Everyone had needed something from her today that made her life difficult. No one had gone, Annie, what do you need? Otherwise, she would have been able to say – what do I need? Oh, I need reliable childcare, so I can do the interview and hang around with the film crew afterwards. And I need not to be so worried about my husband's head being turned by a foxy French cellist that I had to go sneaking into her court-yard and then go into her apartment – although, to be fair, Sylvie's wardrobe had been a definite result.

This is all my fault. This is all on me.

She looked out of the cab window, then at the phone in her lap. Apart from Ed, there was no one she wanted to even think about speaking to until she had her babies safely in her arms. They were safe, weren't they? What if that had been the police telling her something much more sinister? She listened to the message once again. Not understanding the language well meant she was jumping and snatching at phrases, hoping she'd got the right end of the stick.

Here she was, the taxi was pulling up and this was definitely a police station.

And there, to her surprise, was Ed, running at speed up the staircase.

She paid as quickly as she could and then hurried up the staircase after him. By the time she got to the reception desk, he was already talking quickly in French with the woman at the desk. And for a moment, Annie hung back. It seemed dreadful to be here in a foreign police station because she and the nanny had made such a complete mess of a handover.

But every other thought vanished when a police officer came out from behind the desk with a beaming and even laughing Max and Minette.

'Daddy!' they both shouted, catching sight of him first, but this was quickly followed by cries of 'hello, Mumma!' too, as they caught sight of her before he did.

Ed wheeled round momentarily to look at her, but then they both focused back on the children again.

'Babies!' Annie exclaimed with love and relief. And all four of them were folded into a family hug.

'The man took us to the police station because we had your phone numbers in our shoes, but no one would answer,' Max began.

Minette said, 'I think that man thought we'd been abandoned, but we knew you wouldn't do that, Mumma, would you?'

The two children burst into laughter at the thought.

'Did you forget about us?' Max asked, looking right up into Annie's eyes and she thought she might just die of guilt, embarrassment, shame and sadness right on the spot.

'Of course not... I didn't forget about you. I forgot about the time. I got here as quickly as I could... I got completely stuck and my phone was dead and I think that's because...' She petered out. There wasn't going to be anything to gain from trying to blame Max for playing on her phone earlier for his very small part in this.

'I'm so sorry, buddies. I am so, so sorry...' she pulled Max and Minette in towards her again, as Ed began talking to the woman at the desk. No doubt there were probably forms to fill in and questions to answer. But they wouldn't be in any kind of trouble, would they? Surely this would be understood as a genuine mix-up.

'Don't be sorry, Mumma. We've had a great time,' Minette assured her.

'We've been in a police station. They gave us hot chocolates from the machine and they tasted like melted biscuits,' added Max, high-pitched with the excitement of it all.

'You're sure you're OK?' Annie asked. 'Samia left you in the park with a parent and he brought you here?'

'He tried your phone a lot,' Minette said. 'We waited for absolutely hours.'

'Well, it can't have been hours because...' Again, she petered out from defending herself. 'It must have felt like a very long time and I am just so, so sorry about all this.'

Max beamed up at her and shrugged. 'Never mind,' he said. 'We didn't get kidnapped or anything.'

Maybe he was trying to be funny. But Annie looked up at her husband, met his eyes and saw how absolutely furious he was.

* * *

The twins spoke to both their parents on the taxi ride home. But their parents did not speak to each other.

Annie took up her phone and began to make the dreaded calls to Elodie, the film crew and then to Tamsin, grovelling for all she was worth.

Every now and then she glanced over at Ed, hoping he was listening to her explanations too and realised how bad she felt about everything.

'Oh my God, I am so sorry. I just can't believe I've missed the interview and messed everything up. The most bizarre thing happened...' she told all of them in turn. 'I tried to take a shortcut because I wanted to be there in plenty of time. And... I was following my map, thinking I was taking a shortcut, but I got locked into one of those Parisian courtyards. The door back into the building locked behind me, the wooden door out of the courtyard was locked with a padlock. No one could hear me calling and knocking. And my phone ran out of battery because...' she glanced over at Max, 'well, I didn't realise how low the charge was when I set out.

'I was stuck there for over an hour and I couldn't even phone anyone to say what was going on. It was a nightmare.'

'Look... is there any chance of rescheduling our slot?' Annie asked Elodie. 'Even just for ten, fifteen minutes of her time? Any place, any time, we can organise it.'

Elodie made it clear that the answer was absolutely not. 'I can't believe I am even picking up the phone to you. This afternoon was a fiasco! I will not let Katie Rock-Thomson speak to you, not today, not tomorrow, not ever. Goodbye.'

And with that she hung up.

'Look...' she apologised once again to the film crew lead, once he'd listened with some incredulity to her explanation, 'I am so sorry. I never do this kind of thing. This is the first time I've ever not showed up for a shoot. Please forgive me, please don't bill the production company too heavily for this balls-up and I hope we'll be able to use you for something else very soon.'

To Tamsin, who was also not sounding too sympathetic about the locked-in-a-courtyard plight, Annie explained, 'I hope I'm never, ever in a situation like that again. It was awful. I was stuck and completely helpless. I know you must be so angry we've missed the interview. And believe me, I have tried to get a reschedule, but that PR is... a nightmare,' she sighed heavily. 'But there is at least one piece of good news to come out of it.'

Tamsin's, 'Here's hoping,' sounded doubtful.

'The woman who rescued me from the courtyard...

I went into her flat and she has the most perfect French wardrobe of outfits you can possibly imagine... it is the Holy Grail of French Chic. And she said we could film it and we can interview her too. I mean, the everyday Paris wardrobe – I am excited just thinking about it.'

There was a long pause.

'I'm not quite ready to forgive you for missing KRT.'

'No,' Annie agreed, 'I can understand that.'

'But... that does sound good,' Tamsin agreed.

'It's bloody amazing, darlin',' Annie added.

'And she's happy to do this?'

'Yes, totally.'

'OK, can she send me some photos of her wardrobe and some outfits? And if I like what I see, we can get a film crew lined up.'

'You will definitely like what you see. OK, speak soon.'

So, the phone calls were finished just as they pulled up outside the apartment.

Ed paid the driver and helped the twins out of the cab, while Annie got nothing but a glowering look.

She knew exactly where he was supposed to be this evening – his school concert. She looked at the time and tried to gauge whether he was supposed to be there right now.

It was heading towards 7 p.m. Yes, Ed was definitely supposed to be there right now.

'Erm... Ed?' she ventured. 'I can take it from here because you probably want to go back to school.'

'Yup...' he said tersely. 'That would be good. What with all the practising we've done for weeks to prepare for tonight. Yes, it would be quite good to go back there and make sure the person who has had to stand in for me at incredibly short notice when the police phoned the school directly isn't completely out of their depth.'

She could hear the quiet fury in his voice.

Although the twins had already run towards the building's front steps, Annie and Ed were still on the pavement in front.

'I am so sorry this happened, Ed,' Annie began. 'I am really, really sorry. I was locked in. And then, yes, I admit, I got caught up in something else and I genuinely forgot I'd arranged to pick the twins up in the park.'

'I'm going to catch that cab before it leaves,' Ed said, and with that, he was away.

* * *

'Lift or stairs?' Annie said to the twins, once they were through the front door.

'Stairs please,' Max replied, 'the lift is scary.'

So, she led the twins up the many stairs and apologised all the way for the mix-up, while they kept on telling her that it was fine, an adventure even.

She rummaged about in the kitchen cupboards and fridge and found enough to rustle up a supper for them. After this came a relatively peaceful bathtime before she snuggled them up in their beds and sat on floor cushions between them to read their bedtime story.

'Are you having a nice time in Paris?' she asked them both, adding, 'Well, let's not include this afternoon. That was a bit of a drama.'

'I like being with you, Mumma,' Max said. 'It's much funner.'

'When you didn't come,' Minette added, 'Samia swore a lot into her phone. A lot! Some of it was in French, but some of it was not.'

'Oh...'

'Yes, and we know French swearing, because sometimes Daddy swears in French...' Max added.

This made Minette laugh. 'Yes, he goes *salope!* Or *putain de merde* and then he says "excuse my French!"'

Both of them went into full-on giggle mode at this.

'And do you know what those words mean?' Annie asked, eyebrows fully raised.

Max told her, 'We asked Owen and he searched it up on the Google and said he couldn't tell us and we shouldn't use them, but they are very rude.'

'And Samia used them and a lot of other ones...' Minette added.

'Oh dear... I've made everyone really angry this afternoon: Daddy, Samia, you two, the people I was supposed to be meeting... it's been a complete disaster.'

'Poor Mumma,' Minette said, and put her arm around Annie's neck. 'You are very silly sometimes.'

Max turned his sweet little face up towards her and asked, 'Did you really get locked in a court? For all that time?'

'Courtyard...' she said. 'It's like a garden at the back of a building.'

In Annie's long experience of bringing up children, she knew that keeping it as simple and as honest as possible was always the best policy. Those 'white lies' or attempts to fudge the truth with complex explanations always came back to bite you on the behind at some point.

'And I did get locked into the courtyard for about an hour,' she began, 'and my phone was dead...' She raised her eyebrows almost imperceptibly at Max, but he understood immediately.

'Ooops,' he whispered.

'But the person who saw me out there in the court-yard, and unlocked the door... well, she turned out to be a teacher at Daddy's French school...'

'Really!' Minette sounded almost as excited at this news as Annie had been.

'Yes... I was so upset about being locked in and missing my important TV interview, and I was very hot and thirsty. This nice teacher, she let me into her apartment and gave me some water, and let me use the loo because I was desperate by then... and I know this sounds really, really bad, but I was so upset about missing the interview and my phone being dead and not being able to tell the TV people what had happened... that I... well, it went out of my head that I was supposed to come to the park to collect you from Samia. I mean, it's not that I forgot about you both – I could never *forget* about you.' She leaned over to give them each a big kiss in turn. 'I think about you every few minutes, all day long. But I forgot about the arrangement...'

Max put his hand into hers and said soothingly, 'It's OK. It was funny to be at the police station. We got to sit on their chairs that spin round.'

'I was talking to the teacher,' Annie went on, 'and... I didn't even notice that another hour had passed and then, you can imagine how worried I was when I realised what I'd done. But I was sure Samia would stay with you. She should have stayed with you. I never imagined for a moment that she would leave you with someone else. That was just... crazy of her. Completely crazy!'

'Is Samia going to look after us again?' Minette wondered.

'No,' Annie said firmly, 'definitely not.'

'Oh well, that's good, because she was OK, but you are funner,' Max said, leaning back against his pillow, looking pale and in need of sleep.

Annie told them not to worry about anything, gave them another round of hugs and kisses and left the room, so they could snuggle down.

Then she went into the kitchen to make herself some food. Surely Ed wouldn't still be as angry with her when he got back tonight?

22

LES TALONS HAUTS – HIGH HEELS

There is a mania for high heels, but I do not understand it. I swear, I can tell from a woman's face if her shoes are uncomfortable. I love to walk the street of Paris, so my shoes of choice are lace-ups, loafers, ankle boots, ballet pumps, even le sneaker.

— M.M.

* * *

It was much later when Annie heard the key turn in the door, well after 11 p.m. She had been sitting up, scrolling, waiting and wondering when her husband was going to get home. She very much doubted the school concert had gone on for all that time, so she guessed that he'd gone out afterwards with his colleagues. Maybe that included Sylvie and maybe he now knew she'd been at Sylvie's.

'Hello,' she called out when she heard he was inside the front door, 'had a good evening?'

There was no reply, but she could hear his footsteps coming towards the sitting room. Then the door opened and Ed appeared. He looked handsome... that was often her first thought when she saw him these days. He was older, yes, than when she'd first fallen in love with him. But he was also more together, more grown-up than he had been back then.

'I'm still very angry with you,' he said, without raising any kind of smile, without giving her any sign that there could be a hint of forgiveness in the air, 'and I know where you were this afternoon. It turns out you were in Sylvie's apartment, trying to persuade her to be on your programme.'

'She didn't need much persuading,' Annie said defensively. 'She loves fashion. She has a beautiful wardrobe and she loved the idea of showing it off to our viewers. Don't make me sound like some kind of undercover reporter.'

'But... let's set aside for a moment the fact that you forgot to pick up our twins and they ended up in a police station... why were you in her apartment?' Ed asked. He closed the door behind him but remained standing.

'Why were you locked in her courtyard?' was his next question, but he didn't wait for an answer. 'I remember telling you where she lived,' he went on, 'and I think you were... well... did you follow her there, Annie? Were you *spying* on her? I can't believe I'm even asking you this question because why would you do something like that?'

Annie looked away. She could feel the warm prickle of a blush spreading up across her cheeks. She wasn't sure what to say. How did she sum up all the building feeling that she had lost some of her hold over him? That she just wasn't quite as important to him as she had always been. And that she was deeply worried he had developed feelings for someone much younger, much more attractive than her?

How did she say all that? She needed to think this through... she didn't want to go blurting everything out. But then all her anger and anxiety about the whole situation rushed up and before she could think about it, she was blurting: 'Why was I following her? Oh, I dunno, maybe because she's hot and sexy and seems to think you're hot and sexy too. And maybe because I keep finding things in your pockets that make me extremely worried and extremely suspicious.'

'Things in my pockets? Like what?' Ed demanded.

'Like notes with love hearts and... and phone numbers... addresses and *condom wrappers*! Yes, I found a condom wrapper! So, what do you have to say about that?'

'What?!!'

She could read the expression of shock on Ed's face clearly enough. But was it shock that she had found out? Or shock that she was accusing him of something so ridiculous? That was what she couldn't tell.

Ed stepped forward into the room now. In a quiet, but still infuriated, voice he added, 'And let's keep it down, or we'll have the twins in here asking what all the fuss is about.'

'What all the fuss is about?!' she repeated. 'I'm sure you would make a fuss if you found wrappers like that in my pockets. Or do you not care about what I get up to any more?'

'Of course, I care – but going by this afternoon, you get up to a whole load of mischief and nonsense.'

'Don't talk to me like I'm some badly behaved pupil of yours,' she said, outraged.

'Then stop acting like a badly behaved pupil.'

Now they were glaring at each other in what looked like fury.

'So, you don't have anything to say for yourself – no explanation?' she demanded.

'I don't owe you an explanation. I haven't done anything wrong,' Ed insisted. 'I have no idea what you're talking about.'

'Shall I go and get them then, the notes and the wrapper?'

Even as Annie said these words, she realised she might sound angry, but she didn't feel angry. She felt overwhelmingly sad. This was just sad, sad and damaging. Every word coming out of their mouths was like an axe blow to their trust, their friendship, their love and understanding. How had this happened? This was Ed, the person she had completely loved and trusted absolutely. What had they done, or not done, for her to be waiting alone all evening, full of suspicion, and for him to unable to tell her what was really going on?

This was what it meant to drift apart.

It had happened so slowly at first. They'd hardly even noticed the distance building up between them. They'd assumed it was temporary and would pass, would somehow get better without either of them having to do anything about it.

And now this is where they were. There were important parts of his life that weren't available to her any longer. She genuinely did not know if he was involved with someone else or not. Now, they were in this angry, sad, mistrustful place and it would be so much harder to sort anything out from here.

'Don't get anything. Go to bed,' Ed insisted. 'I've had a very long and very stressful day. I'm not talking to you about anything. Just leave me alone.'

Annie left the room in silence.

It was much later when Ed finally came into the bedroom. But Annie, lying on her side of the bed with her back turned to his, pretended to be asleep.

But she knew that this was no good. And this wasn't them. Why had they not tried to sort these problems out before? Why on earth had they assumed Ed going to Paris would magically heal everything?

Now, lying side-by-side in silence, Annie wondered if she would get any rest before her 6 a.m. alarm call, when all she could think about was Ed. And the fact that their marriage was in deep danger.

23

LES CHEVAUX — HAIR

A good hairdresser will work with you to find styles and colours that make you look your best and will encourage you to update your look regularly. I believe in treating my hair gently, like my best cashmere sweater. I like the contrast of a more casual outfit and hair that is carefully 'done', or, the Parisian classic, a smart outfit and casual, rumpled hair.

— M.M.

* * *

By 7.30 a.m. the following morning – a Saturday, so Ed could be at home with the twins – Annie was in the hairdresser's reception area when a sleek, black SUV pulled up at the door and the driver leapt out to open the rear passenger's door. There could be no doubt that this was Svetlana arriving.

A high-heeled foot emerged, followed by a bare tanned leg, a knee-length pale skirt and then, Svetlana herself. The big black shades were a typical accessory, but the enormous caramel-coloured turban was not. It gave Annie a jolt. If Svetlana was wearing a turban to get to the hairdresser's, the hair must be bad.

'That's Svetlana,' she told Stephan, the salon's star stylist, who was here ninety minutes before opening for this special session. Meanwhile, Pierre, the grouchy cameraman was already all set up with lights and camera at the chair where Stephan would work on Svetlana's hair.

'Good morning! Good morning, everyone,' Svetlana exclaimed as she strode in through the front door. She shook hands all round, then bent down from her towering heels to kiss Annie on the cheek, twice on each side. Although she seemed to be enjoying the attention of the arrival moment, she immediately whispered, 'I don't want to talk about the damage. I don't want the right side of my head to be filmed. Is that agreed?'

'Right... OK, I'll go and speak to Pierre. Let's see what we can do to make you comfortable,' Annie said, deciding on the spot that whatever Svetlana needed to keep her in the chair for this haircut, Svetlana would get.

So, Annie went to explain the situation, as Svetlana and Stephan made some introductory small talk.

Soon Svetlana was settled in the chair with Pierre and the camera to her left, Stephan behind making eye contact via the mirror, while Annie stayed out of shot and out of the way on Svetlana's right.

'OK,' Stephan began gently, 'would you like me to take the turban off and we can look at your hair?'

As Svetlana gave a curt nod, Annie couldn't help leaning forward. What on earth was this going to look like?

Stephan put one hand on either side of the turban and slowly eased it upwards. As it came off, Svetlana's hair began to fall down. Annie had never seen her without her hair up, so this was fascinating. The hair was long, well below shoulder length and it dropped down in chunky, caramel-blonde tresses. But on the right side of Svetlana's head, well, it was startling – a major chunk of hair was missing, almost up to the level of her ear. In place of the long tress that should have been hanging there was a frizzy frazzle, which stuck out, completely out of place on this blonde, polished, thoroughbred of a woman.

Annie restrained herself from gasping, although that's what she instinctively wanted to do. It was just such a significant amount of hair. She had thought maybe Stephan could incorporate the damage into soft layers around the face, but this was major.

'You are so lucky you didn't get burned, darlin',' Annie told her.

'Yes, I know. I am not wanting to use hairspray again for a long time, so maybe this helps to make the decision to change my hair easier for me.'

Stephan had a brush with widely spaced bristles and he was using it to gently work through the locks. He was feeling the hair, evaluating the texture, condition, thickness, the way it might fall in a different style. Then he moved to the burned area of hair and held the frazzle in his fingers.

'Do you have to cut off all my hair?' Svetlana asked in a voice barely above a whisper.

Stephan smiled reassuringly, before explaining, 'It's going to be shorter than you might want, but maybe not as short as you fear. And hair grows. It forgives us all our mistakes. If we go short at the front, but graduate down, we can keep to almost shoulder length at the back.'

Svetlana turned to Annie at this point, who quickly smiled and told her, 'It's going to be sensational. I can't wait!'

'You're not frightened to lose the hair?' was Stephan's next question. 'You don't look like a woman who is easily frightened.'

With these words, he was daring her to do it. And Svetlana always found it hard to refuse a dare.

'No, I'm not frightened,' she said completely neutrally, as if it was nothing, as if she was not even related to the woman who had previously refused to come out of the taxi and set foot into the salon.

'Cut off the hair,' she said.

And so, surprisingly quickly, Stephan brushed the hair out straight, so it fell behind the chair, then used an electric trimmer to make a clean, straight line right at the top of her shoulders.

* * *

It was a blunt bob, cut a bold two inches above the shoulder line, with a wide, curving fringe at the front which dropped down in careful layers to meet the longer hair at the back, so that all the burnt and frazzled hair could be removed. Stephan had spent a long time cutting, shaping, trimming to make sure the style was full of life and movement. Then he'd lifted the colour from the yellowy, caramel tones Svetlana had worn for years, to a lighter baby blonde.

He'd made her sit with a conditioning mask on her head for twenty minutes and advised her to do this once a week to keep her hair sleek and smooth. After he'd applied some miracle product, which she was to buy – along with the shampoo, conditioner, and mask, of course – he had just blasted her hair with the hairdryer, shaping it roughly with his hands. No curling brush, no tongs, nothing complicated.

'You can use tongs, of course, to make waves, to make ringlets, whatever you like...' he'd told her, 'but it's beautiful hair, so I want it to be free.'

When he was finally done, he went off in search of a finishing spray, as Pierre moved in to film the end result. Svetlana and Annie sat looking in the mirror, transfixed.

* * *

As Svetlana looked at her reflection, she realised that her hair hadn't been this length since she was maybe twelve or thirteen. At that age, her locks had been close to this colour, too, bleached lightest blonde by the fierce Ukrainian summer. So, it was a disorientating effect. Instead of the tied back, controlled updo, there was soft, flowing hair moving round her face, touching her jaw, swishing when she moved her head from side to side. It was brand-new, but it also revived memories of way back then, when she was young, carefree, bold, determined and so excited for the adventure of life.

She smiled at herself, no, she grinned at herself. She swung her head from side to side and the hair swung with her. She took her hands and ran them over the back of her head, mussing up the hair and making it more rumpled and puffy at the back.

'I can't believe it,' Annie said. 'You look incredible. It is a work of freaking genius.' And this was all completely true. Svetlana always looked younger than her age, but now she looked softer and fresher too. She looked more relaxed, more fun even.

'What will Carlos think?' Annie ventured. 'About 16 inches of hair has hit the floor here today!'

'I think he will be happy for me. Maybe he would have made more changes if I had let him,' Svetlana admitted.

Stephan was back to squirt some potion onto the locks and give them a final scrunch and tweak.

'*Et voilà*,' he said, taking his hands from her head and admiring his work in the mirror, 'we are rid of the burdened rich-lady look and have set you free.'

Svetlana blinked and swallowed, while Annie panicked that the hairdresser had overstepped the mark here. Svetlana really was a rich lady, not some wannabee. There was now a danger that she would throw off her cape and make an imperious exit.

But Svetlana looked at her reflection and felt the truth of his words. She was rich, she was burdened and she did want... well, maybe to be set free was the best description. Even though she didn't know what it was yet, she did want the freedom to live her life differently to how she'd lived it before. She didn't have to live the way her mother wanted her to, or any of her previous controlling husbands. She did have a brand-new freedom but she didn't yet know what to do with it.

From her late teenage years until the day Igor's hard-fought divorce settlement had made her a very wealthy woman in her own right, every moment of Svetlana's life had been about pleasing the important men she wanted to impress, to captivate, to influence.

So, the idea of being set free... the idea of somehow capturing some essence of the person she was before all that, was very attractive.

'I last had hair like this when I was twelve,' Svetlana said finally, 'straight, and very blonde with the sun. I had a short fringe and my hair was halfway up my neck maybe. My mother hated to brush it, so she cut it into this style.'

With one haircut, Stephan had dismantled the image she'd maintained for decades... and maybe this would help her to remember who she *really* was and who she had wanted to be all those years ago.

'You don't look twelve, of course,' Stephan said, and Annie was worried again – what was he going to say now? Please don't make her angry or send her rushing off in search of more surgical solutions.

'But you remember the spirit of twelve,' Stephan added. 'We're often well-formed at that age and begin to know who we are and what we want, no?'

Svetlana smiled at this, and Annie gave a little laugh of relief.

'Do haircuts in France always come with such a generous slice of philosophy?' Svetlana asked.

'*Naturellement,*' Stephan replied.

'It's wonderful. I absolutely love it!' Annie enthused.

Svetlana swished her head from side to side once more.

'Me too,' she said. 'This is beautiful work, Stephan. And now we have to go, on to our next appointment.'

As Svetlana's cape was unclipped and the final loose hairs brushed from her neck and her clothes, she caught another glance at her reflection and couldn't help thinking of Coco Chanel's words: 'A woman who cuts her hair is about to change her life.'

24

LE STYLE PERSONNEL – PERSONAL STYLE

Yes, it will take trial and error, but gradually, if you pay attention, you will build your signature style. Learn from experience the colours that make you look alert and refreshed, the styles that you feel at home in, the fabrics that you love. Once you've found your look, build on it, develop it! Allow yourself to project on the outside the you that is inside.

— M.M.

* * *

Out on the street after the haircut, walking along the pavement towards her waiting car, Svetlana immediately felt different. Lighter, freer... how had she not realised before how the updo weighed on her head? Made her walk in a certain way, holding her shoulders rigidly back?

Now, she felt as if her head could move, her shoulders could drop, she could have more swing to her stride. She wanted to take longer steps, walk faster, swing her arms and her shoulders. She kept looking for those glimpses of herself in corner windows and glass doors and she hardly recognised herself. The skirt-suit was the same, the big sunglasses were the same, the high courts, the status-symbol handbag, but this swish of bright blonde hair. This free, soft and shiny hair... it changed everything. She wanted to laugh. She wanted to skip in the street. She felt directly plugged in to the spirit of twelve-year-old Svetlana. Bold, mischievous, determined, smart, strong, resourceful, and laughing. Laughing a lot. At all kinds of things.

'You look fantastic!' Annie told her. 'Thank goodness for the candle incident! Your hair is better than I could ever have imagined.'

Svetlana put her hands up to the edges of her short bob again. 'It is making me think of all kinds of things,' she admitted, 'especially of young Svetlana. Young Svetlana, she was a force of nature!'

'Of course she was,' Annie agreed. 'Older Svetlana is a force of nature too.'

'But I have let life change me too much,' Svetlana said. 'I need to go back to the essence of that girl. She was so strong and so capable. She could do everything and anything and no one told her what to do.'

'Not even her mother?' Annie had to ask.

'Well… it's true, my mother was a very big influence,' Svetlana admitted, 'but young Svetlana made her own decisions, made her own way. She was her own person.'

With these words, Svetlana stood stock-still in front of a large window and looked properly at her reflection. She was tall in her heels and still skinny from a lifetime of careful eating, but she was also strong, the way she had asked her personal trainer to make her. This head with its short and fluid blonde bob no longer matched the body in the pernickety skirt suit and spindly heels.

'A new life is coming,' she told Annie. 'I need different clothes for the new life.'

'You do,' Annie agreed, 'which is good, because that's exactly where we're headed.'

* * *

The two women swept in to the glamorous, bang-on-trend boutique, highly recommended by Emmanuel, which was expecting them. The doors had not been closed to other customers, but a generous fitting room had been reserved for them and the cameraman was already one step ahead, setting up, and looking not one tiny bit more cheerful than at the hairdresser's.

'Shall we look around?' Annie suggested once she and Svetlana had said hello to the staff and introduced themselves.

'Of course. But I must tell you that I've not been shopping for a long time,' Svetlana admitted.

'Really?'

Although Annie knew the couture outfit Svetlana was wearing dated from a good many seasons back, she couldn't imagine Svetlana not shopping at all. This was a woman who had once needed both her driver and several store assistants to transport all her purchases back to her car.

'Yes, I wear some new things from Perfect Dress, and I bought some swimsuits for the summer holidays, but shopping, planning a new season... not for a long time,' came the revelation.

'Well, you just have to start slowly... ease yourself

back in,' Annie advised. 'Let's walk around and enjoy the colours and maybe run our hands over a few things. Don't overthink it.'

So, they did just that, pulling out a silky top here and stroking some cashmere there.

'What would young Svetlana like?' Annie asked playfully, definitely not wanting to start any kind of crisis of the 'what am I going to do with my life?' variety.

'Ah, I like this idea,' Svetlana said with a smile. 'Young Svetlana... she wants clothes that let her move! Clothes that don't need Maria to take them to the dry cleaner. Clothes for wearing, clothes for living, but still beautiful... you know?'

'Oh yes, I know...' Annie was still looking at the careful displays. Svetlana must have been young in the eighties, maybe even the seventies. Luckily, there was a sort of seventies/eighties vibe to this season's fashion.

'Trousers?' she suggested. 'We never have you in trousers. Maybe you need to try some on... and what about suede? Soft and slouchy suede? Although, obviously, that does need the dry cleaners now and then.'

She flitted around with one of the assistants and together, they came up with an armful of choices.

And thinking of Sylvie and Yves Saint Laurent, Annie went over to the reassuringly expensive selection of jeans.

Could she even *imagine* Svetlana in *jeans*? But maybe this was exactly the lightning bolt change that she needed.

'To the fitting room, my darlin', let's try and make Pierre the cameraman smile.'

* * *

For the next hour or so, everyone's attention was lavished on Svetlana. They put her into beautifully tai-lored wide-legged trousers in caramel cord. They even coaxed her into the dark, soft, Italian-fabric jeans. They swathed her in sumptuous Missoni, skinny, multi-coloured sweaters and scarves.

'A little bit of 1970s vibe, oh yes! That is what we want,' Annie encouraged, sure that this would help with getting in touch with the inner twelve-year-old. The one who grew up in the vivid yellows, greens, or-anges and earth shades of that decade.

A sheepskin jacket, a suede coat, a soft, puff-sleeved denim blouse, low-heeled knee-high boots, a luxurious version of a school satchel, gold earrings and bracelets studded with chunky stones – these were all suggested by Annie and the tireless assistants.

Then came soft, knitted fabric A-line skirts that let Svetlana lengthen her stride, and nubbly cashmere sweaters that embraced her, instead of jackets which constrained and structured her.

'Annah, I have missed finding new clothes with you,' Svetlana gushed, looking at herself in the changing room mirror in the first pair of jeans she'd worn for decades. They were wide at the bottom, tight and high waisted with patch pockets at the top. She hadn't worn jeans since her very early twenties. She'd completely forgotten how flattering they could be and how anonymous and universal, yet also individual, and even slightly rebellious. Going from couture Chanel to jeans... in Svetlana's book, that was definitely rebellious.

Underneath the jeans, she was wearing conker-brown ankle boots with a block heel. And above the jeans, a silky, slinky knit in multi-coloured shades of wine, bright-blue, silver and rust. Then came a generous scarf in the same vivid multi-colours, draped round her neck, and a short swingy suede jacket on top. The wine-red satchel was over one shoulder. And then her soft, bright halo of chopped blonde, blonde hair.

'I love this outfit,' Annie told her. 'I love you in all of it! Young Svetlana would love this, wouldn't she?'

Current Svetlana had to nod in agreement.

'Young Svetlana would be able to run, climb, walk, even hitchhike in this outfit,' Annie added.

She had caught the bus out of her village at sixteen... Svetlana remembered. What if she had headed not to a beauty contest, not to decades of trying to please very demanding men... what might have happened instead? Maybe she could have caught a different bus. Maybe she could have gone off in the direction of university and a different kind of life altogether.

But Svetlana stopped herself from pursuing this train of thought. Lately, she had spent too much time looking back. She looked carefully at her reflection in the new clothes.

'I don't want to look back, or go back, Annah.'

'No, of course not,' Annie agreed. 'You can nod to the past. You can treasure the past. But it's time to look forward.'

Svetlana took out her phone and snapped a selfie. For a moment she thought about sending it to Harry, but no, she wanted to surprise him properly, reveal her new look to him when she was back home and the moment was exactly right.

The new Svetlana with her decade-erasing hairstyle, said yes to almost all the fashion-forward clothes and shoes she'd tried on and asked the girls to pack them up for her. 'The satchel, too, please.'

* * *

Afterwards, coming out of the boutique felt like a triumph, felt as if one whole episode of *How To Be Fabulous* had been created. Annie had plenty to worry about, but she at least felt less tense about the future of the series than she had done in weeks. Tamsin would love what they'd done with Svetlana. The viewers would love it too. And if even Svetlana could lose her fashion way and need some help to find her direction again, then so could anyone. And Annie and her show were here to put things right again. Paris style.

'Where shall we go next? Let's go and drink some Champagne!' was Svetlana's suggestion.

But although Annie had been able to park her domestic woes for the hair and shopping sessions this morning, glancing down to see her phone alight with family messages, the woes all came rushing back. She would have to say goodbye to Svetlana and get back to the apartment.

'Let me just see how things are with Ed and the twins,' she stalled as Svetlana's large black car swept up to the pavement, ready to whisk her on to her next destination.

Annie opened on message number one and was astonished to read the words sent by Ed:

I've packed all your things up and booked you and the twins onto the train to London this afternoon.

'Oh, babes,' Annie glanced over at Svetlana, 'I've had such a great time, but I have to get back to base.'

'Are you sure?' Svetlana climbed into the car and beckoned Annie to come and do the same. 'We should go to The Ritz to celebrate, have cocktails in the bar where the stars of Paris saw out the war.'

'I love being your friend,' Annie told her and it felt as if the smiles between them did finally put to rest what had gone wrong earlier this year, 'and we will do that, my darlin'... but not today.'

No, today, Annie had something much more urgent to see to – the state of her marriage by the sound of things.

25

LE CONFORT – COMFORT

Coco Chanel taught us almost everything we need to know about dressing well. The most important lesson from the woman who took us out of corsets and into trousers and bathing suits was that we must be comfortable in our clothes. They must fit us, not the other way around. Nothing should be tight. Everything must be wearable and soft, with pockets!

— M.M.

* * *

When Annie arrived back at the apartment, the twins rushed to greet her, wrapping themselves around her legs and up into hugs, as if she'd been away for days.

'Daddy says we're going home today,' Minette enthused.

'On the train!' added an excited Max.

And Annie could see that all their bags were lined up in the hallway ready to go.

Ed hung back in the doorway of the sitting room without a smile on his face.

Directing her question at the twins, she asked, 'Would it be OK, my buddies, if you could go to your room and play for just a little bit because there are some things I need to talk to Daddy about? Could you do that? I can even give you my phone,' she said, handing over the bribe.

So, then she and Ed were in the sitting room alone. And it felt just as angry, sad and confused as last night.

'Are you going to explain what's going on then?' was Annie's opening question.

'I don't owe you any explanation. I haven't done anything wrong. I have no idea what you were talking about last night,' Ed insisted, 'and I think you should go home.'

'But I can't just go back to London now. I'm already

trying to set things up for next week... and do the research.'

'Well, come back, funded by your TV company, when you need to. But right now, I want you to take the twins home. I want to be in Paris by myself, the way we planned.'

Annie stared at him, momentarily too surprised to speak.

He really did want her and the twins to go home today, without sorting any of this out, without trying to help move the two of them back to a happier place. She'd never expected this to happen.

'Why?' she asked. 'Why do you want us to go?'

And now he was running both hands through his hair, the way he did when he was agitated. 'Just give me a break, Annie. Can you do that? This was supposed to be my time away. This was supposed to give me some headspace, a chance to think about my career, and my music, and... yes, maybe myself. And I was hardly here for any time at all before you arrived to fill up the apartment and fill up my head. This is not the way I wanted it to be.'

'Oh, I'm *sorry*,' she said with more sass and sarcasm than she had perhaps intended, 'am I supposed to put our family and my career on pause while you have some quiet reflection time... some *you* time?'

'Well, yes, right now you are,' he replied. 'When you're back to full-time filming, I pick up all the slack on the family front, so yes, right now I want to be a bit selfish and concentrate on my stuff. I'm not a house husband. I have a career too. I'm the head of music at a very competitive school in case you hadn't noticed.'

She didn't see how she could argue against that. It was true, during her filming months, she was away for twelve to fourteen hours a day, and she did rely on him to pick up not every single bit of family life, but a lot.

Completely deflated, she answered with a still angry, 'I see.'

But that just didn't convey the half of it. She was totally upset, her questions were unanswered, and she had no idea what else was going on in her husband's head. But right now, they were both far too angry to continue this conversation. Maybe her going back to London was a good idea – for now.

'Well, I better go and check the bedrooms, make sure you've packed everything,' she said, preparing to sweep out of the room.

'Good idea,' was Ed's maddeningly calm reply, as he sat down and switched on the TV.

Good idea... *good idea*?

Oh God, there were occasional moments in a marriage when you wondered how on earth you could have picked such an infuriating numbnut to be your life partner and how could you possibly unravel it all as quickly as possible.

So, fired up with hurt and fury, Annie went to the bedroom and noisily banged the wardrobe and bathroom doors open and shut as she made sure that all her and the twins' belongings had been gathered up.

'What time is *our* train?' she shouted into the hallway for Ed's benefit.

'I'll order the taxi now.'

'Are you going to see us off?' she wondered.

'No, I've got to go to a meeting.'

'A school meeting? On a Saturday?' she had to ask.

A terse 'yes' was all the information she got.

'So, this is *au revoir*, is it?' she asked, annoyed, upset, confused. He was practically throwing them out and he had never been so harsh, so unwilling to discuss anything ever before.

Was he fed up with her? Was he having an affair? And now she was being sent home so she couldn't even dig about and try to find out what was really going on, let alone talk to him properly.

Ed wanted her to go. Ed wanted rid of her. How had this happened? Was it his fault? Her fault? Her feelings of distress and fury were so strong, she couldn't even protest, could think of nothing to say. Maybe she did have to go. Maybe they had to part now before they could work out what to do next.

26

Les Couleurs – Colours

The colours I love on myself and to see on others are all the neutral tones – from creams and beiges to shades of brown, grey and black – but with jolts of the deep, true colours, such as emerald-green, scarlet-red, or cobalt-blue. I can never get so excited about pastel tones like salmon-pink or pale-lemon. But each to their own. If you adore a colour, you should probably wear it.

— M.M.

* * *

When the taxi arrived, Ed at least helped to take the bags down to the front of the building.

'Have a good journey back,' he offered and she got a kiss on the cheek, although the children were hugged, squeezed and twirled around in the air as he promised them he would speak to them every day.

As soon as the taxi set off, everything became very grumpy very quickly. The twins began to whine about 'do we have to go back home?' At the sight of the Eiffel Tower in the distance, they complained bitterly that they'd never even been to see it, followed by, 'Why do we have to leave Paris, and Daddy?' And then further whinging about being too hot, or too cold, or feeling sick. Her half-hearted attempt at playing 'I spy' was completely ignored.

The station, on her own with the twins and so many bags, was just as tricky to negotiate as when she had travelled from London. But finally, she wrangled a trolley and managed to get them onto the train, even squeezing in buying two chocolate croissants on the way down the platform.

Alas, the train was running late... and once they were finally onboard, double, triple alas, all the alcohol was sold out, so there was no chance of a soothing glass of wine. To add insult to injury, when she gave in to the demands and bought Minette and

Max packets of crisps for 'lunch' instead of sensible cheese sandwiches, a very well-dressed elderly French woman sitting in the seat across the aisle from them actually leaned over and told her off!

'This is not good food for *les petites*,' she began, with a firm-but-fair expression on her face, 'they need to learn to enjoy good food when they are young and you are responsible for this.'

For a moment, Annie was too surprised to say anything, and then she thought she might cry. Finally, regaining some composure, she tried something along the lines of... 'Well, travelling, everyone is a little bit upset, it's not like at home.'

But the senior lady was having none of it. 'You can't give in to all these demands. You must be firm and very predictable. Strict even. Especially when it comes to food. This is the problem with young people nowadays, they have no discipline around food. It is all snacks and junk everywhere!'

Annie decided, whatever her thoughts on the matter, it might be best to just thank the woman for her well-meant advice, rather than get into any kind of debate. On the plus side, Max and Minette were looking at the lady, open-mouthed with surprise and Minette actually folded her crisp packet shut and pushed it over towards Annie.

'Thank you, that's very helpful,' Annie told the woman contritely. 'I will give them a good meal when I get home.'

Then there might have been a long and awkward silence between her and this elegantly dressed woman, who looked to be around the late sixties, maybe even seventies mark, but Annie wanted to clear the air and be friendly, plus she'd noticed an intriguing detail.

'You're wearing a beautiful brooch,' she said, pointing to the creamy enamelled piece of jewellery on the lady's jacket lapel. It didn't escape Annie's notice that it was in the shape of a camellia.

'Oh, thank you,' the woman replied, brightening immediately, 'it represents a camellia.'

'Yes,' Annie said, 'I'm guessing it's vintage Chanel.'

'You are correct,' the woman said, 'bought as a gift for me many, many years ago. And do you know why Chanel liked to adorn women with real and jewel-shaped camellias?'

'I always thought she must have loved the flower. And they are white, one of her favourite colours. But are you going to tell me another reason?'

'Oh yes, apparently, when Chanel was a young woman, women pinned camellias onto their gowns

when they were mistresses who had become... available.'
The woman raised her eyebrow gently. 'So maybe it was
a little joke of hers to have all the respectable women of
Paris pinning this sign of availability onto themselves.
And, of course, it is a beautiful flower and so elegant.'

Now Annie noticed the vintage Chanel scarf
tucked in under the woman's jacket lapel, and the
small brown alligator handbag set down beside her
heeled loafers. Unfortunately, just as Annie was
thinking that she and this French fashion lover from a
different era could have quite the delightful chat all
the way back to London, Max announced that he felt
'really sick this time' and Annie had to spring into
action.

* * *

Despite everything that had happened in France, it
was still lovely to be home, especially as Dinah and
her family were currently staying there and Dinah, the
domesticated goddess, appeared to have cleaned and
organised every last dust-bunnied nook and spider-
webbed cranny.

Annie hugged everyone hello very gratefully, especially Owen, and there was tea to be drunk, home-

made biscuits to be eaten and all the very latest chat to catch up on.

'Couldn't you just move in?' Annie asked her sister as they were all folded up into the huge corner sofa in her sitting room. 'I want to live in a family commune. It would be so lovely. We could share the cooking and the cleaning, then some nights, I can palm the twins off on you and have Billie all to myself...' Annie said, cuddling her niece in close.

Billie squeaked with delight at the thought of this and began a little chorus of, 'Can we, Mum? Can we...? I could have Lauren's room...'

While Minette interrupted with, 'No, Billie can share with me and Max can go somewhere else...'

Prompting Max to fall face down onto the sofa shouting, 'No! I want Billie in my room, not stupid Minette!'

'Calm down, everyone,' Dinah said, taking charge of the impending mayhem. 'This is a beautiful big house, but maybe not quite big enough for two families. Oh my goodness, calm down,' she repeated, scooping Max up into a hug. 'Annie, you send the twins to me as often as you like, and of course Billie can come to you whenever you want. Can I just remind you, Billie, that when we do go home, we're going to have a brand-new bathroom? So maybe you'll feel a bit less like moving in here.'

'But here is fun!' Billie insisted, nestling up between Minette and Max and shooting a grin at Owen who was perched on the end of the sofa. 'With lots of fun people.'

'Right...' Annie caught sight of her older son's pensive face and remembered that she needed to make time to take him aside for the big talk about how his decision about what to do or what to study next year was coming along. Music or economics? Classical music or something much more contemporary? Poor Owen... all the stress of this big decision.

And bloody Music... bloody Ed... bloody Paris... bloody cello-playing, siren Sylvie.

* * *

27

Les Ceintures – Belts

Don't be frightened of belts! Think of them as jewellery for your trousers and your skirts. Slim shiny belts in complementary colours will dress your outfits up. Chunky leather will add interest to your casual look. Where would a wrap coat be without the luxurious tie belt to complete it?

— M.M.

* * *

Svetlana was back in London, back to sitting in her residents' garden in Mayfair in her all-new outfit of jeans, luxury sweater and suede, still wondering what to do with the rest of her life. One thing she was not back to was smoking her favourite Sobrani cigarettes, or any kind of cigarette at all. There were only so many brushes with death that you wanted to invite on yourself in a year.

She'd had some surgery – minor tweaking to the neck under local anaesthetic, instead of the planned facelift and breast reduction. It had been successfully completed three days ago and was healing up nicely, but just hours after the surgery she'd suffered a blood clot in her leg.

Pah, she tried to shrug off the memory. It was over, they'd treated it, she was back on the pills. Best not to think about it. Now... back to the Rest of Her Life.

She twiddled her fingers and tried to think. Nothing at all inspirational came, so she was very glad when her phone rang and she could see Annie's name on the screen.

'Svetlana, how are you doing?' Annie began.

So, Svetlana gave her friend the latest update, minus the clot detail, but ended with the words, 'My health is good, my stitches are healing, I like my new clothes, my new hair... I look good on the outside, and

Harry thinks so, too, but Annah... my soul is still in Siberia.'

So Annie began to talk in her usual positive, cheering way, about how Svetlana needed to find something not just to do but to give her purpose.

'We've sorted you on the outside, my darlin'. Now, we need to sort you on the inside,' she said. 'What's really important to you?' was Annie's next question. 'You need to do the thing that's really important to you...'

It wasn't as if Svetlana hadn't thought about this question. Her family was very important to her, of course. Her beautiful home was important to her, along with keeping herself extremely financially secure forever. All of these areas were in a very good place. Then there was Ukraine, of course. But she already wrote cheques, she already paid for two families who had moved to London temporarily. There was not much more she felt she could do here. She had even asked Igor what influence he could bring and he had promised he was doing what he could.

It was what else was important to her. That was the question... and...

'I'm not going to help out at a soup kitchen,' Svetlana told her friend. 'I don't think I would be very good at this.'

'Noooo...' Annie had to agree. 'I can't really imagine that. What about a pet?' was her next suggestion.

Svetlana made a disdainful sound and added, 'I am not going to be one of those women with a little dog.' No, definitely not a little dog. 'It is difficult for me to explain...' Svetlana began. 'I want to do something that is important to lots of people, that is big and visible. I want to be able to help hundreds of people. Not one little dog.'

'Become a politician?' Annie suggested, but Svetlana could hear the light-heartedness in her voice and they both laughed at this thought.

Annie made her promise she would prepare her financial slot for the TV series, because as Annie reminded her, Svetlana loved doing that slot, the audience loved her and it was often very helpful advice. Then, promising Svetlana that the good idea would come if she just kept looking for it, Annie rang off, but not before they'd arranged to meet again soon.

'We'll think of something,' she'd promised Svetlana.

After the call, Svetlana looked around her surroundings properly. The weather was chilly and damp and this garden, surrounded by multi-million-pound houses was utterly dreary and lacklustre. The featureless lawn was already scattered with twigs and leaves. Several tall plane trees commanded the centre of the space and the boundary, marked by high iron railings, was surrounded by a neat but struggling hedge.

There were no flowers... no fruit trees... no blossom in the spring... not even any nettles or dock leaves. As she breathed in, it occurred to her there wasn't even the smell of a garden. Or the buzz and busy hum of a garden. She rarely saw birds or squirrels in here.

And now she was lost in thoughts of her mother's garden. There had been a large plot for vegetables, of course. This was the main aim of the garden, to keep her and her mother from going hungry and to stretch out her mother's meagre earnings as far as they could go. Carrots, potatoes, squash and courgettes were grown in the deep raised beds. Then there were fences made of cane and chicken wire which grew broad beans, green beans and peas upwards. Her mother had always said farmers never thought about all the vertical space they owned, too obsessed with their horizontal acres.

In the hot summers, tomatoes, cucumbers and grapes grew up in a patch that got the early morning and late evening sun but were shaded from the fierce heat of midday. Then there was salad, so much delicious salad – cos lettuce, radicchio, tender spinach leaves, lamb's lettuce, rocket, and all the herbs her mother used to snip and sprinkle over the leaves: chives, oregano, basil, mint, dill. Her mother's salads, with homegrown tomatoes and cucumber, sprinkled with herbs, still with a slight tang of fresh earth, drizzled in the co-operative's olive oil and home-made vinegar from a neighbour – no starred restaurant she'd ever eaten in had been able to recreate those salads.

There had been two apple trees, one cherry tree and one plum tree with yellow-fleshed sweet plums, another with the zingingly sour plums used to make those early autumn flans. She'd never been able to find the like in the UK.

There were flowers too of course, to attract and feed the bees. A clambering rose, lavender, and tall sunflowers, all the seeds carefully picked out of the heads by Svetlana at the end of the summer.

Svetlana could feel a tear slipping down her cheek, which she quickly brushed away. Now that she was a mother of older children, now that she feared they would flee the nest and barely ever return, she wondered how she could have stayed away from her own mother for such long periods. It must have hurt her so much. And when her mother had died, unexpectedly and much sooner than Svetlana could ever have anticipated, she had still not returned home because that would have been far too late.

Instead, she'd sent lavish flowers, shipped in from the best florist in Kiev; she'd paid for a proper dinner with plenty of wine for the entire village to enjoy after the funeral. But then, the house and garden had been sold without Svetlana ever visiting again. So now the garden existed only in her imagination.

She turned her head upwards and took a deep breath in to stem the tears. She had called her mother often, she consoled herself. Every single week, they had spoken at least twice. And her mother had been so proud of her and loved to hear about the life she was leading – so far from the village and so close to all their dreams and aspirations.

She had spared her mother too many details about the painful divorces, the legal wrangles over money and her children. She'd always painted a wonderfully rosy picture. And, of course, she'd been able to make her mother's life comfortable in all the little ways her mother had allowed – a monthly allowance, a wood-burning stove, warm clothes, shoes, blankets. But she wasn't allowed to send her mother flights or holidays, because she wouldn't come, or buy her anything really showy, like a new car, or a bigger home – because her mother didn't want that, didn't want to feel different from the other people in the village who were her community, her family.

Her mother's desire to be the same, to fit in, not to raise her head above the crowd was strong. Her ambitions had all been channelled into her daughter – she hadn't wanted any of it for herself.

Svetlana was sitting so still on the bench that the gardeners who had come in some ten or twenty minutes earlier were now raking leaves in the bushes behind the bench and were talking companionably within her earshot, but perhaps unaware that she was there.

'All right for people who live round here,' one of them said in an accent that was London mixed with some other corner of the world. 'They're not worrying about the heating bills this winter, are they?'

'Nah,' the other guy agreed, 'they probably leave the heating on and go off to all the other homes they've got all over the world.'

Ja... Svetlana thought to herself, *I am one of the fortunate ones. And what can I do to make even a small corner of the world a little better?*

* * *

That night, Svetlana had what felt like a long, deep and vivid dream. She was at home, a young girl again, and it was high summer in the garden. She was walking with grass at her feet, and the scent of fresh herbs in the wind. Then she was kneeling in the earth, picking tender spinach and sorrel leaves and collecting them in the yellow plastic colander that had been in the house for her whole lifetime. Two of the village cats were perched on the garden wall looking down at her. She could hear her mother's voice, and although she couldn't see her, or make out the words, she felt deep happiness and contentment as her hands worked carefully over the leaves, pulling out those ready to be picked with a gentle tearing sound.

It was so happy and peaceful that when she woke up at the end of the dream, she found herself lying on her back with her hands folded on top of her heart and a smile right across her face.

She knew, as soon as she was fully awake, before she had even moved a muscle, that the first thing she was going to do next, was transform that residents' garden. There would be flowers, and bees, and flocks of birds, even bats. There would be dock leaves and nettles and thistles, along with the show-pony flowers. There would be apple trees, rare varieties, cherry blossom, squirrels, roses climbing up pergolas, but roses complete with greenfly and blue tits, caterpillars and butterflies. In a garden, as her mother had always said, there couldn't be beauty without dung. There couldn't be butterflies without caterpillars.

This oasis in the heart of London would lead the way. Then surely other gardens would follow when they saw how beautiful, how full of wildlife and how fruitful this one had become. It would have public open days, school visits and word of how to reinvent outdoor spaces would spread. And she would do this in memory of her mother.

There was no time to lose, Svetlana wanted to make a start straight away this morning. She would begin by contacting the right people and finding out what the steps needed to be.

Finally, she felt as if her mind had shifted. The gloom was beginning to disperse and she could feel her old energy and enthusiasm return. The memories of her past had awakened and now they were pushing her forwards.

28

Le Denim – Denim!

*If you hate to dress up, I have a solution for you –
darkest blue jeans, in the classic straight leg with a low to
mid rise. With elegant shoes, a dark silk blouse, jewellery,
make-up and your hair done, you will look as though
Yves Saint Laurent himself has dressed you.*

— M.M.

* * *

Annie had been in London for almost a week now and
she had heard nothing from her husband. She had

messaged him several times, but no response. Late last night, she had cracked and called him, but he hadn't picked up. As a result, she'd had a few choice things to say in her voicemail, along the lines of: 'This is just ridiculous, I can't believe you're being so juvenile. If you've still got some things to say, then please say them. I know I still have some things to say. This, Ed, is sulking. We are too old for sulking.'

Now she was approaching a fifth evening without any word from him and her head was full of troubling thoughts: maybe he would leave her... maybe he and Sylvie were a real thing... maybe Ed would stay in Paris forever, and maybe this was all her fault.

Had she appreciated him enough? She wondered. Had she applauded his fitness drive? Made enough of a fuss about his Paris achievement? Over the years, he had, OK sometimes grudgingly, worn most of the clothes she'd bought for him, but what had she done to learn about music, the one thing that he truly cared about? She twisted her wedding ring around on her fourth finger and felt guilty, sad, and convinced that she had brought this disaster about all by herself.

She absolutely loved him. He was the constant in her life. Not instant fireworks, but slow and smouldering passion. Yet over the past two years, when the twins had turned three and then four, when Owen and

Lauren and all their teenage and young adult emotional demands had taken up so much time and energy, when work gobbled up all the other ounces of attention, care, creativity, what had been left over for Annie and Ed? Not very much, she realised, not much at all.

The time she had spent on him over the past year... it had mainly been at her laptop buying him nice clothes on the internet. There had been no meals out that she could think of apart from the Italian football night disaster... no cosy couple weekends to get away from family life and concentrate on one another. In fact, she couldn't even think of an event they'd been to together that had involved dressing up, looking good, and eyeing each other up with appreciation.

It also couldn't be denied that the once so spicy love life, one that had even involved the family dog running around the house with the love toy he'd managed to snaffle from the bedroom, had definitely toned right down. Even in Paris, in a different room, different bed, new apartment – something that would have provoked all kinds of steamy passion before – well, that time had passed without a single sexy moment.

What was to be done? Well, she better blooming well get her act together and start doing something, that was for sure.

'Owen!' she called out from her quiet and gloomy corner of the sofa. No reply.

'OWEN!' she yelled again, louder this time, and then regretted it as she did not want to wake the twins.

She could hear footsteps on the stairs, but luckily, just Owen appeared in the sitting room several moments later.

'Hello, babes, how are you doing?'

Owen looked a little surprised to have been summoned from his room.

'Do you have just a little bit of time to help me out? There's no one else who can help with this the way you can.'

'Hmmmm... depends...' Owen said, sounding suspicious.

'I want to learn a bit more about classical music.'

'What?!' Owen's eyebrows shot up and he looked vaguely horrified at the thought.

'What's wrong with that?' Annie protested.

'Well, A, Mum, why would you want to learn about something you have literally no interest in? And, B, Mum, it's not the kind of thing you can pick up in an evening. I mean, it's not like when I showed you how to create a spreadsheet on your computer – and then you were done.'

'No, I know, I know that,' she insisted, 'but I

thought maybe we could start with something small. Something that would give me a little bit of a clue. And I could do some listening, to your suggestions, and sort of build from there.'

Owen looked dubious.

'And we have to start tonight... now?' he asked.

'Well... if you have a bit of time,' she said. 'If you've finished your homework and the important stuff.'

'S'pose I have some time,' Owen decided.

Annie cast a long maternal and protective look over him. He was getting tall, just over six feet now, so he had long ago overtaken Annie, then Lauren, and then Ed on his journey upwards. He was filling out too, the shoulders and chest growing broader, bigger hands and feet, more muscle developing. Sometimes, she caught little glimpses of her late husband, Roddy, Owen's father, who was there for the early years of his life. And sometimes she caught phrases, expressions, hand gestures that were pure Ed – the father Owen had known since he was in primary school. But mainly, Annie saw her son. His own person. Sometimes, he looked a little older than his years, with shades of worry, concern and sensitivity on his face. Sometimes, he looked goofy and so much younger, as if he wasn't at all ready to grow up yet. That's how it would be for a good many years – pushing and pulling between developing into an adult and still wanting to retreat into being a kid.

'OK... let me get my guitars,' he said.

When he came back into the room, he was carrying his two guitars – the shiny blue electric and the glossy wooden acoustic. Owen did play the violin, too, not to mention drums and the xylophone, but really his heart and his musical talent now lay with the guitars.

'I thought I'd play you some rock 'n' roll first,' he began, 'then explain how the same kind of chords and even melodies are at work in a classical piece. Does that sound like a plan?'

When Annie nodded enthusiastically, he added, 'This is just one, tiny lesson though. Don't get too excited, you aren't going to learn it all in an evening.'

'No,' she agreed, 'but I've got to start somewhere.'

'You could go on YouTube,' he offered.

'Owen, the point is I want to learn from you. I want to know more about what you, and Ed, are interested in. My music knowledge – apart from pop bands of the 1990s and disco divas of the seventies – is—'

'Woeful,' Owen finished her sentence.

He plugged his guitar into the amp, struck a chord, then fiddled around to tune the strings.

'Sometimes, I think half my practice sessions are

just tuning,' he said, a look of deep concentration on his face. But a few moments later, the opening chords to fifties classic 'Johnny Be Good' were blasting out over the sitting room.

'I love it!' she laughed. 'But turn the volume down, the twins!'

So, Owen tweaked the volume and then an intriguing hour followed, as Annie tried hard to pay attention and really listen to the sounds and Owen's detailed explanations.

She had thought that maybe she could watch Owen play both types of music and then help him with his big decision about what to do after school: where to study, what to study... or if studying was even the right thing for him.

But as she saw his total absorption as he played first the rock 'n' roll classic and then a piece by Villa-Lobos on the acoustic guitar, she understood the problem. He really did love all kinds of music. He also loved both instruments. He loved the sounds they made, the detail that went into producing each note, the finger movements. He fell so naturally into the concentration required and as he explained how chords were held and played for the acoustic guitar versus the electric one, she began to understand his level of knowledge and dedication too.

'Could you play the classical piece again for me, Owen?' she asked. 'And explain again how the tune repeats and changes key and then repeats in a slightly different way. Just so I can try and fix that in my mind.'

He did as she asked and she listened. For so long, she'd brushed classical music off as 'not really my thing'. And she'd stopped going to school concerts and turned down Ed's many offers of taking her to see something orchestral and interesting in London. Contemporary music, fashion, the new, the exciting, the fresh – that's what she liked, that was her world. She associated classical music with fuddy duddy frumpiness, boring evenings and... well, school, probably.

'What would be the best way to start getting into classical music?' she asked Owen, feeling a tiny bit shy and stupid about it.

But Owen smiled and said encouragingly, 'You already know more than you think you do – there's loads of music on adverts and all over the place. But I think you'd like opera, Mum, lots of colour, drama and fabulous costumes. I think sitting watching people play instruments is probably not for you. But maybe, when Dad's back, we could go to the opera.'

She loved the enthusiasm on his face as he added, 'We'll pick something really well-known, we'll get you listening to it for a few days before and then you'll be blown away.'

She had to admit, it was a great idea.

Owen went on. 'People think we're always playing the exact same things in the exact same way, but there's as much reinventing the classics that goes on in music as in fashion... probably.'

And for Annie, those words were the beginning of the click.

'Really?' she asked. 'Reinventing the classics...? Now, I know a lot about that in fashion, so maybe it's not such a jump.'

'Yeah, absolutely, when you start listening to different recordings by different musicians, or conductors, you really start to hear the variety, all the reinterpretations.'

'That is so interesting,' she said, and she meant it. The classics... reinventing the classics... clever Owen to see what was the same for music and fashion.

'So... how's it going with your big decisions about next year?' she had to ask at the end of her first music lesson.

Owen held his guitar in his lap as he said, 'Dad told me not to worry about it too much. Said to keep visiting different colleges and universities, get a feel for the places, the people... where would I like to be, who would I like to be learning with. And if I can't find it, don't force it. He said maybe a year out might help. I could work for a band, or a club... or a venue. He said there's lots of time, no need to rush.'

'Very good advice,' Annie said, aware of the lump in her throat. Why wasn't Ed giving her good advice? Why wasn't he even replying to her messages?

'Yeah,' Owen agreed, sitting down on the sofa beside her, 'it's helped me calm right down. St V's is in a frenzy of UCAS forms, and grade predictions and Oxbridge application meltdowns...'

'Yeah...' she knew just how intense it got with the ambitious St Vincent's parents, 'I bet.'

'But I am doing my research, Mum,' he added. 'You know, looking up courses and stuff, thinking about it... trying to decide.'

'Yeah, I know you are. Try not to stress,' she said, seeing the concern on his face. 'You can talk to me anytime... anytime, especially when you're stressed about it. Look,' she pulled out her phone, 'I'm going to set an Owen ringtone. No matter what, when I hear the Owen-tone, I will answer.'

'Mum?' Owen began and she could hear the hesitation in his voice. 'Is everything OK with you and Dad?'

'Yes... of course... what makes you say that?' Annie

asked, at once fibbing and needing to know a little more.

'Well, I didn't expect you back from Paris so soon and... when he was speaking to me today, Dad didn't ask about you. And he always asks about you...'

* * *

Annie and Dinah were already one glass of Prosecco down when the doorbell rang in the jaunty way that let Annie know it was Connor. Gorgeous Connor, one of her best friends, a truly 4-ply cashmere jumper of a friend. He went with everything, he made everything a little better and with proper care and attention, he was going to be around forever. Plus, she had inherited him from Roddy. Connor and Roddy had once been young actors together, vying for the best parts, helping one another to land the roles and learn the lines.

After Roddy's death, Connor's career had grown and flourished – maybe like Roddy's might have done too. At first, Connor had landed a long-running TV starring role, then several film parts in the US and lately, regular, extremely well-paid lead parts in West End theatre and musicals.

He had become the kind of star who has 50,000 followers on Instagram, is sent freebies, is regularly recognised and asked to pose for selfies, but he still found time for the old friends he thought of as family. And there was no danger of celebrity going to his head when Annie, Ed and Dinah were around to burst his ego at every turn.

'Darlings!' he gushed as he stepped into the large kitchen where drinks, snacks, supper, small children and larger children were all scattered about. Snacking, sipping and chatting were the order of the evening. The twins rushed at him, Owen high-fived him, Annie and Dinah both got hugs and kisses and the mood in the room, which had already been cheerful, amped up several notches.

'How is our superstar?' Annie asked, when Connor was settled in a chair and supplied with a generous glassful.

'Exhausted,' he sighed, leaning back theatrically. 'Audiences demand every single ounce of me. You can see why every thespian I know is into hot yoga, sleep-scheduling, green smoothies, green tea and being tee-total.' Although he finished this with a big glug of wine.

'How's the love life?' was Annie's next question.

'A complete desert,' he replied. 'Honestly a desert landscape with tumbleweeds blowing through.'

'Is that what we're calling the late-night hook-ups now? Tumbleweeds?' she couldn't resist joking.

'Not what I meant, but I like it,' he laughed showing perfect white teeth and crinkling the skin around his eyes. Connor was such a beautiful, not to mention successful, man that it was hard to imagine he was single for any reason other than it suited him to be single.

'You could always go back to Hector,' Annie told him. 'I liked Hector the best.'

Connor shook his head. 'Has a husband and a baby now, like he always wanted.'

'Ah.'

'So what about Paris?' Connor asked to change the topic. 'Tell me all the news. What is happening from the *Champs-Élysées* to the *Rive Gauche*?'

'I think it would be fair to say... the news is mixed,' Annie admitted, shaking out more tortilla crisps into the already emptied bowls. 'I have made some amazing contacts. We've got a brilliant Svetlana makeover in the bag. I have got some potentially good filming arrangements in the pipeline. But there have also been some complete disasters...'

Connor looked at her with a shade of concern. 'Such as?'

'So... I may have mortally offended Katie Rock-

Thomson and her entourage forever...' Annie con-
fessed. She hoped he didn't ask for any details because
she wasn't ready to go into the specifics of creeping
about a courtyard looking, firstly, for her husband's
possible girlfriend, then for an exit... and then for the
Holy Grail of French Wardrobes, even if it did belong
to her husband's possible girlfriend.

'KRT?!' Connor asked, eyes wide. 'Uh-oh. She is
huge in starry circles. Huge. And you have mortally
offended her?'

'Yeeees... but that's a long story that I'm not ready
to tell you yet.'

No, she was definitely not ready to tell him, not
when she was trying as hard as she could to erase
every single one of those excruciating details from her
mind.

'Oh no,' he said, 'was it an Annie disaster?'

'Might have been... slightly.' She picked several na-
chos out of the bowl and crunched down on them for
comfort.

'I don't know what it is about you – you're charming, smart as a whip, one of the most competent
people I know at just about everything—'

'Awww, Connor, that's very nice,' she interrupted.

'But...' he went on, 'sometimes, you can summon

complete bloody chaos from the universe. And it builds and snowballs...'

'Well... let's not dwell on that. It's sort of a work in progress what's going on there...'

'Work in progress?' he repeated. 'Does that mean you're still cleaning up?'

When Annie's response to this was a defensive glower, Dinah chipped in with a breezy, 'So, who's in the new show, Connor? Who are you working with?'

'Ooooh, now,' Connor began, but not before scooping up some olives and taking another big glug of wine, 'well, we have...'

He reeled off several well-known TV names, which impressed Dinah, Annie and even Owen, who'd just swung back into earshot. Then Connor added, 'And to be honest, they are all fine, very professional, great to work with, but the star casting is this old lady from Paris and I swear to God she is one of the most interesting people I have ever, ever met.

'We sit down with her after rehearsals,' he added, 'and she drinks *"une tisane"* and gives us gossip from the sixties and seventies that would make your hair curl.'

'Ooooh, such as?' Annie asked.

'Yeah...' Dinah added, 'you've got to fill in at least a few blanks for us.'

'Does she know any musicians?' was Owen's question.

Followed by, 'We went to Paris,' from Max.

Followed by Minette's revelation. 'Daddy told Mumma she had to go home and we had to go with her because he wants some time for himself.'

At this, Connor glanced at Annie, but she rolled her eyes to head him off from commenting.

'So, this elderly lady...' he went on, 'Madame Moreau, was a couture model for Yves Saint Laurent.'

'No!' Annie and Dinah said together.

'Yes, so she has stories to tell about him and being in the big shows, going to Marrakesh for wild fashion parties... she's met all the biggest fashion designers, Andy Warhol and for your benefit, Owen, she made Jimi Hendrix dinner when he came to Paris to perform in 1966.'

'Oh wow... Jimi Hendrix!!'

'Used to play the viola, but then changed to the electric guitar...' Annie dropped in casually, because she'd put in some late-night googling in a bid to try and help her son with his music studying dilemma.

'Really?' Owen asked before beginning some thoughtful pitta bread chewing.

'She is so cool,' Connor added. 'She looks like a prim and buttoned-up as Miss Marple, but next thing you know, she's telling you about how Jimi Hendrix was hopeless at blowing smoke rings when it was his turn on the joint.'

'Cover your ears, children, cover them right up,' was Dinah's instruction to Owen, Billie and the twins.

Meanwhile, Annie couldn't help feeling that maybe this could be the beginning of another very good idea. And perfect for the older demographic she was supposed to now appeal to.

'So, she's from Paris?' she began. 'And she was a model for Laurent... she's met all the greats, even Jimi Hendrix... how does she dress?'

'Quite like Miss Marple, but in a French way. I think the word would have to be...' Connor paused thoughtfully for a moment, 'immaculately. And apparently, back in the 1980s, she wrote some bestselling French style guide called *French Dressing*, or something like that.'

'I have to meet her...' Annie said, 'and preferably with a film camera. I don't suppose you have a picture of her?'

'Course...' Connor delved in his pocket for his mobile, scrolled through photos, then brought up a selfie of his ruggedly handsome features right next to a face that was aged, yes, but, oh, the bone structure! Not to mention the perfect application of glowy foundation and berry lipstick.

'She is so beautiful,' Annie said. 'And... so familiar.'

'Really? I don't think she's done any films in the past twenty years or so. Well, maybe a character role or two.'

'No... much more familiar than that,' Annie said. 'I think I had a little encounter with her on the train back to London...'

'Uh-oh...' Owen chipped in, 'what did you say, Mum? What did you do?'

29

LE PULL MARIN – THE BRETON SWEATER

Ah, surely this is the quintessential French item. And if it suits you, voilà, you can wear the timeless top beloved by Bardot, Chanel, Audrey Hepburn and so many others. In my opinion, this top suits a slimmer frame with a defined waist, but Picasso would disagree with me!

— M.M.

* * *

'Are you happy with the lighting?'

Madame Moreau smiled and shaded her eyes with

her elegant hands. 'I know young people think old faces need to be spot-lit to best effect, but I prefer something a little more flattering.'

Annie smiled and asked the two-man crew if they could oblige.

She was delighted that this had all come together so quickly over the course of only a few days. Connor had charmed Madame Moreau into saying yes to the interview and Tamsin had given it her blessing, especially as madame was perfect for the 'older demographic'. So, now, a cosy little set had been created in one of the dressing rooms at the theatre where Connor and this French legend were performing. Connor had even invited himself along and was perched on a chair well out of shot, promising he would be silent, even though Annie suspected this would be hard for him.

'That looks nice,' Annie told the crew after they had dimmed the brightness of the lighting and amped up the warmth.

'Candlelight is the most flattering light of all,' Madame Moreau added, 'but, I suppose that's not practical for television, so as you will.'

Annie and this opinionated septuagenarian had already had a laugh about their earlier encounter on the train.

'I don't want you to worry,' Annie had assured her.

'I made the twins an extremely nutritious breakfast before I left to come and meet you today.'

'Now, that is good to hear,' madame had replied, touching Annie gently on the arm, which Annie took to mean: 'Please forget about that, we're here now.'

So, here she was, Madame Madeleine Moreau, perched on a chair in front of Annie in a TV-friendly boat-necked claret red dress that matched her lipstick perfectly. A gold and pearl brooch and a pair of unusual, curled shell earrings caught the camera lights. From the tip of her defiantly golden-brown bob to the base of her chestnut lizard skin court shoes, she was as Parisian as a plateful of garlicky *escargots* or a blast of Chanel No. 5.

'We're so excited to meet you Madame Moreau,' Annie began, and gave a summary of madame's fascinating biography – couture model for Yves Saint Laurent, child of sixties and seventies Paris, actress, author of a French style guide, and now starring in the West End with Connor McCabe.

'What a fascinating life you are leading,' Annie told her with an encouraging smile. 'My first question for you is do you have any advice for everyone who wants their lives to be a little more exciting?'

'Of course...' madame began, tilting her head and flashing a charming smile, 'at this age, especially, it's important to stay interested, dress thoughtfully and make sure to get out of the house! This way you can see, be seen, and meet new people. I always say "start with the arts", as this is where all the interesting people are. The creative ones. So, take yourself out to galleries, join a film club, or a book group. If you look interesting and you make interesting conversation, then interesting people and an interesting life will follow.

'And...' she leaned forward conspiratorially, 'I find interesting outfits are a conversation starter by themselves. How many times have I gone up to someone and said – "this is a wonderful necklace, I'm sure there's a story to tell here". And then a conversation has opened up and maybe a friendship has followed, or even an opportunity. Plus, if you like someone's taste, you will almost always like them too.'

'That is so true,' Annie said, and she smoothed over the folds of her fuchsia-pink silk skirt.

'This colour is so becoming on you,' madame added. 'You are one of the people who lives for bright colours and looks fully alive in them. Never forget this! No hiding your light under navy-blue or, heaven forbid, shades of beige or grey. Even if they are so perfect on someone else.'

Thinking back on her attempts to look classic in

the beige raincoat and matelot top, Annie couldn't agree more. When she was in a red dress, she was as happy as other women appeared to be in a black one.

'So, what do we need to know about French style? True Parisian chic?' was Annie's next question.

'*Tiens*...' madame began, 'this is not a, how you say it, "soundbite"? This is a long list. French chic takes practice, dedication, time and daily effort. And also, it is not to everyone's taste,' she added. 'It would be a boring world if everyone dressed like the people of Paris.'

'But if we wanted to look totally Parisian, where do we start?' Annie prompted.

'Two most important principles,' Madame said, holding up two fingers, one encircled with a gold and ruby ring, 'grooming and quality. By this I mean quality items, from your coat to your bag to your T-shirt to your underwear. It does not matter if it is expensive or cheap, as long as it is good quality. In fact, every French woman lives for things that are top quality for a very fair price. This is why we love lambswool jumpers, cotton trench coats and well-made jeans. I love jeans,' she revealed. 'I still have two pairs of Levi's from the sixties.'

'I am learning that classic jeans are a Paris cornerstone,' Annie added.

'*Exactement!*' Madame replied.

'And the grooming part?' Annie wondered.

'Shoes polished, clothes clean, nails well-tended, light make-up, neat brows. As soon as items are too worn out, then repair or replace. I think the only exception is that we like our hair to have very natural movement. Even to be a little bit – this is one of my favourite English words – rumpled.'

The way she said it, rolling her 'r', brought a fresh smile to Annie's face.

'And then,' Madame held up her finger once again, 'and this is a big secret.' Her voice dropped down conspiratorially, and from the corner of her eye, Annie could see the microphone being brought a little closer.

'But you're going to tell us...' she encouraged.

'Of course...' Madame cocked her head a little to the side and, like the pro she was, looked directly at the camera, 'there must be some grit in the oyster.'

Well, this was as charming as it was baffling. *Grit in the oyster*? Annie thought she had some inkling of what was meant here, but...

'To make a pearl, you must have some grit, no?' Madame Moreau began, her hands and face animated now. 'Everything in the look cannot be too perfect, there must be a little grain of grit, a touch of mustard, a drop of vinegar. This is the secret recipe.'

'Can you give us some examples?'

'Yes... and Yves, he was the master of this. He was the first to say black does go with navy-blue and then he would add maybe a bright-yellow clutch or a too-pink lipstick. There must be something that is different, notable, not quite in keeping. Something to throw the look slightly from its orbit, so that it is not boring. Perhaps, you are very soberly dressed but you are wearing a black bra that shows through your white blouse. Or you have an immaculate black satin skirt and heels but a slouchy sweater. Or, the Paris classic, a smart, buttoned-up outfit, but wonderful long, rumpled hair, artfully curled. And this little sprinkle of salt, you can't learn it. You can't read it in a book. Like a chef in the kitchen, you have to practise in real life. And sometimes, you get it wrong. But no matter. Fashion is for fun, no? It is not serious.'

'I can spot your touch of grit now, madame,' Annie declared. 'It's the shell earrings! I've been looking at them, wondering if they were a holiday purchase and thinking how cleverly they combine with the gold and pearl brooch.'

'Yes! And it is this mix-and-match,' madame enthused. 'The antique brooch, passed on from my mother, and shells, bought on the beach...' she shrugged, 'maybe ten years ago. It is very Coco Chanel to mix your real jewels with cheap ones.'

'And do you think British women dress well... or badly?' was Annie's next question.

'Both, of course,' came the reply. 'Sometimes too scruffy, sometimes too boring, sometimes far too formal – the wedding outfits, *mon Dieu*! But there are so many British characteristics that I love *absolument*.'

'OK, we are all ears,' Annie said, although, after the train experience, she wasn't quite sure what was about to come out of Madame's plain-speaking mouth.

'English girls will never be French girls and this is to be celebrated. English girls are too irreverent and full of humour. They do not care too much what anyone else thinks of them. They love high fashion and shocking looks and "a night out with the girls", *non*? In a way that no Frenchwoman will ever understand. And this is all good. It should be celebrated. Burberry, Vivienne Westwood, Marks & Spencer – *vive le style Anglaise* and *vive la difference*.'

'Oh, I love this,' Annie told her. 'And it is so true.'

'And you, my dear, I have been told...'

Uh-oh, Annie did not like the way Madame was fixing her eyes on her. It was a little bit too like on the train. It was serious and more than a little teachery... something not good was coming. And wait... she could hear Connor shifting in his seat behind her. Oh no, did he have something to do with this?

'You have suspected your husband of having an affair,' Madame Moreau announced.

Oooft, bombshell, and on camera too. Annie could feel her breath rushing from her body.

'But Englishmen don't have *affaires*...' madame added with a theatrical roll of the 'r' now.

'No?' Annie almost squeaked.

'*Non*, they have hobbies.'

Everyone laughed. Madame Moreau, the cameramen, Connor and even Annie. But she did turn and send Connor a glare that said, *Just you wait until afterwards!*

30

Les Sacs à Main – Handbags

How many handbags do you need? I find three well-chosen handbags should cover most eventualities. First comes my workhorse tote, capacious enough for note-books, documents, scripts, a purse, keys and all the other necessities required to keep me 'on the road'. Mine is classic tan leather with a zipper and two straps just long enough to go over my shoulders, but it also looks chic carried in the crook of my elbow.

— M.M.

* * *

'Wasn't she wonderful?' Connor gushed as he and Annie left the theatre once the interview was all wrapped up and they'd guided Madame Moreau into her cab, so she could go back to her Airbnb apartment for a 'restorative nap' before curtain up this evening.

'She was, but I can't believe you told her—'

'Now, Annie,' Connor cut in, 'don't get mad. You know that I live for gossip and not only was it too good to resist but it gave you the best line of the whole interview! You can't be angry with me for that.'

'The best line at my expense! No way are we keeping that all in.'

'And where's the drama in that?'

'Sometimes I'd like a little less drama, quite honestly.' She sighed.

'So, what's the latest Ed news?' was Connor's next question.

Annie took a few moments to answer because it wasn't easy to talk about. She and Ed still hadn't spoken since she'd left Paris. Over a week ago now.

She'd messaged, she'd tried to call and he'd not picked up or replied to anything. It would be fair to say that her most recent messages had been pretty frosty... to say the least.

'We've not spoken since Paris,' Annie said simply.

Connor wheeled around to face her. 'That does not sound ideal.'

'No.'

She locked eyes with her oldest friend and suddenly felt like she might cry. In all her time with Ed, there had been nothing like this. They had always been able to talk everything through. This silence, this refusal by him to engage with her, it was weird and worrying and deeply hurtful.

Last night, she had sat alone in their bed scrolling through the hundreds of photos of much happier times and she could only wonder helplessly what they had done wrong. How she had let this past happiness slip so easily through her fingers? Then her tears had fallen freely.

She'd texted Ed, saying:

I miss you. I really, really miss us.

But there had been no reply.

'Right,' Connor checked his watch, 'I have a hair appointment, and I can't cancel, but in ninety minutes exactly, we will meet in my favourite Soho bar for dry martinis and crisis talks. OK?'

'Martinis... at 1 p.m.?' she asked.

'Crisis talks,' he repeated.

Annie considered the plans she'd made for this afternoon and thought they could probably be rearranged because she probably did need crisis talks, not to mention a dry martini.

'Connor... are you qualified to give marriage advice?' she had to ask. 'You're single and... all the rest.'

'Never mind my qualifications, I'm going to listen and then I'm going to give you the advice you need!' he insisted. 'Now, off you go, I'm sure you can think of plenty of ways to keep busy round here. I mean, we're a stone's throw from The Store. And I know that fashion always inspires you to live your best life.'

* * *

Fashion... Annie wondered as she headed instinctively, like a homing pigeon, to the beautiful high-end department store where she'd worked for years, first as a shop assistant, then as their top personal shopper. Maybe a little burst of fashion inspo might help. It definitely wouldn't hurt.

Fashion was the pull of the new. It compelled you forwards. It made you look to the future, not to the past. It urged you to update, to imagine the new you, the future you, the one who would attend that event and look wonderful, considered, absolutely pulled together. Fashion was always nudging you towards the next chapter of your life. It was there to remind you that it's OK to let go and to grow, to burst, reinvented, from your latest cocoon. Fashion never failed to make her feel that she could face the future and shape her destiny.

As she walked, she thought back to the darkest days when she had lost her first husband. She could still remember the very first thing she'd bought as a widow, crying in the changing room at the thought that Roddy would never see it, never run his hands over it and purr, 'I love this and when can we take it off?'

It was a simple summer dress, mainly white, but patterned with sprigs of green and little pink flowers. A print like that wasn't at all her usual style, but in that dress, she felt as if she was telling herself and whoever saw her – yes, this really is a terrible, devastating time, and I don't feel any sense of hope yet, but I'm hoping that I will. I'm hoping for the very first signs of feeling better. I'm hoping for hope.

Right now, everything between her and Ed felt so much more complicated than it should be. Had they taken each other for granted? Of course they had. Did any parent of small children, confused adolescents and demanding young adult children not take their nearest and dearest partner for granted? She didn't know of any.

Ed had always loved hiking and camping. And now, so busy at work, so busy concerting and parenting his socks off with all his children, he never got the time to do the things he really enjoyed. Instead, he'd started whizzing to and from school on a bike and then disappearing off for a few hours at the weekend with the bike club. Was that so bad? She asked herself. It kept him fit, it kept the dreaded middle-aged midriff at bay and it probably meant he was less grumpy and stressed than he might otherwise be.

But working, parenting and Ed's new biking hobby left them with even less time to be together as a couple. Something they should have noticed and talked about like grown-ups before it all blew up to where they were now.

And then there was Sylvie... she couldn't ignore the Sylvie question. Ed had been on nights out with her before Annie arrived in Paris... and maybe there was more. Sylvie was a gorgeous, free-spirited, much younger woman who clearly thought Annie's husband was attractive and fascinating. And what about those notes, and that bloody wrapper? There had still been no word from Ed. No explanation. And surely she deserved that?

All this walking and thinking had brought her to the shiny glass windows of The Store, full of luxurious autumn clothes set out in a luscious display with pumpkins, tumbling copper leaves, rustic baskets and piles of second-hand books in autumnal shades.

She felt a little surge of excitement. No, it would not solve any of her current problems, but it also wouldn't hurt to go in, say her hellos, find out what the latest news was and take just a little glimpse at whatever delightful new collections were hanging on the rails.

* * *

Usually, Annie preferred wine and she was never averse to a bubble or two. But today, she thought she'd join Connor on the hard stuff, so she ordered two dry martinis then chose a corner table in this lovely bar. Soon afterwards, Connor walked in, causing that ripple of fuss that came with being a well-known face.

People's smiles were just a little twinklier for Connor and the serving staff were always extra-attentive. Connor took it all in his extremely charming stride. He must be in his early forties now, Annie thought with a jolt. But, fresh from his haircut, he looked fit, deeply handsome and – wait a moment –

suspiciously dark-haired. She would have to tease him about that as soon as she got the opportunity.

'Hello again, gorgeous,' she greeted him, standing up to give him a hug and a kiss.

'Did you do some morale-boosting shopping?' he asked.

'Unfortunately not... I managed a tour of the ground floor, but then in came an urgent call from the production assistant, so no more window shopping for me.'

'Alas!'

Then there was a clinking of glasses and some light-hearted teasing about his jet-black hair before they got onto the main topic.

'Ed and I... well...' she began, 'this is not just about drifting apart, babes. Or having a little strop with each other and doling out the silent treatment. We had a big row in Paris. It all blew up because he accused me of being careless about the twins, which I was, Connor. There's no getting away from that. But I accused him of seeing someone else. And when I say seeing... I mean...'

'We all know what you mean, darling,' Connor said quickly.

'Connor, babes,' Annie's voice dropped low so she was in no danger of being overheard, 'I found a condom wrapper in his pocket. No sign of the condom.'

'Well...' Connor took a swig of his drink, 'thank goodness for that.'

And, despite herself, Annie let out a burst of laughter.

'What do you think I should do?' she asked. 'I never had this worry with Roddy.'

And Connor's had to laugh again.

'Yes, you did,' he insisted, 'you were jealous of any woman who came within a twenty-foot radius of the man! I'm surprised you didn't buy an actual bargepole, to keep them at a safe distance. And as for when we went away on location! If you'd been able to buy electronic tags at that time, you'd probably have made Roddy swallow one.'

'Oh...' Annie took a sip of her martini, then tried not to cough because it was so much stronger than she was used to. Yes, well, now that Connor mentioned it, she did vaguely remember having some of those feelings.

'And did Roddy ever leave you?' Connor asked. 'Of course he didn't. He adored you.'

'Did he ever cheat?' Annie asked.

'I can't answer that one,' Connor said, 'and that's not because I'm hiding anything. To my knowledge, he flirted, he enjoyed the company of gorgeous women, and he never cheated, but no one can know everything about everyone. And maybe that's a good thing.'

Annie looked at him and tried to understand what he was saying here. 'Do you think Ed might be cheating and I should just ignore it?' she asked.

Connor paused and seemed to consider his reply carefully. 'Ed is fantastic, I love him. The two of you are brilliant together and you have this gorgeous family...'

'I feel there is a "but" coming...'

'It's not a but, it's just an admission of reality. Maybe we shouldn't be so judgy, maybe we shouldn't hold people to impossible standards. If my very long-term, very committed life partner had a tiny-weeny little fling with an absolutely willing grown-up and he made every effort for me not to find out and not to be upset... maybe I could just consider that a part of life. A part of growing older, wondering what else is out there, and what you might have missed while you were very busy building this incredible relationship and family.'

Annie took a bigger mouthful of the cocktail now. *Gah*! That stuff was strong.

She didn't know what to say in reply to this. It was not the conversation she had expected at all. She'd thought Connor would be full of 'go and get your man' type advice. She'd also expected Connor to be much more robust in his defence of Ed. She'd expected to hear that Ed would never do something like this; he would never, ever cheat on Annie and how could she even consider it.

Instead, Connor was being far more realistic. Here he was telling her that Ed may have had a little fling. His head may have been turned. And was that the end of the world? Did that make him a terrible person? Did that undo all the good things that had come from their years together creating their family?

Connor propped his lovely face up on his hand and told her, 'Look, I'm gay. I've heard all the gay propaganda – we're more highly sexed, we're more promiscuous, we don't like to settle down, we can't do long-term relationships, we "turn" everyone else gay – you name it, I've heard it. And I've been in and out of love, in and out of relationships... and all of this has made me much less judgy of other people and what they do. The relationship rules are impossibly rigid... and people are human. You and Ed love each other and if we love someone, doesn't that mean we should be understanding and forgiving and there for them? Even if they don't always do exactly what we want.'

'Oh... I don't know,' Annie said finally.

'I don't know either,' he added. 'But I do know one thing. The two of you should not be in separate countries fuming about each other. You should be together, trying to work out whatever is going on and how to take it from here.'

'But he wanted alone time...' she reminded her friend.

'Well, he's had his alone time. Now he needs Annie time,' Connor insisted. 'Round two?' he asked as both their glasses had been drained.

'I think I better change to coffee... I've got a lot of thinking to do and turning up at the nursery gates full of cocktails is never a good look,' she replied.

'Fair,' Connor agreed, 'but don't mind me,' and he waved the waiter over to make the new order for one more martini and a bracing cup of coffee.

'You two will work all of this out,' Connor said, 'I know you will. And sex, by the way... I find it gets more and more complicated with...' he dropped his voice to a whisper, '*age*. Even I'm not as keen as I used to be. Plus, you have to admit, always doing it with the same person does get a bit—'

'Don't say it,' Annie interrupted. 'No one needs to hear it and it doesn't help. At our age...' she began.

'*Our*?!' Connor said cheekily. 'You've still got a few years on me.'

'Yeah, yeah... whatever... hormones dip, saggy bits droop...'

'No, I wasn't going to say that,' Connor insisted, 'there's no sagging or drooping going on here yet...'

'We can't all have personal trainers.'

'Yes, you could, Annie Valentine, TV personality, you could go on the biggest health kick of all time and it would be amazing for you. And amazing for Ed, probably.'

'Uuuuurgh.'

'And Ed...' Connor added, 'you have to admit, he's looking great. Anyway... to finish my train of thought here...'

At this point the waiter arrived with the martini and coffee on a tray. 'So sorry,' he said, setting the drinks down, aware he was interrupting a moment.

'At *our* age,' Connor went on, once the waiter had departed, 'sex is much more in our heads than in our bodies.'

Annie let that thought wash over her.

He did have a point, this older, wiser Connor.

She had come to him expecting to get different advice. But she was getting something much more sensible instead. And wasn't that so, exactly true? If she and Ed could be in the right place in their heads, then wouldn't everything else fall much more easily into place?

Connor put his hands over hers. 'Annie, please don't be one more couple to go through a horrible, painful break-up because someone had a quick roll in the sack. A tumbleweed,' he added with a little laugh. 'I've seen far too many lovely couples split up lately, when they maybe could have worked it out, and now they're bitter, resentful, and regret everything.

'I don't care what Ed's done,' he added. 'So, maybe he wanted to check he was still virile... he's still got it. And maybe you shouldn't care so much either. Maybe you're allowed to go off and do something wild, too, so then you will be even. You guys are a great, *great* couple.' He almost pleaded with her now. 'And you give me hope that love can last. So please don't blow it.'

At this, Annie felt a conflicting rush of emotions. Plenty of anger – was she just supposed to turn a blind eye? Is that what Connor was telling her? But she also felt upset and almost tearful. They *were* a wonderful couple. It was far too soon to even think of giving up on that.

'He won't return my calls. He's not replying to my messages. I don't even know if he's opening them,' she told Connor.

'Then you need to get on the Eurostar.'

'I have children... and work.'

'But this is an emergency. And, Annie, maybe drop in on The Store again. Get into your spiritual home – the changing room – and give yourself your own best advice.'

* * *

Annie took a good, long look at herself in the floor-length mirror. Red was so her colour. In a structured red dress like this, which hugged the good curves and draped artfully over the not-so-amazing ones, she felt as if she could do anything. Red! Vivienne Westwood! Cut for a woman who knew her own mind and wanted to go places.

Annie hadn't intended to try anything on, let alone buy a big-ticket number like this. But, in this dress, which fell to just below the knee, big slit up the back, perfect neckline, she suspected she could go back to Paris with her head held high. She could bag all the filming she still needed to secure, even inside the venerated House of Chanel. She could turn up with her head held high at Sylvie's home to record the beauties of her wardrobe. She could have whatever showdown was needed with Ed.

This was the dress. And although she could think

of the coat and the one-off handbag at home that would definitely work with it – the bag providing the all-important touch of 'grit' – there was a shoe-sized hole in this outfit that would most definitely have to be filled.

'Divine, my darlin',' she put her head round the curtain to draw the attention of the wonderful shop assistant who wasn't just looking after her, she was giving Annie the five-star treatment, 'sometimes you just need a red dress, don't you?'

'Oh my God, yes!' Divine told her. 'You do.'

'So, this beauty is coming home with me,' Annie told her. 'And we're going to need some shoes.'

Divine clapped her hands together and gave a little squeal of approval.

31

Les Objets Vintage – Vintage Items

Markets, charity shops, vintage boutiques – these are wonderful places to buy quality items that still have plenty of wear left: leather jackets, garments made of tweed, beautiful knitwear and special occasion dresses. Ideally, you want to air these garments outside, then treat them to careful dry cleaning or handwashing, and even a fortnight inside a freezer to make sure they don't come with any unwelcome insect life attached.

— M.M.

* * *

It had been extremely difficult for Svetlana to source an outfit appropriate for gardening from her extensive wardrobe, which (not including the items in storage) was spread out over one walk-in wardrobe room, for everyday use, and two bespoke built-in cupboards that took up entire walls in a bedroom and a dressing room. This was the downside of having enough money to buy anything and everything you could ever want, you had to develop an in-depth storage and cataloguing system to house it all.

To find the kind of things she was looking for, she'd had to delve deep into the depths of all her closets. Finally, she had emerged with a pair of tweed plus fours, bought on impulse when Igor had hosted a golfing competition in the furthest reaches of the Scottish Highlands, plus matching woollen socks and an ankle-high pair of Prada Wellingtons. On top, she went with a designer T-shirt, a cashmere cable knit and a short waterproof cape, which she vaguely remembered had been bought in the Hermès shop on a rainy day in Venice.

The ensemble was far from perfect, but it would have to do for now. Later in the week, she would have to go to one of those proper country and outdoor shops to get herself kitted out for the garden. And tools, it occurred to her, she needed something to chop and prune and dig with. She wasn't sure if there was anything. She would go and look in the small back garden of the townhouse. There was a shed there, tucked in behind some trellising and a canopy of clematis. Maybe it contained a spade, a fork, or some other useful implements.

She had now set all kinds of plans and changes in motion for the residents' garden, but she didn't just want to sit on her chaise longue in the sitting-room window and watch it happening down there below her. No, she wanted to be part of it. She was determined to be back in a garden, digging the earth, pulling up weeds, mixing dung and other good things into that sticky London clay.

In memory of her mother, and to relive all those happy memories of time spent with her, Svetlana wanted to go down there into the garden and get involved.

Once she was dressed in her unusual outfit and had found several useful tools in the shed, she was about to head out of the front door when she realised she needed to keep her hair out of her face, so she pulled on one of her son's beanie hats.

'Unrecognisable,' she told her reflection and for a moment, she wondered how she would feel if she ran into one of her extremely rarefied neighbours – the man who owned the household-name clothing company, for example, or the tech wonder-child, or the Hollywood celebrity, who had bought the house two down from hers as her 'London bolt-hole'.

'Tschaaa...' she said, shrugged her shoulders and told herself, *so what? I am gardening now. I have to be practical and, anyway, they won't recognise me.*

So, down to the garden she went, Wellingtons rubbing against her woollen socks, cape flapping a little in the wind and the beanie hat a touch itchy.

The gardeners, who were making a start on chopping back the tedious evergreen laurel bushes to begin installing the new wildflower beds, glanced up as she came into view.

'I am planning to dig up that corner where we are planting the three new fruit trees. This does not disturb or get in your way, no?' she asked them.

There was a momentary beat, while they made a mental note of who she was and squared up recent conversations with the glamorous head of the project against this woman in a cape, plus-fours and a beanie.

'No, Ms Wisnetski,' the man she knew as Joe answered finally, 'all help very welcome. Do you have a good fork? Or do you want to borrow one of ours?'

'Let me see if yours is better,' Svetlana decided, and went over to investigate the tool collection. After careful consideration, she decided that hers was more suited to her after all.

'But thank you,' she told them. 'I haven't dug in the earth since I was a child, so I better start slowly.'

When she was over in her corner, sticking the prongs into the earth, pushing down hard with her right foot, she was surprised at how naturally the movement came to her, although she hadn't dug anything for decades.

The gardeners were still just within earshot, but thought that they weren't, and she could hear Joe say to the other guy, 'She's like some billionaire's ex-wife or something, but you know what, she's all right that one.'

The other voice replied with a half-hearted, 'Lucky for her, eh? I'd be all right too if I lived round here with billions in the bank. 'Specially if I'd got shot of the old man.'

This made Svetlana laugh quietly. She thought the other man's accent sounded Eastern European too. Maybe he'd had a childhood like hers, under the fierce, inescapable heat of the summers and then the brutal cold of the winters. Oh yes, she may have lived in Mayfair for decades, but she could still remember winter in her mother's little house, when they would stuff gaps in the windows and walls with newspaper and hand-knitted draught stoppers, anything to try and keep the freezing winds out. She knew what it was to be cold. So cold you couldn't sleep, you couldn't even think and you dared not move from the circle of warmth around the fire.

* * *

Svetlana carried on digging, pushing rhythmically into the earth, levering it up, turning it over, breaking the clods down with the prongs of the fork. She did this movement many more times, completely concentrated on the job, amazed at how easily it all came back to her, how quickly she remembered from watching and doing at her mother's side.

Her mind was totally focused on the fork and the earth, completely taken up with the task, not thinking about anything else.

And then... there it was.

The big idea.

The one she had been waiting for, longing to find.

It seemed to arrive all at once, in a rush, almost completely formed. And she knew this was the thing she would do next. She could do it and make an enormous success of it.

Of course, the garden was a big and important

project that she had set in motion and she would enjoy seeing it through, but this... this would give her focus in the years ahead. She had the time, she had the money, she had exactly the right friends and social circle, and this would give her both purpose and positive influence.

She dug and turned earth for another twenty minutes or so as the idea expanded in her mind, filling out with further detail and colour. She asked herself questions and came up with good answers, and then even better answers.

When the picture was much clearer in her mind, thanks to all the digging and the thinking, she knew it was time to go and talk to who else but her beloved husband, Harry.

As she left the garden and approached her own front door, Svetlana felt almost nervous. It wasn't that she was asking for Harry's permission, or even his approval. She knew she didn't need that. She could start this up all on her own today if she wanted to. But he was so considered and such a grown-up about everything that if he thought it was a good idea and could work, then she would be much more certain.

The downside of this thought was, if he considered it hare-brained and half-baked, then she would be uncertain too. And she didn't want to be uncertain. Because she loved this idea. Was sure she could make such a success of it.

'Harry?' she called out from the entrance hall, wondering if he was within earshot.

'Still in the little sitting room, my darling.'

She hurried across the hallway and into the gorgeous room, all soothing shades of beige and cream, hung with a crystal chandelier and some of her favourite paintings.

There, she saw Harry sitting in his favourite armchair, reading what appeared to be his second newspaper of the morning, as the distinctively pale-pink *Financial Times* was folded on the table beside him.

'Harry, you know I've been wondering what to do with myself next...' she began and realised she didn't want to sit down, she wanted to stand before him to deliver this outline. If necessary, she might even need to pace around the floor as she talked and thought.

'I've had a very good idea, and a useful idea too...'

'That sounds very promising,' he encouraged, 'and are you ready to tell me about it?'

'Yes!'

'That sounds fantastic, but, darling girl, I'm going to have to stop you because my taxi will be here in two minutes and if you're going to give me the details of your amazing new plan, I want to have time to listen to you properly.'

He stood up and came over to hug her. 'I'm very sorry if that's disappointing news.'

'It is disappointing,' she admitted, 'but two minutes is not enough.'

She smoothed a hand over his hair and ran a dusting hand over his jacket to remove a minute particle of fluff.

'You look very good,' she told him. 'Busy day ahead?'

'Busy as a bee,' he said with a smile. 'But I'll be home at 7 p.m. sharp. So why don't we ask Maria to make my favourite supper and get us all set up in the dining room? Then we can discuss your idea in all the depth it deserves, accompanied by a nice Malbec.'

She smiled at him. 'Good idea. Steak pie and Malbec in the dining room at 7.30? I will tell Maria.'

The faint sound of the downstairs doorbell could be heard, followed by the sound of Maria going to open the door.

'Time to go,' Svetlana said, landing a kiss on his cheek.

'I love how much we've changed since we married,' he said, gathering up his papers and briefcase.

'No!' she insisted proudly. 'I have not changed at

all. Well, maybe I learn to like this steak pie meal that you are so crazy about,' she added with a shrug.

'I've changed,' he said. 'I was just a crusty old lawyer before I met you. I've learned how to take my work much more seriously, much more professionally. My office runs like an efficient machine thanks to your suggestions.'

'Harry, you were the best divorce barrister in London when I met you,' Svetlana reminded him.

'Well, I'm still better than I was and you...' Almost at the door, he paused and took a long, last look at her. 'I'm delighted to say you are moving, just ever so slightly, from international glamour queen to eccentric English lady.'

'What are you talking about?!' Svetlana demanded, as if she wore woollen socks, tweed knickerbockers and a rainproof cape every day of the week. But she couldn't help her own secret little smile.

32

LES HOMMES – MEN

If you want the man in your life to be better dressed, there is only one icon to follow – Cary Grant. Whether he was headed for the beach, in bright-white swimwear, or the boardroom, in a perfectly tailored suit, this screen idol was always impeccably turned out.

— M.M.

* * *

One small leaving-the-house Max meltdown, one delayed Eurostar journey, one long taxi queue and taxi ride later, and Annie was once again standing in the street in Saint Germain, outside Ed's apartment building. As she still hadn't heard from him, she'd decided to arrive unannounced. Maybe a surprise visit would answer some of the questions she had.

Standing on the pavement, she felt strangely nervous, but there was no turning back now. Looking up, she could see the light was on in the apartment. So, hopefully, that meant her husband was there, inside his Paris flat... alone. Hopefully, Ed was reading a book, or maybe watching French TV, or marking a pile of essays.

But there was also the possibility that he was up there Not Alone.

Before her mind went into overdrive about who else might be there, she rang the bell. And waited, heart hammering a little too hard. Although that might also have to do with the buckets of caffeine consumed to propel her through all the organisation that this day had involved to get her here, in one piece, with luggage to hand, with children cared for, wearing the knockout dress, albeit toned down with ankle boots and a swishy coat.

'*Entrée*,' she heard Ed's voice instruct, '*quatrième etage, s'il vous plait.*' Before the entry-phone clunked down again.

She realised he must be waiting for a food delivery and now, she faced having him open the door completely unprepared... onto... his lonely essay-marking self? Or his love nest with the French minx?

She rang the bell again, so she could at least warn him it was her. But this time, there was just the buzz of the door-opener, so she pushed the heavy front door open.

Gripping hold of her small trolley bag, she saw the lift wasn't available, so she started to take the many generous sets of stairs up to the top floor.

Finally, she was just rounding the corner onto the final set, not even puffing too hard, because her previous stay had obviously built up her tolerance to a French apartment-stair workout, when she heard the click of a door latch unlocking. Her first instinct was to stop in her tracks, go backwards even... and seriously reconsider if this was such a good idea. But, no, it was too late for any indecision, she had to keep going forward and find out what the heck was going on.

So, she carried on up the stairs. As soon as she had rounded the last corner and the front door was visible, she saw Ed standing there. And Ed saw her. Funny how when you know someone so well, you can just tell.

She could tell straight away that he was happy to

see her. Her heart lifted with the thought that it was going to be OK.

He was in old chinos and a shirt that she knew was a comfortable, old favourite. His hair looked rumpled, but as if he had been running his own hand through it – pondering difficult questions, answers and marks – not as if anyone else had been rumpling it. And he looked surprised, yes, but also kind of relieved to see her.

'Annie!' he exclaimed. 'What on earth are you doing here? Are you here on your own? Why didn't you tell me you were coming? Have you just arrived?'

The questions came thick and fast.

'You're not answering my calls. You're not even opening my messages! What was I supposed to do?' she began.

By now, she was at the top of the stairs, walking towards him, heeled boots holding her straight and giving a few extra inches, coat open, swishing a little, sensational dress visible underneath.

'You're looking amazing,' he said, as they both held out their arms and she hugged him tight. So, it was a pretty enormous surprise when she heard an unmistakable French-accented voice call out from inside the apartment, 'Is that the pizza?'

Annie stepped back and met Ed's eyes.

Under her breath, she demanded, 'What the actual freak, Ed?'

Then came those words. Oh God, those words that every single man ever caught red-handed has to utter, 'It's not what you think, Annie.'

Annie could feel her heart sinking to her knees, which suddenly felt a little wobbly and unstable. She needed to go. She had to get out of here.

But, before she could turn and run, her phone began to ring. And it was the special ringtone she'd put in for Owen, assuring him he could call anytime, especially when he was stressed, and she would always pick up and listen.

'I have to get this,' she told Ed, giving him a fierce glare. 'Hello, Owen, sweetheart, are you OK?'

'Yeah... not too bad. Have you got to Paris yet?'

'Yeah... just arrived at the apartment.'

'How's Dad?'

'He's fine... look, never mind us right now. It's all OK. So, I'm here and we can talk about whatever you like, because that's why you phoned, isn't it, darlin', because you're worried? We can talk about the serious stuff... or if you just want to take your mind off it all, we can talk about what's on TV, or what the twins refused to eat for supper... or whatever will be helpful for you.'

She heard Owen's little laugh of relief and his big sigh.

As Annie talked, Ed turned and gestured for her to follow him, so she walked behind him into the hall-way, where she dropped her bag, and went straight on into the sitting room.

One ear on what Owen was saying, she could still hear Ed announce, 'It's not the pizza... it's my wife.' He said the words very neutrally, as if he wasn't fazed, or angry, but as if he wasn't entirely happy either.

And there was Sylvie, sitting on the rug beside the low coffee table. It didn't escape Annie's attention that the lighting in the room was low, there was a bottle of wine on the table and two glasses with only a small amount left in one.

Sylvie was in a skimpy white vest top... her shoes kicked off underneath the table.

'So...' She tried to keep her attention on Owen and what it was he wanted to tell her.

But she also quite wanted to gasp and turn and run, because she couldn't bear the humiliation of this and surely Ed wouldn't lie to her, not right here in front of... what else but, '*that* woman'.

But...

But... wasn't that a big pile of jotters on the coffee table? Wasn't one of them open and filled with handwriting? And was that a biro that Sylvie was holding in her hand?

Could this possibly be a teachers-meeting-to-get-some-marking-done scene? If it was, it was still a pretty sexy marking scene.

Her eyes went again to the white vest top and the peek of cleavage coming from the top of it.

'Ah, Annie! *Bon soir!*' Sylvie's face split into a wide, completely unflustered, and not at all guilty smile. 'Ed did not expect you tonight, no? Has your TV company sent you back here early?'

'Hello... sorry... I'm on the phone,' Annie said, glancing from Sylvie to her husband and back again.

'Hello, Owen!' Ed called out, then added, 'Maybe you'd like to go to the kitchen, Annie? Speak to Owen there.' Ed's voice, again neutral... no, maybe she could hear some hint of anger emerging. 'There are a few things Sylvie and I need to get finished off for tomorrow. Then you will have my undivided attention.'

'Sure,' Annie said, coolness of her own emerging. 'I'll just dump my coat in the bedroom,' and she just about dived for the bedroom door because it occurred to her that if there was going to be any evidence in there, she needed to get to it before Ed did.

Door open, she threw on the light. The room looked military neat. Like it never did when she and

Ed were together. The bed was made, pulled tight, pillows undented. The bedside rugs were completely straight on the wooden floor. No wild, unabandoned shagging had gone on in here that was for sure. But she still didn't absolve him.

Closer inspection of the dim sitting room was going to be required. Meanwhile, she could go and snoop for any further signs in the kitchen. But first...

'Owen, I'm so sorry, I was just arriving, but I'm sitting down now. Totally ready to listen,' she said, setting herself down on the side of the bed.

'I'm phoning to tell you that I'm feeling OK, Mum...'

'Oh, that's good. That's really good to hear,' and it was true, just those words were helping the knot in her stomach to unclench a little.

'In fact, think I might have come up with an answer...'

'That's brilliant, Owen. Well, tell me, I am all ears.'

'Quite a funny expression when you think about it.'

'Yes.' She gave a little laugh. Surely, they were marking, Sylvie and Ed. Marking with wine... and maybe something else on their minds for later. But... hadn't Sylvie looked quite pleased to see her?

Maybe she was acting.

Maybe they were snogging right now... with that thought, Annie had to get up off the bed and actually peek through the bedroom doorway. To her annoyance, she couldn't see anything, but she could hear low voices, not enough to make out the words.

Anyway, right now she had to concentrate on Owen.

'I can study Economics and Music... together. Joint honours. That degree is available in London, at Royal Holloway, and in Glasgow.'

'Glasgow?' she repeated, suddenly horrified at the thought of Owen not being in his bedroom and within shouting distance for at least some portion of his day.

'Yeah... and it's the quite serious type of music, the degree stuff. But I thought if I kept up my weekly guitar lessons and went to gigs with all the other kinds of music I like... with my student discount, obvs... then that's all going to keep me learning and helping me decide where the life path will lead.'

'Wow... that sounds amazing, Owen... the life path, I love that. So, can you visit Royal Holloway... and Glasgow? Maybe you'd like me to come? Or would it be better if it was Ed?'

'I think it would be nice if you both came. Dad can make sure the music teaching is sound. But you can be on the alert for bell-ends and tell me if I'm going to like it there.'

'I'm honoured... well, you need to find out when the visits are and book us all in...'

'OK, I'll let you go, Mum. I'm feeling like... mega-relieved. You have a good night.'

'Owen?'

'Yeah...'

'The twins, Dinah... is everything OK?'

'Yeah... yeah. There's been some screaming, dunno what that was about. But all seems to be OK now.'

'Oh... are you sure?'

'Yeah. Have a good night. Love to Dad.'

With that, he hung up.

Annie stood up and looked herself over in the mirror. Time for the coat to come off and for a touch-up of lipstick. She also brough her bags in from the hallway, then swapped the ankle boots for the brand-new shoes... in for a penny and all that.

So, looking like this, she would just walk through the sitting room and into the kitchen. Not saying anything, not interrupting the 'marking' session. Just, you know, walking through on three-inch heels in a knockout red dress.

As she made her entrance and then walked slowly and showily to the kitchen, she saw both Ed and

Sylvie look up from their work and follow her with their eyes.

'Much more to do?' she asked.

'No...' Ed spoke first.

Sylvie followed this up with, 'You know, I should go. I can do the rest at home. You must want to catch up and maybe make some plans for the evening.'

Ha! Yes... Annie couldn't help thinking. *Plans to murder my husband, but not before I've tortured him very slowly and thoroughly.*

In the kitchen, going to the cupboard, going to the fridge, pouring herself a glass from the bottle of chilled white wine in the fridge door, Annie kept a close ear on Sylvie as she packed up and prepared to leave.

'Goodnight, Annie,' she called out from the hall-way. 'We'll speak soon about the wardrobe filming.'

'Sure...' Annie said, not at all sure that this would ever happen.

'Goodnight, Ed, see you tomorrow.'

Mwa... Mwa...

She heard the kiss, kiss that came before the close of the door. And her thoughts were conflicted... they have just kissed, they are obviously lovers, or they have just kissed – why would they do that if they had anything to hide? Maybe they have kissed just to pretend that everything is normal... oh my God, like everyone who's ever suspected infidelity, I am losing my mind!

The door was shut. Sylvie had gone and now Ed and Annie would have to face one another.

She picked up her wine glass and stepped back into the living room.

Ed walked in from the other doorway.

For several long moments they just stood looking at one another, then both seemed to burst out at once.

'Annie... I—'

'I think you—'

'Why don't you go first?' was Ed's suggestion.

For a moment, Annie took a breath and tried to get her thoughts in line.

'I don't want to be lied to,' she began.

Ed tried to start up with an, 'I'm not—'

But she cut him off. 'You know what, I'm going first and you're not going to interrupt because you need to hear me out.'

'OK,' he agreed.

'You need to tell me completely honestly what has been going on and what is going on. Complete honesty. No skipping over anything, no sugar-coating the pill. I just want to know exactly. And then we can work out where we are. And before you ask, yes, I did deliberately walk through the door of Sylvie's apartment block that day. Yes, I did stand in the courtyard and peer into her window trying to work out what was happening. Yes, full disclosure, I did go into her apartment when she invited me in and truffle through her wardrobe in search of further clues. I did that... because I was, no, I *am* very suspicious,' she admitted. 'My suspicions began when you went on lots of nights out with her, when you didn't seem very keen on me and the babies coming over and the icing on the cake came when I found notes with times and locations in your pockets and then, of course, the condom wrapper. I mean, that's quite a piece of evidence, Ed. No wife wants to come across that.'

She heard the wobble in her voice and tried to steady herself because she wasn't quite finished.

'Plus, you just packed us off,' she added. 'Without an explanation. And you've been out of contact ever since. So, now, I've come back here for your full and frank explanation. Whatever has been going on, I need to know about it, so we can handle it like grown-ups. OK?'

She stopped there and folded her arms across her chest to let Ed know she was ready for him to talk now. She could just about feel her heart thumping against her arms, as she now felt frightened. This was why people turned a blind eye, and didn't want to know what their partner was really getting up to, because it risked everything.

Maybe, as Connor had suggested, she could admit that Ed was only human and he had thoughtlessly had a fling. Maybe they could go back to their normal family life when Paris was over. But she wasn't so sure. Surely an affair would change everything. Everything would be different between them after this. Maybe they would have to break up. And as she looked at her husband standing just a few feet from her but feeling miles and miles away, she wondered why she was insisting on a truth that could be so damaging and so painful.

Ed folded his arms across his chest too. His eyes went down to the floor and he looked upset and guilty enough for Annie to have a very bad feeling about this.

A long moment passed before he said the words, 'I'm glad you're here... because I do want to explain it all.'

Her heart dropped.

33

LE MOUCHOIR – HANDKERCHIEF

Always carry a clean handkerchief, preferably made of white cotton or linen. Every now and then, noses must be blown, tears wiped away, cuts covered, or spills blotted.

— M.M.

* * *

The candles in the ornate, solid silver candelabra between them were lit. Maria had served out the old-fashioned steak pie with salad on the side for Svetlana and mashed potato and sautéed carrots for Harry. The wine was poured. They were alone in the smaller of the two dining rooms and it was time to talk.

'So, tell me all about it,' Harry began, picking up his knife and fork.

For a moment, Svetlana hesitated. She didn't want to care so much about her husband's opinion but found she couldn't help that she did.

Then she reminded herself about everything she had done so far in life. Why was she worried that there wasn't more ahead? And that really, she could probably do just about whatever she set her mind to.

'I want to sell all the clothes and accessories from my collection that I don't wear any more. Not just sell, Harry, I want to have a big celebrity auction, once a year. I want to encourage everyone I know to sell their things too. I mean look up and down this street... rooms and rooms full of things that people don't use any more, don't wear any more. I want to raise lots of money for charities to help other women.'

Svetlana held his gaze, feeling steady and determined. She looked at him expectantly. His expression hadn't changed but there was a pause. She hoped he was thinking carefully, and she knew he wouldn't speak until he was ready.

She could feel her heart beating expectantly. He

would like it, wouldn't he? He would think it was a good plan... he would want her to do this?

'My darling...' he began, 'this will be a great deal of work. And I do have one question...'

She nodded.

'Are you willing to commit. To really commit to this?'

'I'm going to give myself some time to think about it in detail. But I believe I am.'

'I think it's a fantastic idea,' Harry said, 'and when the beautiful garden you are creating is made, it would be a wonderful place to hold a fundraising auction,' Harry added.

Svetlana pictured a marquee in the grounds, Champagne and auction guests, the bidding and the excitement and all around, the flowers, trees, even the swooping of a tiny, nocturnal bat or two. Her in charge of all of this and for such a good purpose too.

'Harry – I love it. I love all of it.'

'I love you,' he said gently, 'you are one of the wonders of the world.'

'Thank you,' she said with a smile. 'I won't do it on my own, of course. I need to tell my friend Annah all about this plan. She knows fashion. She knows all the most important shoppers of the last... two decades.'

She waved her hand airily. 'She will have all the best ideas to help me.'

Svetlana looked at her husband.

'I think about something else too, Harry,' she added.

'There is no stopping you today,' he said with a smile. 'Go on.'

'I think we should buy a nice house close to the boys' school in Scotland. We can go and stay there whenever we want and have the boys for weekends, let them bring their friends too. You can play more golf, my darling. And I want to learn to sail a yacht, not just pose on the back of one.'

This made Harry laugh.

'We need to enjoy our lives,' she added, reaching over to hold his hand. 'We've worked so hard to get where we are. I want to enjoy being happy with my boys and with the man I truly love.'

Svetlana knew that Harry was far, far too much of an old-school Englishman to let his emotions, let alone any tears, run away with him.

But still, he suddenly had to pull the immaculately ironed handkerchief out of his pocket, turn away from the table, give his nose a manly blow, then insist that there seemed to be 'something caught in the corner of his eye'.

34

LES SACS À MAIN (ENCORE) – HANDBAGS (AGAIN)

Alongside my tote, my second handbag is a smaller, structured, flap-topped bag, ideal for non-work outings. I can fit keys, purse, sunglasses, lipstick and mirror in here. It has handles, but also a long, slim strap when I want to be hands free. This bag is leather in a beautiful shade of violet, which seems to go with all of my outfits, no matter the season.

— M.M.

* * *

'So, when you say "explain everything"...' Annie began and she did not like the sound of her voice. She wanted to sound clear and firm, but instead, she sounded dangerously close to tears. 'I want you to be completely honest, Ed. Totally honest. I have to have that. We can't go anywhere from here unless you give me that.'

'I understand,' Ed said, then he sighed deeply and began. 'When I first got here, I went out with Sylvie and the other staff members a lot. It was exciting, being somewhere new, meeting new people, being social, going out. I haven't had any of that for a long time. For years now, it's been hard work at school, and hard work parenting and not much else.'

Annie gave a curt nod. She just wanted Ed to get on with this. She wanted the worst to be over.

'Sylvie is lovely,' he added. 'You've met her, you know that. And she's very...'

Don't say sexy, please don't say sexy.

'She's fun, light-hearted, touchy... there's all that French thing of kissing and hugging and sitting in... close contact. Sexy, I suppose. She's very sexy.'

And there we go... he's said it. Yes, she's totally sexy. I mean, who wears a vest top to a marking session?

Annie made another very frosty nod.

'I was...' Ed gave a shrug that at least seemed

vaguely embarrassed. 'OK... I was completely bowled over. I had the kind of crush I haven't experienced since I was a teenager.'

Annie felt weirdly disconnected from her body. *Really? Was this really happening? Was Ed about to tell her that he was having an affair with a colleague who was at least ten years younger than him. Oh God, oh God, oh God.*

'And then that progressed, did it?' she asked just wanting to know, wanting the Band-Aid off and as quickly as possible.

'No!' He looked her right in the eyes now. 'No, no, of course it didn't progress! But I will in all honesty admit that I wanted it to.'

'I see... so what...?'

'That was when you arrived with the twins and I was... furious, to be honest. And confused... I wasn't quite so sure about what I wanted and—'

'You sent us home,' Annie concluded.

'Yes...'

'So, what happened after I left?' she asked, feeling as if she could almost be sick. The freaking Band-Aid moment still hadn't happened.

Ed suddenly sat down and put his head in his hands, while Annie continued to stand, even if she was wishing she'd not put on brand-new shoes with a three-inch heel.

'I'm not exactly proud of sending you home, or of what happened afterwards.'

'Just tell me, please. I'd rather know.' She had no idea how she could sound so calm.

'I went out with Sylvie and her friends that night. We had plenty to drink and I told her that I wanted to be more than friends.'

Here it comes... try to brace yourself. Don't be judgy, Connor said. Oh bloody hell, I am going to be so, so judgy. I am going to be the judgiest person who ever lived.

'And...' Ed went on, 'that didn't go well... because... it turns out that I misread all the signs. And Sylvie, well, she couldn't have been more charming about it... but she has a girlfriend, although it's the "non-exclusive" kind of thing all the young people are into.'

Wait. What?!

'And for the rest of that weekend... in fact, ever since then, I've only been thinking about what an absolute tit I've been. No, "tit" is too nice... I think I should probably go with arsehole.'

The fact that Ed never, ever swore because he'd trained himself out of it as soon as he'd started teaching made this word all the harsher to Annie's ears.

'You can totally believe me that this,' he gestured to the wine glasses and the books on the table, 'this is honestly a school night with a colleague.'

'Oh boy...' Annie sighed the words out. 'I'm not sure what I expected, but I don't think it was this...'

She really wanted to believe him, but she was not going to be hoodwinked. Didn't she have actual evidence that there was more to it than Ed was telling her.

'So, on the condom wrapper front... why am I still not getting an answer on that? Or maybe you'd like to explain the mysterious phone number, address and "kiss, kiss" notes first?' She heard how headmistressy she sounded. But this was a very important question. It felt as if everything might depend on that one little piece of foil-coated packaging.

'Oh God,' it was Ed's turn to sigh now, 'I really am going to have to confess every little detail...'

'Yup...'

'Well, the notes are easy enough...' he began. 'I go around the school picking up bits of rubbish and stuffing them into my pockets. Whenever I see a bin, I empty my pockets out. The notes... I forgot to throw them out.' He paused.

'Why didn't you just say that when I mentioned them?'

'Would you have believed me?' he asked.

'And do you expect me to believe that you picked up a condom wrapper in the school playground and forgot to empty it into a bin?' She raised an eyebrow to let him know there was absolutely no chance.

'It's worse than that...' he admitted, dragging his hands through his hair.

'Well... is it, "*I shagged the gorgeous French music teacher worse*"?'

'Without going into details... I am not going into details.' He looked up at her now and did seem to be cringing with embarrassment. 'I'm just going to say, it's been a long time since I... well, we don't use condoms... so I wanted to make sure... in case I...' he stammered, 'this was before...' he tried to explain, 'before I knew that Sylvie had a girlfriend and I was an absolute dickhead.'

Annie looked at him with astonishment.

'Oh my God. So, you're telling me you bought a packet of condoms and tried one on for practice?' she wanted to clarify. 'In case you and Sylvie decided to—'

'The school has a vending machine... you don't need to buy the whole packet,' he added ruefully.

Oh, she really didn't want to think about this. And she realised that she almost wanted to laugh.

Laugh! Why on earth did she want to laugh? Because this was all such an incredible relief, that was why. Nothing *real* had happened between Ed and Sylvie... just a whole load of stupid, mortifying, midlife-crisis type stuff had been going on inside Ed's stupid, mortified, midlife head.

'Bloody hell, Ed,' she burst out. 'Why on earth didn't you throw the wrapper away along with the blinking practice condom? And then this conversation would never have had to happen.'

Ed shrugged and shook his head sadly. 'What an absolute prat I've been,' he added. 'You're never, ever going to forgive me for this, are you?'

When he looked up at her now, even in the dim light of let's-do-marking-with-wine, she could see tears forming in his eyes and the look of utter distress on his face.

'So, there was flirting and a massive crush on your part?'

He nodded.

'And you asked her if she was interested in more?'

He nodded again.

'But she wasn't.'

Another nod.

'Plus, one condom was bought, but not used... well, not for shagging purposes anyway...'

Another curt nod followed.

'And are you feeling deep, complete and utter regret for being such a complete arsehole? For not thinking about me... and our family? And our future?'

'Oh my God, yes,' he whispered. 'That is all I've done since you've been gone. Especially looking at you now. You are absolutely... magnificent.'

'So, why didn't you call, or reply to any of my messages?'

'I didn't know where to start. I didn't know what you were thinking, or what you would believe. Or where to even begin explaining...'

Annie let out a long sigh. She was still tempted to laugh, but it was too soon. First, she had to make sure he was completely and utterly sorry.

'And do you absolutely swear this is the truth, the whole truth and nothing but the truth, so help you... if I ever find out you have fibbed, even slightly, I will... I will... let's just say some kind of intense testicle torture will be involved.'

When he answered this with a heartfelt, 'It's completely true. I am so, so sorry. I've been a complete pillock from beginning to end. Do you think you can ever forgive me?'

For a moment, she paused. Then she asked, 'Do you want me to forgive you?'

'Yes! Oh God, yes. I can't think of anything worse

than not being able to come back to you and our family.'

'The testicle torture would be worse,' she had to warn him.

But then she considered everything he'd told her for a long moment.

That condom story was so embarrassing, she almost wished Ed and Sylvie had done the deed. She could already imagine telling Connor about the 'practice condom' when she'd had one dry martini too many and he was wheedling all the details of Ed's Parisian adventures out of her. No, no. She wouldn't tell anyone about this, not even Connor. (Let's face it, she probably *would* tell Connor. He already knew far too much about her trip here.)

'Ed... we need to pay close attention to what this means. We need to pay really close attention to *us*...'

And now she sat down, too, not on the sofa beside him, but on the armchair close by, so their eyes were level with one another.

'When I left for Paris... and when I was here before you came, all I could think about was how bored I was,' he admitted, 'how fed up, how much I just wanted to do something different, have an adventure. But now... I just want to be your husband, boring Dad, doing all the usual things... that sounds completely perfect to me. Can you forgive me?' Ed asked, very humbly.

Annie looked at him for a long moment. There he was, her Ed. The one who had been missing-in-action for quite some time now. There he was at last.

'Of course, I'm going to forgive you,' she said, Connor's words ringing in her ears. *We're all just human and if you love someone, doesn't that mean you should be understanding and forgiving and there for them.* It suddenly occurred to her just how much understanding and forgiving Ed had done for her over the years, when she'd been so caught up with work that he and her family had taken a complete back seat.

There was a moment where her words hung between them and Ed seemed almost confused, as if he couldn't quite believe it. It was funny, but his reaction reminded her of the very first time they'd kissed, when he'd been so completely surprised, as if he couldn't believe his luck.

She couldn't stop herself from closing the distance between them, so she moved to the sofa and wrapped her arms tightly around him. She closed her eyes and wanted to hold him tight, his arms around her too now. He smelled of washing powder, that ferny cologne, wine and a slightly sweaty undertone that suggested just how anxious he'd been.

For several long minutes, they just held one another.

'I am so sorry,' he added.

'I'm sorry too... we haven't seen each other. We haven't made time... we haven't been close,' she added.

'That is all going to change,' he said against her ear. 'Thank you so much for coming to get me. I love you.'

'I love you too.'

And then they began to kiss. She pushed in against him and for a couple who hadn't made really top-notch love in months, it quickly began to feel interesting... pretty hot in fact.

She kissed his neck, to let him know that this was not just a kiss and make up. This was going to be a proper rekindling of the fires because that was what she wanted. That was what she had hoped for when she came all the way to Paris in the beautiful dress and shoes.

'OK,' she whispered against his ear, 'you may have put this on for Sylvie, but you do look very good in that shirt.'

'This dress...' he was saying against her neck, as his hands moved down her back and pulled her more closely against him, 'do you think you can wear it every day? Because I think that could very quickly get our marriage back to where we want it to be.'

'Vivienne Westwood. She's the Queen,' Annie said.

'No, you're the Queen.'

'So, have you been dreaming up any new moves you were going to use on your French crush?' Annie dared, wondering what effect this might have.

'Oh my God!' he exclaimed. 'You can't say things like that. I'm going to wilt away with embarrassment.'

'No, no! No wilting,' she countered, moving an encouraging hand down into Ed's trouser pocket.

Then there was hungry, hot kissing – the kind that had been missing for some time now.

'I've really missed this and you,' Ed said.

'Funny way of showing it,' she teased. 'I've been here all along.'

'How did we forget that?' he asked with a hint of sadness.

'We'll just have to try and do much better.'

Then came some hasty undressing and there wasn't any time to retreat to the bedroom, but that was more than OK because the lights were flatteringly low, the sofa was generous and two people who wanted to love each other, who wanted to be back in love, who brought their first time, their best times and this time right here to their lovemaking, could still fully let go and hold nothing back.

The jokes, irritations, mistakes and missteps on the surface of life were put aside for this deep reconnection at soul level. And when souls are involved, then there are no wrong moves between bodies.

And what reminded her so much of the very first time they made love was that she had almost forgotten how glorious sex could be, and once again, it was Ed who was here to remind her.

Afterwards, for long, blissful minutes, there was not one word that needed to be said.

* * *

Sooner or later though, real life had to intervene again. So, Annie and Ed moved to the bed for comfort and were soon deep in discussion about Owen's possible degree choice.

'Economics? He's a dark horse,' was Ed's comment. 'I thought he might skip uni altogether and join a band.'

'Ed!' Annie warned. 'If our sensible boy wants to hedge his bets with music and economics, I'm definitely not going to discourage him.'

Then they both realised how hungry they were

and Ed sat up to ask, 'What the bloody hell happened to that pizza?'

'Oh, the let's-do-marking-with-wine pizza?'

'Are you ever going to stop using that phrase?'

She shook her head. 'I'm afraid your French crush has given me material for years' worth of teasing. Now...' she sat up and smoothed down her bedroom hair, 'get out your phone, babes, and cancel that delicious bad boy because I have the dress, I have the shoes, I have the exciting lover and we're in Paris. So, we need to go out!'

'Out?!'

'Yes! Sounds like you know where all the smoochy jazz clubs are and the romantic river walks...'

He groaned again. 'Could we at least limit it to one French crush teasing comment per day?'

'Per hour maybe, for at least the first month.'

'And there's absolutely no one that I can tease you about in return?'

'Absolutely not a one... although...' she cast her mind back to a certain holiday many years earlier, 'I will admit to being a little bit smitten by Mr Bellissimo in Italy.'

'I knew it!'

'What can I say? My head was turned by his uh-mazing handbag outlet store.'

'OK, let's get dressed and I will show you the sights.'

A bleep from her phone caused both of them to look over at it with instinctive parental anxiety.

'Uh-oh,' Ed said. 'Now what?'

'Could be anything... Owen's changed his mind and run away to join a band? Lauren's got engaged to someone random for a visa... the twins have accidentally hacked into NASA with my old iPad... let's find out.'

Pulling her phone from the bedside table, she was astonished to see she had a message flashing that appeared to be from:

Karl Lagerfeld press

She clicked it open to read the surprising words:

Choupette, Karl's cat, could make herself available for interview tomorrow morning. RSVP ASAP.

35

LA ROBE – THE DRESS

I love separates and the many outfits that they can create, but sometimes one wants to wear a dress. The best dresses are the ones that suit you and your lifestyle. If you are tall or petite, speciality sizing will help. If your waist is not so defined, you may find an empire line, or a ruched cut is more flattering. Never overlook the power of some strategic alterations to tailor the fit just for you.

— M.M.

* * *

They were on a bridge, of course – Paris is all about the bridges – looking out over the lights. The lights on the buildings, the reflection of lights glimmering in the water and, in the distance, the twinkling of the Eiffel Tower.

They had stopped, with their arms around each other, to take in the view. Every other couple on this bridge seemed to be much younger, busy taking selfies and kissing.

'Watch out, that's what I want to tell them,' Annie said to Ed. 'One minute you're in the big romantic dream, kissing on a Paris bridge, the next, you're waist-deep in nappies, tantrums and work emails, wondering how the sexy dude on the bridge turned into such a boring old Dad.'

'OK, hint taken, but we're going to work on that, aren't we? We're going to promise to spend more proper time together. Us time will be carved out of the busy schedule. OK?'

'OK,' she agreed.

'I should have taken you to the bridge where romantics carved padlocks with their initials and locked them to the wire, but they've taken all the padlocks away and replaced the wire with Plexiglas.'

'Ah... but you know, I never liked that idea,' Annie

told him. 'Being locked together forever with the key at the bottom of the Seine.'

'No?'

'No. I think it's far more romantic to know that we are free. We're individuals. We choose to be together every day. How does that sound, boyfriend?'

Ed smiled at her. 'It sounds pretty good, girlfriend.' He kissed her and then said, 'Annie? I'm going to find out if I can wrap up this exchange term early and come home in a few weeks' time.'

But at these words she shook her head emphatically. 'No, no! That's not what this is about. You're going to be totally fine in Paris now. I've got you right back in my orbit. I'm not worried,' she said light-heartedly. 'It's going to be fine. I'll be over again for filming. You'll come back for half-term. We'll make it to Christmas, no problem. But could we maybe up the sexy messages game? More sexy messages please and less of the updates on your gas after onion soup issues.'

Ed burst into laughter. 'OK, I promise. What an idiot!'

'Enjoy some time out of the hurly-burly of the family. Get your head right into the music. And I think you should know that just for you and Owen, I've been starting to learn about classical music. Owen thinks the two of you should take me to the opera – because that is where music meets fashion.'

'Owen is a genius,' Ed said, and he scooped Annie in close. 'I've been doing some studying too. I can tell you something about the top five fashion classics...'

'No!' She grinned at him. 'Really?!'

'Oh yeah, are you going to find that sexy?'

'Definitely, so what do you consider the top five?'

'The Chanel tweed suit – did you know that she was obsessed with real Scottish tweed and the company still sources from little weaving mills in the Scottish borders?'

'Wow... I'm impressed.'

'Then there's the Burberry "trench-warm" coat, originally designed to keep our boys cosy and weatherproof in the First World War trenches. Yves Saint Laurent's *le smoking* is my number three. I think you'd look pretty smoking in one of those...'

'Would you now... even though I don't do black or trousers?'

'Four – the Hermès Birkin, designed for Jane Birkin, English actress and singer who spent her life in Paris.'

'I would definitely do a Hermès Birkin, my darlin', please put yourself down on that waiting list. Ed, I am beyond impressed... what's your number five then?'

'Number five is my favourite… it's you. You are definitely my best fashion classic.'

Just like the other loved-up couples on the bridge with the Eiffel Tower glimmering in the background, they kissed long and lovingly.

'And wait…' Ed said, when the kiss was over, 'I've made you a Classics for Annie playlist. And I think you should hear the first song right now.'

And with that, he took his phone from his pocket, found what he was looking for, turned up the volume and pressed play. Then, even though it was phone music, slightly thin and tinny, the most beautiful woman's voice began to drift out over the bridge and the water.

'"*O mio babbino caro*" by Puccini,' Ed said against her ear.

'It is absolutely gorgeous,' Annie told him.

'She's pleading with her father to let her marry the man she loves.'

As Annie turned in to kiss Ed again, she could feel tears welling up in her eyes. And maybe other people were hearing the music too and feeling completely moved by the voice, the song, the twinkling lights and being right here in the heart of one of the most beautiful cities in the world. But for whatever reason, people began to clap.

And for Annie and Ed, whose love had always

been in a family with children and chaos and work and every other kind of demand around all the time – it was suddenly one of the most moving and romantic moments of their lives.

When the kiss and the aria and the clapping was over, they held hands and walked off the bridge without a word, in the direction of home.

When it was finally time to speak again, she had to ask, 'So... any other good moves you want to try out in the bedroom?'

'Oh definitely, but we can't stay up too late. You've got an interview with a cat tomorrow, so you need to look fresh.'

36

LES SACS À MAIN (ENCORE) – HANDBAGS (AGAIN)

My third handbag is for evening outings. It is big enough for purse, keys, glasses, lipstick and mirror. I wanted a clutch bag with a decorative, even whimsical feel, so this bag is made of exquisite, devoré *velvet in shades of emerald-green. I have had it for years. I love to bring it out. It feels beautiful to hold in my hands and, again, seems to complement every outfit.*

— M.M.

* * *

'I am so sorry, I got here as quickly as I could!' Annie apologised, pulling out her chair at the table for two in this lovely restaurant where Ed was already waiting for her for lunch.

'It's fine, but I've already ordered for us, because there's only so long I can be away. I didn't know how much the cat would have to say,' was Ed's reply.

'Choupette is a gorgeous, gorgeous cat. I get it. I completely understand why the late, truly superb, Lagerfeld was obsessed with her,' Annie began, glancing at the menu.

'It's OK, I ordered steak with béarnaise for you because I knew I couldn't go wrong.'

'And relax...' Annie smiled, leaning back in her chair, 'the husband has made the right choice.'

There was no doubt that the last hour of her life had been one of the more bizarre ones. She'd been in a beautifully decorated and furnished hotel suite talking to a cat... on camera. At least Choupette's agent had thought to give Choupette a little task. Large swatches of coloured fabric had been set out around the cat and as she picked out one colour or another, there had been some discussion around Choupette showing her preference for the best colours for the season ahead.

Then there had been a display of the Choupette

range of products – a handbag and some eye drops with the feline's gorgeous blue eyes depicted on both.

Then Annie had sneezed quite a lot when holding the cat.

Then the agent had filled some more film time with nice detail about how much Lagerfeld had loved the cat and had often asked for her opinion.

'He believed the cat had superior taste, really excellent taste. On another plane of existence,' she told Ed.

'Hmmm... on the plane of a cat, perhaps?'

'This is very nice,' she said, putting her hand over Ed's and then looking around the beautiful venue, 'but do you sometimes get that little pang... that you'd like to share it with—'

'The children?' Ed asked.

'Yes... the children, all four of them, plus Dinah and her family, and my mum, even Connor, and sometimes, I know it doesn't really make sense, because then you and the twins wouldn't be here, but sometimes I just think...' and now she found her eyes filling with tears. 'Oh dear, sorry... I'm Mrs Emotional Car Crash at the moment... but sometimes I'm in a situation when I think Roddy would love this. And you know, he would love this. He did love a swanky meal in a gorgeous venue... especially if he could do a little bit of celebrity shoulder rubbing.'

'Hey, it's OK. It's fine,' Ed said, holding her hand tightly. 'Of course, you think all of those things, because you're a lovely and very generous person. But just now and then, it's OK for us to be a little bit selfish. And recharge our own batteries, by ourselves... for the sake of everyone else.'

She gave Ed a smile, their hands squeezed together on the top of the table. Then, as Annie's eyes drifted from his face to over his shoulder, that was when she saw her – chic bob, slinky satin blouse, wide smile accentuated with plum lipstick – it was unmistakably Katie Rock-Thomson having lunch... right here in this restaurant.

'OMG,' she whispered.

'What have you spotted? You look like you've seen a ghost.' Ed looked at her with something close to concern.

'KRT – the superstar actress I was supposed to interview... you remember? That day... with the twins and Samia and the *police*.' As if she needed to remind him.

'Uh-oh... you're not thinking of accosting her in the middle of her meal?' Ed looked worried.

'No... not exactly but... maybe I can think of something. Some way to reconnect and...' Getting that interview back, that would be The Dream. Tamsin still hadn't really forgiven her for dropping that ball.

'Let's just eat our food,' Ed suggested. 'And promise me you won't do anything embarrassing.'

'We're in a posh French restaurant, Ed, just about everything I can even think of doing is going to be embarrassing.'

'Well, just don't jump out on Ms Scott Thomas... wait, wasn't she in *The Paris Connection*? I loved that film.'

'Don't turn around,' Annie hissed, 'but she just happens to be looking this way.'

So, they ate their heavenly food, and they talked about the French school and music and fashion, trying to make an effort not to revert to talking about the children.

But then, with a squeak of surprise, Annie couldn't help blurting, 'KRT is headed this way... headed straight for us.'

'I think you'll find that's the direction of the ladies.'

'The ladies?'

Could Annie do it... should Annie do it? Should she follow KRT to the ladies and try to talk to her there? Try to at least apologise? But the ladies... any bathroom encounter was fraught with potential awkwardness. She couldn't strike up a chat before KRT went to the loo but was it any better to make the approach afterwards. Would she have to listen to KRT peeing?

The icon was approaching...

Ed gave Annie a slight kick under the table which probably meant 'stop gawping, try to act normally'.

So, she looked down at her food.

'Oooh, I have that jacket in navy-blue, but it looks amazing in pink.'

To Annie's astonishment, KRT's hand was on her shoulder.

'Hello...' Annie managed.

'You are English, aren't you? Just between you and me, I don't think French woman can really do Westwood justice.'

'Oh my goodness... Katie Rock-Thomson... thank you so much!' Annie gushed. 'I'm Annie Valentine, I was supposed to interview you a couple of weeks ago, but... but I got locked into a courtyard by mistake and couldn't make it. Total disaster... I was gutted.'

'What?!'

The astonishingly beautiful KRT actually bent down and said, 'How did that happen? This I have to hear.'

So, Annie gave it as curt but as dramatic a re-telling

as she could manage, not wanting to take up any of the icon's time, especially as she was on the way to the loos.

'So, you missed your interview?'

'Yes... which is obviously awful.'

'And couldn't Elodie reschedule you?'

'Erm...' Annie wondered how to put it tactfully, 'Elodie is quite strict.'

This made the goddess smile. 'Yes... well... have you got your phone? Why don't you take it out and let's have a little chat for a few moments.'

'Are you joking?'

'No... I've just had a delicious lunch with wine and I'm in a good mood. And who's this good-looking man with you?'

'My husband, Ed.'

'Lucky old you,' she said, giving Ed a look, which made Ed actually blush.

So, with a slightly shaking hand, Annie brought out her phone, as Katie *pulled up a chair*.

'I'm just going to prop it like this and focus fully on you. Is that OK?' Annie asked.

'Of course, but I'm ancient now, so do make sure the lighting is dim.'

'Can I ask you about your favourite French wardrobe items?'

'Good question!' the screen goddess exclaimed. 'First of all, the trench coat and sunglasses – so useful when you're running late and need to make yourself over quickly.'

'My go-to hangover outfit,' Annie chimed in.

'Exactly.'

'Then...' KRT paused to consider, 'I do love a Longchamps *le pliage* bag – the roomy, recycled nylon ones – because you can carry your whole life about in those and still look chic. And Roger Vivier shoes, but the ones with heels. So glamorous, impossibly glamorous. But I think English women and French women should enjoy one another's style, learn from one another, and *vive la difference.*'

'Perfect,' Annie said. 'That is perfect. Thank you so much for your time.'

'OK, my darling, it's been wonderful to meet you.' Katie swept up out of her seat and added, 'Very best of luck with your series and I hope this interview turns out OK.'

'Thank you so much,' Annie gushed. 'I've loved, *loved* meeting you.'

Then, in a faint cloud of expensive spicy scent, KRT was gone.

Annie smiled after her until she was no longer visible, then turned to look at her husband.

Ed was still staring in the direction of the departed star with a smile of quite frankly rapture across his face.

'Ed... Ed!' she repeated when she couldn't get his attention the first time.

'Oh! Yes... hello.'

'I've only just forgiven you for... thinking about straying,' she reminded him.

'No, no, this is nothing to do with straying... I'm just starstruck. But, oh my goodness, wasn't she lovely? That film is all coming back to me... her shoulder blades... she has absolutely perfect shoulder blades.'

'And what's perfect about me?' Annie asked, and Ed turned his full attention on her, understanding immediately that this was a serious question.

He brought his hands up to the table, to take hold of hers. He looked at her for a long moment with love, sincerity, and a twinkle of fun.

'Everything, Annie,' he said, 'absolutely everything.'

37

MODIFICATIONS – ALTERATIONS

Small, inexpensive alterations can make all the difference to how clothes look on you. Almost every time I buy a new item, I visit a tailor to have the waist, or hem length, or sleeve length adjusted to ensure it is a perfect fit for me. Rumour has it that certain royal family members have their occasional 'high street' purchases completely taken apart and sewn together again to their exact requirements!

— M.M.

* * *

'Oh my God, can I just say, I think you may have nailed the glamorous gardening look. You may have started a whole new "glam gardener" trend!'

'You think so, Annah? Well, I am proud because I have done it without you, but only because you teach me so many good lessons.'

Annie had come to the Mayfair garden at Svetlana's invitation to see everything that was happening there, to talk about the filming schedule, and because Svetlana had promised 'exciting new developments'.

But first of all, she had to admire Svetlana's completely put together 'gardening outfit': slim-fit cords, with a white vest-top and little pink cashmere cardigan, then a vintage Gucci belt at the waist and, nice touch, classy suede hiking boots with some posh woollen walking socks in pastel lilac. Trousers tucked into the socks. The finishing touches were huge pink diamond stud earrings ('nothing dangling for bending over in the garden,' Svetlana had told her) and one of those cashmere baseball hats from that exquisite Italian brand that Annie knew cost about £700 a pop. Stealth wealth was back. Every thirty years or so, it made an appearance... the 1990s, the 1960s, the 1930s.

'Oh and your gardening tools!' Annie enthused, spotting the lilac suede gardening gloves and the lilac-handled secateurs. Clearly, Svetlana had decided to go all in with this new interest.

'Now, let me show you everything that we have planted,' Svetlana said, beginning her tour. 'These are the plum trees – Victoria plum because it is an English classic, and damson. Over here, we have five apple trees and they are all old-fashioned varieties with flowers the bees will love. We decided herb beds would be beautiful and useful for all the cooks that live here.'

'You're not talking celebrity chefs, are you, darling? You're talking staff.'

'*Ja*... but no vegetable beds, for Mayfair that is maybe a step too far, no?'

The residents' garden was a work in serious progress, a hive of activity with four gardeners bustling about with wheelbarrows, spades and huge wooden sleeper planks.

'It's going to be incredible,' Annie enthused.

'Wildflowers in banks over here,' Svetlana explained. 'Wildflowers will surround the whole garden, but we will have some more formal planting in the middle – lavender, roses, but still pretty, very pretty and full of insects. We are going to have a bat box... and special swallow and house martin homes are going to be built into the garden too. It is all so fantastic.'

'It is, unbelievable!' Annie enthused. 'And what about the other big thing you wanted to talk to me about?'

At this, Svetlana turned to Annie with a big smile and announced, 'I am going to organise a huge fashion auction to raise funds for women's charities. Every year, there will be a star-studded event; a big-ticket, glamorous auction in a marquee, here in the gardens. Society guest list and wonderful "gently used" fashion for sale. For year one, we go through all my wardrobes, all my items in storage, my darling, and you tell me what is going to go.'

Annie was stunned.

'Who is this woman?' she asked mischievously. 'I mean, gardening? Charity auctions? Fundraising? Celebrity events? Are you sure this is you?! I mean, I love this new Svetlana. She's a powerhouse.'

'*Ja!*' Svetlana exclaimed. 'It's wonderful to be so busy again. So full of good ideas!'

'And be able to make them happen. That's the difference.'

'It is all happening, Annah... all go!'

'My worry is, will you have time to come and do your slots on *HTBF*?'

'Of course I will have time,' Svetlana insisted with a smile. 'They are one of my favourite things to do. Plus, they build profile and, besides, you know you are one of my very favourite people.'

'Thank you, darlin'. You are one of my very favourite people too. I missed you so much when we... well... you know.'

'I know, but arguments are good. If you come back after an argument, you come back stronger, no?' Svetlana asked.

'Agreed.'

The women turned to one another and had to have a spontaneous hug at this.

'And I have to tell you that in New York, we need Lauren back, if she does not already have a better job,' Svetlana added.

'Really?' This was amazing news. 'No, she has interviews but... she'll be delighted! Are you sure? Don't feel you have to...'

'I am sure. Many new plans. Elena will contact her.'

'Perfect. So... you want me to talk you through the new episodes? All agreed with Tamsin and the production company.' Annie couldn't resist a happy smile at this.

It was all back on, thank God. The new French-themed episode ideas, Svetlana's big makeover, the handheld, spontaneous interview with KRT, it had all gone down a storm and the full production money was safely in Tamsin's bank account, so Annie could relax and begin enjoying preparing for shooting, aka spending money on TV-friendly new dresses and increasingly severe pairs of Spanx. (Despite Ed's suggestion – 'Why don't you just take some exercise, eat less pastry and drink less wine?' No thank you very much.)

But in fact, what with their new trying to spend time together, trying to notice each other more, yes, she had gone out for twenty minutes round the park on Lauren's old bicycle, as Ed had kindly slowed his pace right down and cycled encouragingly beside her.

Not that she was about to climb into black Lycra anytime soon, but it had been OK, fine... and yes, she might even do it again next week... or maybe the week after.

'So, the schedule...' Annie didn't even need to look, she knew it from memory now, which was just as well as Svetlana had handed her a hoe, with the words, 'Copy what I do here. We break the top of the soil, make it soft for planting, then we add the dung.'

'Where, oh where, has the Champagne, caviar and blini-lifestyle gone?!'

'Oh,' Svetlana breezed, 'Maria will have that waiting for us when we finish here.'

This made Annie laugh, because she suspected it was true.

'OK, four of the episodes we had planned at the start of the summer – they're all good. But the new episodes are going to be *"Annie In Paris"* specials. So, French style part one, we open with lovely shots of Paris and Madame Moreau telling us all about her fascinating life. There's plenty of opportunity for images of the French style classics and then her idea of "the grit in the oyster". Then we use your makeover and film in some of the beautiful Paris stores and boutiques,' Annie added, still wielding her hoe.

'Oh, I spoke to my friends at Chanel. It's all good. We can film,' Svetlana threw in.

'You are an absolute legend!' was Annie's response to this. 'So... episode two, we do French lingerie and jewellery. Plus, we have the inside story of a real Parisian's wardrobe – don't ask, it's a long story – and what about a money when travelling slot from you?'

'OK, I think about that... it's how to be different, unusual on that topic.'

'We also have Choupette the cat – don't ask, it's another long story! Then we talk about the new season, plus trends and inspiration from art, from animals and everywhere. Tamsin is also keen for you to talk about investing... maybe art/collectibles/financial investments?'

Svetlana gave a serious nod.

'Oh, and no forgetting KRT talking about English v French style, so we're going to run with that. English and French models, looks, street style.'

'I love it,' Svetlana said, looking up from her work with a big smile. 'And maybe we have one money slot in the series when we talk about pensions. And how we're going to be so healthy and live so long in our gardens that we must have good ones. Not that we want to talk or even think too much about getting old.'

'No – but you know, with age comes wisdom... and much better accessories,' Annie said, and they both laughed, then hoed peacefully together for a good ten minutes or so.

'Everything is surprisingly calm,' Annie couldn't help commenting. 'Too calm.'

'Well, this is maybe because we haven't looked at our phones for some time now,' was Svetlana's dry response.

'You're right. Should we look at them?' Annie wondered.

'No, I don't think so, because we are having a beautiful time.'

Annie managed a few moments longer, but it was no use, the seed of maternal worry had been sown. Just look what had happened the last time she'd been out of touch: police... near-divorce... general mayhem.

'OK,' Svetlana conceded, 'we take just a short look, just at the screens to make sure no emergencies.'

Both women returned to the garden bench where their respective handbags were perched and delved for the mobiles.

Annie was not surprised to see a new message relating to each of her family members. Anxiously, she opened the one from the twins' nursery first, but no need to panic, it was a photo of Max and Minette laughing together at the sand box.

Then there was one from Owen... what had he forgotten now?

Just been asked to play the glockers in concert at Royal Albt H. Cool huh

Now Lauren... uh-oh, what was the latest problem from NYC?

Elena called!!!! They want me bk!!!! Screeeeeeeam!!!!

And finally, Ed in Paris:

Went shopping for some very Frrrrench lingerie... happy Annie Valentine's day. Love you more.

'Wow! All surprisingly good,' Annie announced, but as Svetlana looked at her screen, her expression changed from relaxed and unconcerned to completely blindsided.

'Oh, this is just impossible!' Svetlana exclaimed, taking in this latest drama, conveyed in under sixty characters.

'And now what do we do?' Svetlana asked, showing Annie the message and looking to her for advice and support.

Annie threaded her arm through Svetlana's and set a smile on her face. 'Well, somehow, we'll just deal with it, babes, because we always do.'

ACKNOWLEDGEMENTS

Thank you so much to everyone at the awesome Boldwood Books. You've worked so hard to breathe new life into the *Annie Valentine* series and cheered me on to writing a brand-new volume. Special appreciation to my editor, Emily Ruston, copyeditor Shirley Khan, and proofreader Camilla Lloyd, who have all helped to make this book so much better.

Huge hugs and thanks to The Fam: Thomas, Sam and Claudie – for silly messages, teas, coffees, dinners, shoulder rubs after too much typing, and all the other very welcome support and distractions. Honourable mention for new puppy on the block, Bingo!

Thank you to my lovely agent, Diana Beaumont, who has been with Annie V since book one, chapter one.

Thank you also to the friends and colleagues who've been so extra-helpful and supportive over the past writing year – Shari, Sarah, Anne Marie, Julie, Andrea, Debbie, Dannielle, and no forgetting Friday drinks and much laughter with Duncan. Loads of love to you all.

And absolutely no forgetting the Annie fans, who kept asking me for a new book. Hope you'll love reading it as much as I've loved writing it!

ABOUT THE AUTHOR

Carmen Reid is the bestselling author of numerous women's fiction titles including the Personal Shopper series starring Annie Valentine. She lives in Glasgow with her husband and children.

Sign up to Carmen Reid's mailing list for news, competitions and updates on future books.

Visit Carmen's website: www.carmenreid.com

Follow Carmen on social media:

f facebook.com/carmenreidwrites

instagram.com/carmenreidwrites

ALSO BY CARMEN REID

Worn Out Wife Seeks New Life

New Family Required

The Woman Who Ran For The Hills

The Annie Valentine Series

The Personal Shopper

Late Night Shopping

How Not To Shop

Celebrity Shopper

New York Valentine

Shopping With The Enemy

Annie in Paris

LOVE NOTES

LOVE IN EVERY CHAPTER

WHERE ALL YOUR ROMANCE
DREAMS COME TRUE!

THE HOME OF BESTSELLING
ROMANCE AND WOMEN'S
FICTION

 WARNING:
MAY CONTAIN SPICE

SIGN UP TO OUR
NEWSLETTER

https://bit.ly/Lovenotesnews

Boldwood

Boldwood Books is an award-winning fiction publishing company seeking out the best stories from around the world.

Find out more at www.boldwoodbooks.com

Join our reader community for brilliant books, competitions and offers!

Follow us
@BoldwoodBooks
@TheBoldBookClub

Sign up to our weekly deals newsletter

https://bit.ly/BoldwoodBNewsletter

9 781837 516896